DEEP CUTS

DEEP CUTS

A Novel

Holly Brickley

CROWN
NEW YORK

Published in the United States by Crown, an imprint of the Crown Publishing Group, a division of Penguin Random House LLC, New York.
crownpublishing.com

CROWN and the Crown colophon are registered trademarks of Penguin Random House LLC.

Library of Congress Cataloging-in-Publication Data
Names: Brickley, Holly, author.
Title: Deep cuts : a novel / Holly Brickley.
Description: First edition. | New York City : Crown, 2025.
Identifiers: LCCN 2024008156 | ISBN 9780593799086 (hardcover ; acid-free paper) | ISBN 9780593799093 (ebook)
Subjects: LCGFT: Romance fiction. | Novels.
Classification: LCC PS3602.R531255 D44 2025 | DDC 813/.6—dc23/eng/20240515
LC record available at https://lccn.loc.gov/2024008156

Hardcover ISBN 978-0-593-79908-6
International edition ISBN 979-8-217-08623-8
Barnes and Noble edition ISBN: 979-8-217-08778-5
Ebook ISBN 978-0-593-79909-3

Printed in the United States of America

Editor: Amy Einhorn
Associate editor: Lori Kusatzky
Production editor: Abby Oladipo
Text designer: Amani Shakrah
Production managers: Phil Leung and Heather Williamson
Managing editor: Chris Tanigawa
Copy editor: Nancy Tan
Proofreaders: Maureen Clark, Tricia Wygal, and Emily Moore
Publicists: Dyana Messina and Stacey Stein
Marketers: Julie Cepler and Rachel Rodriguez

9 8 7 6 5 4 3 2 1

First Edition

For Danny

DEEP CUTS

Sara Smile

He caught me singing along to some garbage song. It was the year 2000 so you can take your pick of soulless hits—probably a boy band, or a teenage girl in a crop top, or a muscular man with restricted nasal airflow. I was waiting for a drink at a bar, spaced out; I didn't realize I'd been singing until his smile floated into the periphery of my vision and I felt impaled by humiliation.

"Terrible song," I said, forcing a casual tone. "But it's an earworm."

We knew each other in that vague way you can know people in college, without ever having been introduced or had a conversation. Joey, they called him, though I decided in that moment the diminutive did not suit him; he was too tall, for one. He put an elbow on the bar and said, "Is an earworm ever terrible, though, if it's truly an earworm?"

"Yes."

"But it's doing what it set out to do," he said. "It's effective. It's catchy."

"Dick Cheney is effective," I said. "Nazis were catchy."

The grin spread again.

The bartender slid me a beer and I took it gratefully, holding the cold pint glass against my cheekbone. The song ended and a clash of bar sounds filled its void: ice shaking in tin, shuffleboard pucks clacking, a couple seated at the bar hollering in dismay at a TV suspended above the bartender's head. Joe ordered a drink and began pulling crumpled bills from his jeans pocket. I was about to walk back to my booth when "Sara Smile" by Hall and Oates began to play, and he let out a moan.

"What a perfect song." His hand shot into the tall dark pile of curls atop his head, then clawed its way down his cheek as he listened.

Hall and Oates! I loved Hall and Oates! They were a rare jukebox selection for the time—a band whose '80s sound was seen as cheesy by most people I knew, too recent to be recycled, though that wouldn't last much longer. I leaned against the bar next to him and listened to the gorgeous, sultry first verse.

"Actually," I said, unable to stop myself, "I would call this a perfect track, a perfect recording. Not a perfect song." I could tell he already halfway understood but I explained anyway, with a level of detail befitting an idea of far greater complexity: "A perfect song has stronger bones. Lyrics, chords, melody. It can be played differently, produced differently, and it will almost always be great. Take 'Both Sides, Now,' if you'll excuse me being that girl in a bar talking about Joni Mitchell—any singer who doesn't completely suck can cover that song and you'll be drowning in goosebumps, right?"

It was a leap of faith that he'd even know the song, but he gave a swift nod. "Totally."

I ducked to avoid being swallowed by the armpit of a tall guy receiving a drink from the bartender. Joe's eyes stayed on me, focused like spotlights, so I kept going. "Now, 'Sara Smile'—can you imagine anyone besides Daryl Hall singing this, exactly as he sang it on this particular day?"

Joe cocked his ear. Daryl Hall responded with a long, elegant riff.

I jabbed my finger in the air, tracing the melody. "See? The most beautiful part of the verse is just him riffing. A great song—and I'm talking about the pop-rock world here, obviously—can be improved by riffing, or ruined by riffing. But it cannot *rely* on riffing."

Joe didn't look smug or bored, which were the reactions these kinds of tangents had historically won me. He didn't give me a lecture about relativism while air-quoting the phrase "good music." He just lifted his bottle of Budweiser, paused it at his lips, and took a drink.

The tall guy beside us smacked his shoulder and Joe's eyes lit up with recognition, so it seemed we were done. But before I could leave, he turned back. "What's your name again?" He squinted at me rather severely, like I was a splinter he was trying to tweeze.

"Percy," I said. "Bye."

I walked back to the booth where my roommate and her boyfriend were planning a party I didn't want to have. "Finally," Megan said as I scooted in across from them on the honeywood bench. "Do you think one of those jugs of SKYY is enough? Plus mixers and a keg?" She showed me a Post-it inserted into her day planner. "That would be fifty each. Unless the mixer is Red Bull."

Megan was an art history major but seemed happiest when doing simple math. I tolerated her orderliness by indulging in small acts of rebellion: unscrewed toothpaste lids, late phone bill payments—all calibrated to satisfy an inner urge for chaos without disrupting our friendship, which was important to me if only for its rarity, like an ugly diamond.

"I told Trent what we discussed about not inviting the whole world," she said as she took a sip of her cosmopolitan, casting a significant look at the boyfriend. Poor Trent. I had expected them to be broken up by now.

"Is Joey Morrow coming?" Trent said to me, with one eye on Megan. When I shrugged, he pushed: "You were talking to him at the bar, right? He's in my econ."

Megan twisted to peer out of the booth. "Oh, him—Joey and Zoe who both like Bowie. Yeah, they're cool."

I knew this, that he had a girlfriend. I watched him across the bar and thought of a rom-com I'd seen at an unfortunately impressionable age in which a man says, gazing longingly at the female lead, "A girl like that is born with a boyfriend." With Joe it wasn't the flawless jawline, the arching eyebrows over wide-set eyes—those were offset, in the equation of attractiveness I had learned from these same movies, by the hooked nose and gapped teeth, the too-square shoulders atop a gangly-tall body. But the way he held those angular limbs, as if this jerking energy was the obvious way to make them work. The way he smiled so easily, and frowned so easily, tortured by a blue-eyed soul song. A boy like that is born with a girlfriend.

"Amoeba warning," Megan muttered, her eyes darting over my shoulder.

I felt a rush of fight-or-flight but didn't turn around. I knew she was referring to staff members of Amoeba Music, the legendary Berkeley record store where I'd worked sophomore year before switching to its inferior cousin, Rasputin Music, just up the street. Amoeba had been a hellscape of pretentious snobs and one thoroughly horrifying sexual encounter; Rasputin had been fine but boring, and nobody ever talked about the actual songs there either. Now I waitressed at a diner for twice the money and felt lucky to be free of the lot of them.

"Just the undergrads," Megan updated. "The guy with the muttonchops and two others. No Neil."

Of course. Neil would never come to a bar like this, blocks from campus, famous for accepting even the worst fake IDs. My adrenaline eased.

"Should you invite them to the party?" she asked, nostrils flaring. "You have two seconds to decide."

This stumped me—I hated them, but I could talk to them. "Okay!" I yelped, just in time for the Amoebans to pass by our booth without so much as a nod, let alone a conversation. Trent whistled a low tone that could be interpreted as either pity or mockery.

I recognized all three from behind. We hadn't been close as coworkers; they had been too focused on proving themselves to the elder statesmen of the staff, the ones with hard drug experience and complicated living situations in Oakland. There was also an incident in which the muttonchops guy had made fun of me for not knowing the Brian Jonestown Massacre and I'd responded by accusing him of being "all breadth, no depth," a view I still held: music was a collector's habit to those guys, a sprawl of knowledge more than a well of joy. But still. A hello would've been called for.

Megan caught my eye, communicating sympathy with her face. I sent back gratitude. "Let's just get Red Bull for ourselves," I said, and she beamed.

Trent began dropping hints that the two of them should go back to his apartment, even though it was only ten and our names were on the list to play shuffleboard. At least I'd gotten out for a bit, I figured. At least I wouldn't have to keep discussing the relative merits of vodka mixers. He slid me his half-finished pint before following Megan out of the booth. It was the kind of beer that tasted like rubber bands but I drank it anyway, urgently, aware of the clock ticking on how long a girl could be alone in a bar before she became monstrously conspicuous. I feigned interest in a stained-glass lampshade hanging low over the booth.

"Name a song that's both."

Joe was standing at the foot of the booth.

I lifted the beer to hide my smile, thinking fast. " 'In My Life' by the Beatles," I said. "The original cut with George Martin's weird sped-up piano solo. A perfect song with perfect bones, plus they nailed the context."

"Eh," he said, visibly disappointed by this answer. He slid onto the bench across from me. "I would argue the double-tracked vocals were a mistake."

I folded my arms and tried to play the song in my head.

"Lennon insisted on those effects because he hated his voice," he said. "But it's such an intimate song—we should feel like he's just alone, singing to us, don't you think?"

"It's not like he's got a choir behind him," I said. "It's just John, multiplied."

"Oh, like it's his multiple personalities?" He smirked. "Sounds like one of those bullshit things a music journalist would say."

I was starting to wonder if he might be right about the song, but I wanted the last word: " 'Bullshit things a music journalist would say' sounds like one of those bullshit things a college boy would say."

He looked at me over the rim of his pint glass, then smiled a little as he drank. "It's still a perfect song," he said. "That's more important."

"Is it?"

We kept talking and couldn't stop. Time stretched like pulled taffy, dipping and clumping. We took turns selecting songs that the jukebox actually, miraculously, played. The overlap in our musical tastes grew wider and wider until it began to seem infinite: indie rock and Elephant 6, the entirety of the '60s, no guilt attached to pop pleasures. When we finished our drinks he disappeared for a few disorienting minutes, then returned with a teeming pitcher and two fresh glasses and we were right back in it. The booth was like its own room, enclosed on three sides by a wall and the high wooden backs of our benches. The rest of the bar—dark and murky, swimming with normal humans—we would observe occasionally, as if from a great distance.

Casually, I invited him to the party, but he said it was Zoe's dad's birthday. "Do you know Zoe?" he said, leaning over the table, his high eyebrows relaxed now.

"No." Zoe was a tasteful punk—rail thin with narrow hips, baby doll tees and platforms, bleached hair with black roots. They had arrived together that fall as a fully formed unit, transferred into our junior-year cohort from some suburban college, both poli-sci majors.

"I think—" He did a quick survey of the bar crowd before looking back at me. "I think Zoe and I might be a perfect track. We need that context—family, friends, our hometown. I don't know about the *bones* of our relationship."

My initial response to this was guilt, as if whatever issue he had identified with his girlfriend was somehow my fault. Then I felt a stab of panic at the possibility of him being available, which I knew would turn this scenario into something I was incapable of handling. So I backpedaled: "A perfect track isn't nothing! A perfect track can be everything! 'Sara Smile' was killing you, before I started my blathering!"

He nodded, running his thumbnail over a pair of initials carved into the wooden tabletop. "True. And I can't imagine my life without her anyway, so." He patted the table conclusively.

This relieved me enough to ease the panic. I leaned back into the corner of my side of the booth; he leaned into his. I stared at the remnants of beer foam clinging to my glass and thought about his metaphor: a relationship as a perfect track. There was something delicious about it, the way he'd made my little take on a pop song so emotional, so very real-world. I nursed it like a hard candy.

The closing-time lights came on, and his face looked different in the glare—something sad and determined around the eyes, brutally alive. I felt a sudden yawning high in my chest, like a door inside me being pushed wide open.

He scooted to the edge of the bench and nodded at some guys near the door, then turned back to me. "Can I show you a song I'm working on?"

So he was an actual musician. I would spend the next few days processing this news, recasting the night's conversation in light of it, but in the moment it left me stunned. Wordlessly I wrote my address on a napkin and then he was standing, bonking his head on the hanging lampshade, buttoning a ratty navy peacoat. I stayed seated.

"Who'd you come with?" he asked.

"Oh, just some people who tolerate me," I said. "They left."

"Walk with us, then?"

"Nah," I said, then realized I needed a reason. "I don't hang out with musicians."

"And why is that?" he asked with a laugh, walking backward toward the door.

Because they make me unbearably jealous. "Because they always disappoint me," I said, which was also true.

He held the napkin up in a fist. "Challenge accepted!"

I sat in the booth until someone cleared the array of empty glasses and the stunned feeling began to mutate into anticipation. His song was certain to be either mediocre or terrible, but I relished the possibilities anyway: Whispery acoustic? Glitchy blips and bloops? On the way home I bought a slice of pizza which I ate as I walked, grease dripping from the corners of a strangely unstoppable smile.

Somebody Said

The next night we threw our stupid party. It made for an exhausting Saturday—borrowing a car, buying booze, shoving furniture around in an attempt to make our living room, which was my bedroom, suitable for hosting. Megan and I shared a one-bedroom unit in a dilapidated triplex four blocks south of campus, though the name on our lease belonged to Megan's sister's ex, who hadn't lived there since 1994—which meant that our rent was well below market value, and also that we were terrified of raising eyebrows with the property management company and thus did not complain about the non-functioning oven, the shower that took twenty minutes to drain, or the hole in the back of the closet through which a thick tree branch was definitely growing. It was heaven compared to the dorms.

The party spilled out the front door and onto the sidewalk. I spent the night moving between clusters, laughing at things that were funny and laughing at things that were not. I had burned a perfect party mix but of course people put on whatever they wanted; by midnight I couldn't even find my disc in the haphazard piles. I viewed parties like a job: they simply had to be done. Freshman year I'd been lazy about socializing—I'd said no when the heads popped in my door, spent Saturday nights tending to a poorly timed Elvis Costello obsession that dominated my imagination and endeared me to zero percent of my dormmates—but didn't love the crushing loneliness that eventually resulted from this approach. Since then I'd been clawing my way toward a normal college existence, and I was proud of what I'd achieved: an apartment, one actual friendship, an impressive mess of inherited CDs.

The day after the party we cleaned in short, hungover increments until it was time for Megan to host one of her informal yoga classes. I joined out of necessity, since it was happening in my bedroom, and was already brainstorming a reason to excuse myself when I heard footsteps on our porch, the tin lid of our mailbox clattering shut. I stepped over the stretched-out bodies.

A blank disc in our mailbox read "untitled for percy," an email for Joe Morrow scrawled below. The sidewalk was dark. All I could think was had he seen us through the window? The other girls in shiny black stretch pants, me in my sweats?

When I returned to the living room, Megan shot me a curious look from her sun salutation. I mumbled something about having a paper due. I hadn't told her about Joe; I knew she would reduce it all to some boring crush. I gathered my laptop and headphones and set up in the kitchen.

Joe's song was quiet but with full instrumentation, programmed drums, heavy reverb. A little Elliott Smith in the guitar styling. The lyrics were pleasantly inscrutable, with themes of gossip ("The night lit up with talk of your talk"), betrayal ("Let's both be Judases, see where it takes us"), and looming heartbreak ("Awoke to the memory of the possibility of the worst").

I played it again. It didn't suck, which I recognized for the enormous miracle it was. His singing had a striking ease to it, like he opened his mouth and some beautiful, mangled truth just fell out. But the song itself felt overly considered, with plodding verses and a nice-enough melody that seemed to leave my brain the moment the song ended.

After several listens, I began composing an email response. And then the bubble next to his screen name turned green. The yoga concluded; girls began filing into our tiny kitchen to fill their water bottles. I hunched over the laptop, trying to stay out of their airspace, and went for it. IM was a new medium for me but I knew enough. I knew to keep it lowercase, keep it cool.

ileanpercy: hey

joeymorrow: hey!

ileanpercy: it's percy

joeymorrow: did you listen already?

ileanpercy: yeah it's great!

joeymorrow: thanks man i thought you'd like it

ileanpercy: i do wish it had more of a hook

joeymorrow: i think the verses are pretty catchy no?

ileanpercy: oh, sorry, but no way—the melody in the verses is super generic.

ileanpercy: and yet also over-written, somehow? it sounds kind of forced.

joeymorrow: damn

ileanpercy: but your singing is magical, joe, and the bridge is beautiful. so beautiful.

ileanpercy: and weirdly it doesn't sound like a bridge

ileanpercy: there's no big changes or anything, same line-length

ileanpercy: it's just a better melody out of nowhere.

joeymorrow: hah i hate writing bridges, i just tossed that out

ileanpercy: if that's what happens when you toss out a melody, i'm scared of your talent

joeymorrow: hah thanks. too bad it's just a bridge, who cares about bridges

ileanpercy: well that's a dumb thing to say BUT i was thinking . . . could you swap the melody of the bridge with the verses?

ileanpercy: then you would have a hook to end the verse

joeymorrow: what would i do with the current verses?

ileanpercy: recycling bin? they were really boring.

joeymorrow: damn that would be a totally different song

ileanpercy: you could keep the lyrics, just use the other melody.

joeymorrow: interesting

joeymorrow: i'm singing it

ileanpercy: me too.

ileanpercy: i think it works, right?

joeymorrow: dunno

joeymorrow: i'll try it out

ileanpercy: rad.

I realized I'd been a massive asshole almost immediately after logging off. Instead of sleeping that night I revised my end of the conversation in my head over and over, a lifelong pastime I always rationalized as productive since the lessons could apply to future interactions, though that never seemed to happen. I hadn't slept so terribly since the dorms, when I used to spend every night optimizing the thousands of social touch points I'd been forced to have in each cacophonous day.

Eventually I stopped revising and switched to crafting an apologetic speech. It was casual, sincere, amply self-deprecating. My plan was to deliver it on Tuesday, when I ran into him on campus, after the economics class I happened to know he shared with Trent in Haviland Hall.

The run-in worked: he was loping out the front doors of the building just as I walked by. There was a dark look on his face until he saw me, at which point it flipped to sunny surprise. I asked if he was okay and he waved me off.

"Zoe skipped econ," he said. "You want a coffee?"

We went to the Free Speech, a modern café recently installed next to the computer lab, filled with informational plaques about Berkeley's free speech movement that everyone ignored. We took turns ordering coffees and brought them to the outdoor deck.

"The song is so good now," he said as soon as we sat down. "I'm freaking out."

A loosening in my shoulders and neck, the muscles Megan called traps. I scrapped my apology.

"Still tweaking lyrics. They had to be changed a lot to fit that melody." He leaned back against the concrete bench and blew into the hole in his plastic coffee cup lid. "Zoe says I owe you a beer, but a beer seems measly. Two beers?"

"Two beers sounds great. I'm just glad I didn't hurt your, you know, feelings."

"Fuck my feelings," he said loudly, swatting them out of the air.

The girl sitting next to us looked annoyed. She was clutching a pink highlighter and hunched over a thick textbook, which she inched as far from us as our shared table would allow.

"Sorry," Joe said, flashing a smile at her. "I mean, it is the Free Speech Cafe."

Unbelievably, the girl smiled back. She returned to her highlighting noticeably less hunched.

"Hey, can I ask you something?" Joe said to me. "Do you sing, or play, or write at all?"

"No." I took too big a gulp of coffee and burned my throat. "I have no talent, just opinions about people who do."

"How can that be? Did you ever take piano lessons?"

"Yes. I sucked. And I just couldn't. It's too important to me."

He tugged a curl of hair at his temple. "But you're an English major, right?"

"Only by default. I started with theater to get closer to music, but I couldn't stand those cheesy songs, all that jazz-hands enthusiasm." I glanced at our tablemate's book: enough numbers to reassure me she wasn't a theater nerd.

"Surely you've written lyrics?"

"No," I said. The traps were tensing again. "I get paralyzed. I'm actually getting a bit paralyzed by this conversation, to be honest."

He laughed and leaned back. "Okay, okay. Let's talk about something other than music."

We sat in silence for a second, then laughed at ourselves, playacting an old joke. Finally I asked where he was from, though I already knew it was one of those Bay Area suburbs that meant nothing to me, and then we were talking about our childhoods and he mentioned his mom had died when he was young. Diagnosed with melanoma the beginning of the summer before he started high school, then buried ten weeks later, Labor Day weekend. I had to go to the bathroom but I held it.

"Were you okay?" I asked. "*Are* you okay?"

"No," he said. "And yes."

The sun came out, dappled through the low-hanging trees, and he pulled a pair of sunglasses from his backpack.

"Sensitive eyes," he said. I remember this so clearly. The black sunglasses, the pile of curls, the blue sky and shuffling leaves behind him—the image still comes to me at random times. Then his eyebrows shot up over the sunglasses. "I almost forgot! Do you want to write a music column for our zine?"

The zine, he explained, was helmed by Zoe, with contributions from a rotating cast of a dozen or so women. Joe provided the occasional band interview. It was called *Ring Finger*.

"I'm not really a writer," I said.

"Think of it as opinionating. You're good at that."

"Opining," I said.

"Girls opining is basically *Ring Finger*'s whole deal."

"So is it like a riot grrrl thing?" I asked. "Because punk music interests me only up to a point, and that point would come fast."

"Write about whatever you want. As long as the *spirit* is a bit punk—I told her you'd have no trouble with that."

I felt that door pushing open inside me again. John Cale! John Cage? The liberation of Tina Weymouth! Curse words to my heart's content!

We both had class but agreed to meet at the campus pub afterward so he could buy me a beer, which he did, and then bought me another, and then we got burritos and ate them on the side of a grassy hill in the dark.

The next day I bought a copy of *Ring Finger* at the bookstore. The logo featured an ink drawing of a ringless ring finger raised liked a middle finger, with black polish on a bitten-down nail. None of the names were familiar to me, thank God—nobody who had known me in my pre-Megan weirdo days. Zoe Gutierrez had written a long, smart article about her first period, studded with historical menstruation horrors. I liked it, but there was a heaviness to the whole thing, a want for humor and lightheartedness. So I decided to start there. I scribbled ideas in the margins of my lecture notes, on the plastic inner flaps of my three-ring binders, anywhere I could find an empty space. When I wasn't scribbling I was wondering about Joe's song, humming the bridge melody. I had this dreamlike feeling of nearing some place I'd been looking for—a vacancy just my shape, hidden inside an enormous puzzle.

That Friday night after I got home from my shift at the diner, there was an email from Joe with the subject line "DONE":

> *my roommates are out tonight so i can play it for you*
> *if you wanna come over, the brown shingle house on*
> *derby by the church*

I stepped straight back into my boots and walked to his house, a once-gorgeous Craftsman with a deep, creaking porch.

He smiled when he opened the door. "You're here!"

"I'm dying," I said.

He rubbed his hands together like he was about to cook me a really good meal.

His bed was in the living room, a futon folded into a couch, which put us in the same socioeconomic strata of upperclassmen—though a room in an actual house cost a lot more social capital. The mattress was so deep I had to tuck my feet up. I could see a sizable kitchen off the living room and a grand staircase decorated with college-boy mess: hoodies slung over the banister, a greasy bike chain curled on the first step like a snake.

When I looked back at Joe, he was shaking the mouse of a desktop computer. "Oh," I said. "You'll *play* it for me. I thought you meant you'll *play* it for me."

He turned, surprised. "Do you want me to *play* it for you?"

"Yes," I said. "I mean, whatever. But yes."

He shrugged, then picked up a guitar from the corner and perched on the opposite end of the futon. "You should hear the track afterward, though. Beer?"

He seemed nervous. I shook my head, fighting a smile.

"Okay," he said. "It's called 'Somebody Said.'"

He cleared his throat and began. His guitar playing was good, fingerpicking assured. It occurred to me his hands would be rough to be touched by—or do calluses feel smooth, I wondered. The verses sounded as I knew they would with that melody, elegant and right, with a new lyric in the repeated final line that gave the song a clear hook: "Somebody said you said it was over." He flinched when he sang it, voice cracking, and I felt with some certainty that I was watching a star—that the reaction I was having would be the reaction of anyone with eyes and ears, of hordes of college girls and sensitive young dads across America; I was not special. It gave me a surge of vertigo, like I'd leaned too far over the edge of a balcony.

The new bridge brought me back with a predictable chord change, a half-hearted couplet. It would do. A perfect third verse and that gap-toothed grin to finish.

"Holy shit," I said.

He exhaled. "Oh, thank God."

"You need to play shows."

"I'm getting a band together."

"I think my hands are actually trembling, slightly?" I held out a hand for observation and he lunged for it, clasping my fingers awkwardly in his.

"Thank you," he said.

The King of Carrot Flowers Pt. One

I spent that weekend in the library, studying a little but mostly writing for *Ring Finger*. With my Dickies bag full of PowerBars, ripe bananas, and a Vitaminwater bottle that possessed a seemingly endless power to infuse dragonfruit essence into drinking fountain water, there was little reason to leave. I enjoyed myself despite a blooming awareness that I had no idea what I was doing. Each column would focus on a single song, that much I knew, but everything else was in question. Which songs? How personal was too personal? What did I want to say? I kept starting pieces and abandoning them when I found a new way in—there were so many *ways in* to a song!—and then starting over again.

"Surf's Up"

When my mom introduced me to the Beach Boys song "Surf's Up," I was still Eileen.

Do I seem like an Eileen to you? Doesn't it sound like the name of a 57-year-old woman who weighs her food on a scale and calls her jewelry "jewels"? It's so stiff, yet delicate, like an overly starched doily. I swear to God my earliest memories are of lying in a crib, being called Eileen, and thinking, "Are you fucking kidding me?"

One night in high school, at dinner, I announced to my family that I would henceforth be called by my middle name, Percy. Definitely used the term "henceforth." My dad was on board—the name had been a reference to his Greek grandmother Persephone, the star of all his childhood stories and the only extrovert ever to grace the branches of my family tree, from what I could tell—but my mom got up from the table and scraped her plate into the garbage. Offending her taste was the closest I ever got to rebellion, to being the punk I

"Surf's Up"

The Beach Boys have a real punk streak. Stay with me here. When Brian Wilson wrote the songs for their album *Smile,* including my favorite, "Surf's Up," he was radically unconcerned with what the world expected of him. He was giving a gorgeous middle finger to the pop music of the time.

My mom, who introduced me to "Surf's Up," has a similar streak. She sat out the musical revolutions of her generation, aside from a passing interest in '70s Stevie Wonder, a little Joni. As a child she'd played violin so impeccably they let her move to New York as a teenager to study at some academy—but when her dad died and their family's money vanished, she didn't go home right away. She played in quartets and orchestra pits and even dabbled as a singer, covering standards at boat clubs, until something happened, or didn't happen—she never talks about it except to say she met my dad and "chose the simpler life" back in Indiana. But she wasn't like the other Indiana moms.

"Surf's Up"

My mom isn't like your mom. She hates almost everything: restaurants ("How do you know what they're
putting in the food?"), museums ("Art zoos!"), travel
("Bragging rights for sale"), camping ("Trying on
homelessness"). Music is our only common interest,
but she ruins that too by having the world's stuffi-
est taste. Mozart, Beethoven, all those white-wigged
ghosts.

So when she sat me down to play me a song one hot
afternoon at the end of eighth grade, I was wary—and,
when I saw the CD cover, baffled. The Beach Boys? I
had aged out of the oldies. A tinny *Dookie* brayed out
of the headphones around my neck.

"You need a break from that Green Day," she
said, emphasizing both words of the band's name as
if speaking a foreign language. "I'm worried what
it's doing to your brain." She cued up the song and
turned to me. "Anyway, this is not the Beach Boys
you're thinking of. The title is a joke, like 'time's up'—
they were done with the surfing thing. The lyrics are
strange, but trust me, it doesn't need words to make its
point. If you don't like it, that's fine, go back to your
angry pop." She pressed play and went out through the
sliding-glass door to the garden.

Instantly the song transported me somewhere
Dookie could never exist. "Columnated ruins domino"! I turned to look for my mother out the window,
feeling suddenly lonely. I'd never heard the word "columnated" (still haven't), but I could see the image
clearly: the cascading end of a civilization. It made my
sunbaked skin prickle. The second half of the song

was a whole new song out of nowhere, like a bridge that never ended. I heard no closure, none of the resolving chords I'd come to expect, just doors opening to bigger doors that opened to a sky. Look, the song whispered to me, that day in my living room. Life can be so big.

I played it again and felt tears rolling down my cheeks, into the soft pads of the headphones around my neck. Finally, unsteadily, I slid open the sliding glass. "Mom, it's so beautiful!" I called, my voice thick with snot.

Her butt was in the air, her hands in a gopher hole. She twisted briefly to give me a thumbs-up.

"Surf's Up"

My mom was my piano teacher for one stressful year in grade school. Fifth grade? Sixth? Post-boobs, pre-bra. We sat together at the upright in our dining room every day after school for an hour and a half. I could get my right hand to play okay and my left hand too, but they did not seem to work together the way nature intended, and the foot pedal required a level of concentration from me that seemed to cause my mom actual concern, like maybe I had suffered some previously undetected brain damage at birth. When I finally begged out of our lessons, she failed miserably at hiding her relief.

A few years later she played me Brian Wilson's piano demo of "Surf's Up" and I hated her for letting me quit. I couldn't stop wondering how the shape-shifting chords and haunting melody of "Surf's Up" would show up on the map of the piano—wondering, really, how the song worked. I suppose like most young music fans I was at this point still harboring dreams that I could make the stuff myself one day, and cracking the mystery of "Surf's Up" seemed an important first step.

The upright in our dining room had been hauled away by now, but there was a Casio stored on a card table in the basement, an old Christmas gift for my brother he'd barely touched. I pulled up a plastic bin of winter coats to use as a chair, plugged in headphones so nobody could hear, and tried to pick out the song—first the vocal melody, which was relatively easy, then the chords, which were not. I spent a handful of afternoons down there that summer, switching the headphone plug back and forth between my Walkman and the Casio, trying to understand what I heard.

By the end of summer I'd given up. Some chords were impossible for my ear to decipher—and most frustratingly, I couldn't see why Brian Wilson had chosen them, how he'd thought to go from that chord to this one, and how on earth it all managed to sound so good. There were people who could make something like "Surf's Up," I decided—people with talent—and there were people like me who could only appreciate it. But at least I had that. I could appreciate "Surf's Up" so hard. I could live on the way that music made me feel, its endless unfurling of emotion and possibility, like a private magic carpet I could ride into my future.

I shuddered. "Surf's Up" was clearly a bad idea. If I was going to go this personal, it should at least be relatable to my audience. So I started over with the ultimate college band: Neutral Milk Hotel.

"The King of Carrot Flowers Pt. One"

I discovered *In the Aeroplane Over the Sea* as a teenager, when an internet friend burned me a copy on a shiny gold CD-R and sent it to me in the mail. I can still see its Sharpie scrawl: "NMH" was all it said. The absence of artwork or liner notes rendered the music even more magical, more mysterious, like finding some dazzling treasure in an unmarked cardboard box.

I spent my senior year obsessed with the album, desperate to talk about it with someone, anyone beyond the primitive message boards I could access only when my brother wasn't tying up the phone line. That this desperation was mirrored thematically by the album, a visceral treatise on the human need for connection, only intensified my experience of it. As did my family's wholehearted hatred of the album—a shared joke that bothered me more than I let on. "Nobody on this album has any idea how to play their instrument, including the singer," my mom used to say, and oh, how they'd laugh. (Every time *In the Aeroplane Over the Sea* lands on one of those "Best of" lists, which is often—*Rolling Stone*'s Best Albums of the '90s, *Pitchfork*'s Greatest All-Time—a tiny idiot inside me crows victoriously.) The lyrics are dense and intense, drawing inspiration from *The Diary of Anne Frank* and singer Jeff Mangum's traumatic childhood, but shot through with moments so tender and beautiful, they make all the darkness worth it. It was just what I needed as a teenager, even though I had no trauma to speak of beyond a persistent invisibility. (Anyone else have a sports hero for a brother? It takes a surprising amount of family effort to prop up that kind of muscular talent: driving to neighboring counties for games, quizzing him on the playbook, saving for gear. My thing was academics, which required very little of anyone else.)

Through sheer force of will, I did eventually get my only friend to like *In the Aeroplane Over the Sea.* Sandy was sharp and curious and

"The King of Carrot Flowers Pt. One"

My only childhood friend, Sandy, was sharp and curious but saddled with strict Korean parents who barely let her out of the house. Our friendship had been arranged like a marriage by grade school teachers who didn't know what to do with either of us, and persisted over the years as alternatives failed to present themselves.

One of my clearest high school memories is the time just before graduation when she called me up to tell me she liked the first track of *In the Aeroplane Over the Sea,* "The King of Carrot Flowers Pt. One." I'd been trying to get her into the album for months. I talked at her nonstop for an hour. I told her it was the third-best song on the album but still a solid choice. I told her the phrase "carrot flowers" referred to real carrots carved into flower shapes, like my mom used to make as decorative garnishes on party platters; the king of carrot flowers was a child who excelled at making them.

"Hmm," Sandy said into the phone. "Based on the nature setting of the other lines in the verse, I would think he meant the real wildflowers that grow from the tops of carrots when they are mature."

It was obvious. "Oh my god. I'm so stupid."

"Stupid people don't get into Berkeley," she said. I had just gotten the acceptance letter.

I stood and wrapped myself up in the coils of the phone cord. "I'm not ready, Sandy! What if I say something like that at a party, at college?" I was half joking, or pretending to be. "I need more time!"

"That's, like, the ninth dumb thing I've heard you say in twelve years of friendship," she said. "Divided by four years, that means you'll probably say three dumb things at college. Not enough to be statistically significant."

Sandy was the best. We lost touch swiftly after high school.

At college, I discovered that parties were not places where people discussed "The King of Carrot Flowers"; parties were sonically aggressive affairs at which music's essential role was forcing people to shout to be heard. It wasn't until I started working at record stores that I met Neutral Milk Hotel fans. I liked to tell my co-workers the story of how I'd thought the carrot flowers were garnishes, expecting to have a laugh about it, expecting it to launch us all into tales of what the song meant to us—how it eased the domestic tensions we absorbed in our youth by projecting them into the most extreme, colorful drama; how it made sex feel like a deep spring of joy and purpose awaiting us in adulthood. But almost invariably, people would say they'd never thought about the carrot flowers at all and had no opinion on the matter.

By this point I was embarrassing even myself. Whatever vacancy I'd seen for myself in this scene, I knew this was the wrong way to enter it—too gooey, too vulnerable. I saved the document with an inconspicuous name and buried it in an Archives folder, in case Megan borrowed my laptop, then banged out a slight, lighthearted piece about an obscure No Doubt song that had nothing to do with my life. I knew this carried its own risk, to write about a mainstream band, but this was the kind of rebellion that suited me.

It was getting late now; only the hard-core students remained in the reading area, the ones who had covered every inch of their desk area with open books and unpacked pencil cases. I stood to unplug my laptop.

But then I sat down again. I dug up the hidden document, dimming the exposure on my screen so low I could barely read it myself. I didn't even bother to change names.

"The King of Carrot Flowers Pt. One"

Neil and I worked together at Amoeba Music. A recent grad with a nine-to-five schedule, he seemed stuck, socially, between the undergrads and the elders of the place. One day we found ourselves in the break room alone together while he went on and on, as usual, about songs he hated. He loved to talk about how "Let It Be" was sentimental pseudo-religious pap, an opinion he spouted with a frequency that would suggest he was the first person ever to have it. And then he had the gall to attack *In the Aeroplane Over the Sea*.

"Overrated," he said, after lifting the top of my Discman and dropping it quickly, disappointed by its predictable contents. "Their first album was better."

"Congratulations, you have a stupid opinion," I said, and began popping and un-popping the aluminum lid of my Peach Tea Diet Snapple. "But why? Why don't you people ever talk about *why*? How does their first album make you *feel*?"

His lips curled into a smile. "Are you the one who likes Tracy Chapman?"

"The chorus of 'Fast Car' is the most moving musical moment of the eighties. That's all I ever said about Tracy Chapman."

The lip curl moved from one side of his mouth to the other.

Neil is just a few years older than me, but he is deeply rooted in that Gen X hatred of the mainstream, an aversion as much political as it is aesthetic. It's not that I don't get this. It's just that authenticity seems to me only one metric by which to judge music, and I don't see why it should swallow all the other ones, including beauty and fun.

Anyway, Tracy Chapman has more authenticity in her little finger than half the drivel Neil worships. So does Neutral Milk Hotel, in a different way. Their songs simply can't qualify as deep cuts because of their popularity among a certain subset of collegiate, and this makes them automatically suspect to people like Neil. I personally like to pretend the phrase "deep cut" has a totally different meaning, one that has nothing to do with anyone else's opinion. How deep does it cut? How close to the bone? How long do you feel it?

"You haven't answered me," I challenged Neil.

He appeared to be considering the question for a moment, and then he leaned across the break room table and kissed me. I kissed him back as if my mouth were performing a programmed response. It was my first kiss, my first anything, but I felt nothing until later that night, when I was consumed with the bright satisfaction of having passed a difficult level in a video game. Two weeks later he introduced me as his girlfriend at a show; a week after that he allowed me to play Neutral Milk Hotel while he took my virginity, or attempted to, until I pushed him off in the middle of the act ("Communist Daughter," second verse, searing pain). I ran from his apartment without my underpants and never went back to Amoeba on a weekday.

Fight the Power

Joe burned me a disc of his other songs, mostly fragments, and we arranged to meet at his house on a Tuesday night to discuss them. From his front porch I heard loud hip-hop; I had to bang on the door with my full forearm.

"Did not take you for a hip-hop guy," I said as I entered.

I sat down and he went to get us beers. Then he perched on the futon's arm, turned the volume down enough for us to talk, and before I knew it my hip-hop confession had come tumbling out of me: I didn't get it, I needed melody, I was too distracted by liberal guilt to enjoy the parts of it I did like. This was a more acceptable thing to say back then, but it was still extremely uncool. And I went all the way: all those white boys in my high school dressing in FUBU, I said, calling their cheerleader girlfriends "bitches," then going home to McMansions bought with inherited wealth from social programs that excluded Black people—it made me cringe, I said.

Joe's eyes shifted upward; if not quite an eye roll, it was eye roll adjacent. "Don't you think hip-hop artists would rather have your twelve bucks for the CD than your guilt?"

I didn't know what to say. Yes, obviously.

The truth was, I just didn't like hip-hop. But I didn't like a lot of music. I'd take hip-hop any day over techno, or ambient, or death metal, or prog rock, or most jazz, or most country. I didn't even like a lot of the greats—Elvis sang songs that bored me; Sinatra sounded like the smug jerk he surely was, showing off over a bunch of blaring, flatulent horns.

Joe was smiling now, letting me off the hook. "I was one of those hip-hop boys, freshman year. Could barely keep my jeans up."

"No way."

He picked up an acoustic and rested it on his knee as if for comfort. "I wouldn't have cared what you thought about it. My mom was dead, I hated school. Hip-hop felt right to me."

I tried to square this image with the even-tempered, fingerpicking guitarist in front of me. "How'd you get into Berkeley, if you hated high school?"

"Zoe," he said simply. "She wanted to go here, and I wanted to be with her. We took all the same classes at junior college and she helped me. Like, a lot. She still does. She's the only reason I'm here, and definitely the only reason I'm a poli-sci major."

He turned the volume back up as the next song started. "Fight the Power": I recognized it from the famous Spike Lee movie. "At least you didn't go the Rage Against the Machine route," I said loudly.

"Oh, I had that phase too," he said.

"No!"

"It didn't last long—I segued into goth once I met Zoe. But Percy, this is Public Enemy." He turned to the stereo and irritation flashed on his face. Finally: I'd been wondering when my shovel would hit that metal. I shut up and listened.

The production was thick with layers, samples, and shuffling funk rhythms, more of an explosion than a song. At this volume, I could feel shrapnel on my skin. It bounced off the high ceilings of the old house, the dark and dusty crown molding, filling every ounce of empty space. The final, famous verse slayed me: Elvis and John Wayne name-checked as racists, "Don't Worry, Be Happy" reframed as an Uncle Tom jam. When it finished, Joe hit the power button with his toe and it was dead quiet in the house. I heard a keyboard clacking in a roommate's room.

"Amazing," I said. "I hear echoes of—"

He stood up abruptly and faced me, holding the guitar. "I don't want you to analyze 'Fight the Power.' I just want to tell you something, which is that when you're fourteen and the worst thing happens, there's a lot of rage. When your dad starts drinking and you're an only child, there's fear too. There's fear, and rage, and very little giving a shit. I was erupting, like this gigantic, ridiculous volcano of emotion. I needed music that matched it."

I couldn't think of the right thing to say. "I get it," I said finally. "That was a volcano of a song."

I tried to say the rest with my face: I'm so sorry that happened to you, you sweet, beautiful boy. But he just stood there holding his guitar by its neck, suspended parallel to his body. He was wearing an oversized button-down made of some stiff synthetic material and he looked like David Byrne in his big jacket, in that moment, towering in his vulnerability.

"You're weird," I said carefully, "but I don't get rage from you."

"It's still there," he said, and his expression finally lightened. "Mostly in the sense that I don't care. Zoe gets all worked up about grades, about Bush, about her zine. And some part of me always thinks: Your mom could die at any minute. Fucking *chill*."

Yes, this was Joe's brand of chill. I hadn't been able to define that wiry, intense easiness. It was not naïve chill, not people-pleasing chill—it was Your Mom Could Die Chill.

"If the rage is manageable now, it's because of music," he said. "Because of good music that made me feel okay, even when there was a monster inside of me. And sorry to be talking about myself for an hour, but I want you to know this—it's maybe even why I had my high school music blasting when you showed up, come to think of it—God, am I being insane? Does it sound like I'm about to say something really massive?"

"Kind of?"

"Sorry. I'm not." A hand went up in the hair. "I want my music to be good." His face flooded with color; he looked down at the floor as if that would make it less noticeable. "I don't have any other options. I suck at everything else."

I felt an impulse to argue with this—he was smart, he was young, etc.—but I held it back. It occurred to me he might not be getting the best grades.

"The problem is, it's not always easy for me to know what's good, when it's my own stuff. All I know is 'Somebody Said' is the best thing I've written—I'm sure of that, I've never been so sure of anything. And it makes me think I . . . I need your help."

"I'm not a songwriter," I said.

"You don't need to write. Just react. Do what you did with 'Somebody Said.' "

I felt myself smiling. "Okay."

We worked all night. We drank coffee with heaping spoonfuls of sugar. I started by telling him which fragments I liked best and why—I had retained enough from my mom's piano lessons to speak the language of music, albeit with a child's proficiency—and then opened the spigot on my opinions as he worked. He had absorbed some confusing music theory from a handful of three-inch tomes on his bookshelf with names like *How Music Really Works,* all of them swollen and shaggy with Post-its, and he would use this knowledge to explain some beautiful choices and also to defend some extremely questionable ones.

"But I wanted to do the sixth with the diminished chord!" he'd say.

"But it clashes with what the song is saying here."

"But what you're proposing is less interesting!"

"But it works."

He'd play it my way on the keyboard and the guitar and then the keyboard again. Finally he'd plug it into Cakewalk on his desktop, just to prove me wrong, while I did some of Megan's yoga stretches on the floor or read his CD booklets.

"Damn," he'd say, playing it back, realizing I was right. (Not always. Sometimes I made a fool of myself with musically illiterate suggestions; some things he refused to change, trusting his gut more than me. These moments felt initially devastating, but he was so casual about them, moving on before I had a chance to dwell—plus I felt buoyed by our victories, by each time the song would suddenly, in a single tectonic shift, become better.)

At one a.m. a roommate came into the living room and announced in a huff that he was going to his girlfriend's. Joe promised to make it up to him, something about donuts from Oakland.

We had turned his fragments into two almost-songs when I noticed the window had lightened. I became, at the sight of the dawn, crushingly tired. I had Shakespeare at ten-thirty.

"Come with me to get donuts," Joe said, putting the computer to sleep. "Then I'll drive you home."

Outside the air was bluish and unreal. The streetlights were still on, accomplishing nothing. As soon as we found his roommate's car parked four blocks away, I curled up in the passenger seat and rested my head on the seat belt strap.

"Oh, hell no," Joe said as he turned onto Telegraph. "Talk to me. Keep me awake."

"But I'm cozy," I murmured.

"Remember twelve hours ago or whatever at the beginning of this night, when I gave you that speech about Public Enemy—God, was I standing?"

"Yes. The whole time. And holding your guitar like this." I held my arm out.

He laughed. "Well, give me your speech. What's your high school story?"

"I just existed," I said, yawning. "Nobody died. I had one friend, but her parents were strict so I was alone a lot. There was a tendency for people to be"—I used my hands to show opposing magnetic force—"repelled. By me."

He leaned over the steering wheel and looked intently out the window as if he were having a conversation with the road. "And this was in Indiana?"

"Yeah. Madison. Small town on the river."

"One of those places with racists and big-box stores?"

"No. I mean, yes, racists, but historical charm. My mom would never live somewhere ugly. She's a snob."

"No way."

"Yeah, she—oh, you're kidding. Hah."

"Sorry."

"It's okay. I don't see myself as a snob, but I get what you mean."

He glanced at me, seemed reassured by whatever he saw. "What do people do there?"

"My dad makes car parts at a factory. He works hard." I tried to think of what else people did in my hometown, but instead my brain served up an image of my mom scrubbing a spot on our Formica counter with a sponge, then switching to her fingernail. "So does my mom."

"Were you poor?"

"Only moderately, in the context of our town. In fifth grade my dad got promoted to manager—that was the year I got real Keds."

"Hah. My dream was Reebok Pumps."

I smiled, remembering the way a certain type of pubescent boy would crouch down to his shoes, pump up the tongues with a toss of his hair. "Did you ever get them?"

"No. I always managed to get tapes and CDs, though."

"Me too. I got a job at the Dairy Queen to support that habit. The high point of my year would be my brother's games in Louisville or Indianapolis—I'd have my parents drop me off at the HMV and blow my whole check."

"Okay, so, here's my question," he said. "Why? Why'd you get so into music?"

"I didn't get into music," I said. "People who work at Amoeba, they got into music. My mom got into music. I got into songs."

"Mmm. I like that." He drove quietly for a minute and then he tapped my thigh lightly with the back of his hand. "You haven't answered me. Why? Was it your snobby mom? Dad a jerk?"

I laughed. "You think bad parenting is the only reason people love songs?"

"Well—" He laughed too. "Maybe? I mean *really* love songs. There's got to be a driving force."

My eyelids were a heavy curtain above the sky, which was white now with morning fog. I could still sense the presence of his hand; he must have rested it on the edge of the passenger seat. "I think songs gave me a window into a magical life," I said. "Something bigger, or whatever, waiting out there. And I felt like the only way to get there was through the songs. Like the songs, if I listened hard enough, would show me how to get it right."

"Get what right?"

I let my eyes close, feeling the rumble of the car, the heat of his upturned palm near my leg.

"This."

Total Hate '95

The first time I heard Zoe's loud, lispy voice was on my answering machine, when she invited me to a *Ring Finger* meeting. I went to her apartment at the appointed time, the night before everyone left for Thanksgiving. She lived in one of those boxy '70s buildings with sliding-glass doors and bikes on the balcony. The idea was to use the long weekend to work on our contributions for the next issue, but I'd come prepared with my No Doubt piece, the printout still warm in my Dickies bag. I wore my thick-soled Mary Janes because they were the closest thing I had to platforms.

Zoe greeted me warmly. "Joey loves you!" she said in that voice. If there was any complexity behind this statement, any resentment, it didn't show. We hugged, and I smelled the astringent hair product keeping two tangled mounds of hair high on her head.

She sat on a black tufted couch and two girls alighted beside her. Each wore a heavy studded belt on low-slung pants. Another girl and I found spots on scattered pieces of IKEA furniture. Joe wasn't there; it was later revealed he'd gone to San Francisco to see a friend's band. Everyone discussed their travel plans for the long weekend, their one- or two- or six- or seven-hour drives. When I said I'd be staying in town, there was an awkward silence, like they were trying to figure out how to express sympathy without sounding condescending. It occurred to me in this moment that the printout in my bag might actually be quite terrible.

When it was my turn, I handed it to Zoe, hoping nobody noticed my shaking hand. The two girls next to her on the futon bent their heads next to hers, and the third scrambled to the arm of the couch, peering over their shoulders.

No Doubt Is Fucking Good

Oh shut up. I'm tired of being impressed by how much you hate No Doubt. Because before she was a red-carpet gazillionaire Gwen Stefani was fucking rad, with a voice like an ambulance siren and the stage presence of a prehistoric beast. Take "Total Hate '95," from the self-released album *The Beacon Street Collection,* whose cover appears to feature a black-and-white photo of Phil Collins swallowing a bright yellow canary and should thereby prove my point that this band is magnificent, no? PHIL COLLINS SWALLOWING A CANARY. Think of the implications. (There are probably no implications.) (I am also not positive it's Phil Collins.)

"Total Hate '95" features a classic ska breakdown sung by Bradley Nowell, pre–heroin overdose, of the band Sublime. I KNOW I KNOW YOU HATE SUBLIME EVEN MORE THAN YOU HATE NO DOUBT. And his part does include the line "Sublime rockin' No Doubt stylie," which is indefensible. (Doesn't it seem impossible that someone with a heroin addiction could say "stylie"?) But listen to those horns. Listen to Gwen fucking owning this whole giant mess of musicians, the control in her voice, the rich contempt. Listen to all the guitars in the chorus, a descending seesaw of the crunchiest chords that make even me want to mosh, and I am not a mosher, never been a mosher, my boobs are too big.

Listen to something unexpected for once, something uncool, far from the college playlists. Listen just
for yourself.

Listen to the great big beautiful FUN of it all. Ska
was the fun side of punk, the reverse image of grunge,
and of course MTV chewed it up until it was a big
shiny wad of flavorless gum on the underside of a picnic table, but let us not forget the fresh stick it once
was. Please. Get your hands on this song somehow and
play it loud, pogoing on your childhood bed until your
hair is filled with popcorn ceiling, please.

The girl on the arm of the couch looked up. "Uh, okay. Aren't we
more, like, underground than No Doubt?"

Zoe considered this. "I think she addressed that in the first sentence."

The girl glanced down and rolled her eyes. "Fine. Still. The whole
tone just feels weirdly . . . corporate?"

"I said fucking three times," I said, trying to keep my voice light.

She gave me a side-eye. "Okay, I'm not trying to be a cunt here,
but just the fact that you said that. Like who cares how many times
you said fucking?" She looked down the length of the couch for
agreement.

But Zoe's eyes were on the page. "She's calling us out, though. I
like the flippant attitude, the all-caps freakouts, the energy of it. It's
different for us."

The consensus aligned with Zoe, as I sensed it often did. She
nodded and stuck the paper into a folder.

"Any notes, going forward?" I said. "Longer, shorter?"

She looked at the girls, then back at me. "It's a little slight. Silly,
even. Fine for now, but you can go meatier next time."

"I would love to go meatier," I said, and our eyes locked for a
minute. My obsession with your boyfriend is largely platonic, I said
telepathically. I swear she nodded slightly.

. . .

It was my first time skipping my family's Thanksgiving, having finally achieved a level of stability at school that revealed flying home to be the waste of time and money it had always been. I had told my parents that Megan had invited me to her house in Sacramento, leaving out the minor detail that I'd turned the offer down.

It wasn't a terrible Thanksgiving. I blasted music and ate cereal out of unwashed bowls. I made my way through Megan's collection of magazines and *Sex and the City* DVDs, consuming them simultaneously with the tiny portion of my brain required for each. And I worked on my next column for *Ring Finger*. In order to go "meatier" without sliding into the navel-gazing attempts I'd hidden in my Archives folder, I was trying to layer in more sociopolitical commentary—not my specialty, but I'd absorbed enough from two years at Berkeley to push out a subtly pro-Nader piece on Sonic Youth that did not, looking back, age well.

My mom called me on speakerphone in the lull between dinner and pie. She and my dad ranked the turkey against the turkeys of years past, apparently for my benefit, and my brother detailed the various affronts that had been made to the house in our absence: A sewing table in the living room! A duck-shaped throw pillow on the couch! I feigned indignance, playing our long-standing game of uniting against our parents on inconsequential matters just to have something to talk about. He and my dad were being good, sitting at the table instead of the couch, but they were clearly listening to some big game because I was in the middle of describing the incongruously warm weather in Berkeley when they gasped in unison and scraped their chairs away. Mom took me off speakerphone.

"Get any gossip?" I asked, referring to my brother, who was a serial monogamist at the southern college where he played football.

"The Victoria's Secret salesgirl has gone past tense, but I didn't ask for details," she said. "How's school? Did you get that *Hamlet* paper back?"

"Yeah. A."

"Ah." She was always miffed when I didn't get an A-plus, disappointed not in me but in the professor's inability to recognize her daughter's genius. "Should you put Megan's mother on the phone, maybe? So I can thank her?"

I knew this wasn't a real offer—she was just waiting for me to say no, that's not necessary—but it made me feel caught anyway. "I didn't go, in the end."

"Honey!"

"It sounded more awkward than staying here sounded lonely."

She paused, then said, "I understand that." I knew she would.

The day after Thanksgiving, Joe and Zoe called with orders to come visit their suburb. "Not optional," Zoe piped into the receiver Joe was holding.

I wrote down the name of the train stop and began ping-ponging around the apartment, getting halfway dressed before remembering I needed to shower, applying makeup and then wiping it off. On the way there I listened to "Total Hate '95" on my Discman to psych myself up, and it worked: I felt an amount of excitement that bordered on the absurd.

From the platform at the station I could see them in the parking lot, sitting on the hood of an old sedan, smoking. The lot was framed by blue glass walls of office parks, low purple mountains in the distance. I imagined growing up with such easy access to Oakland and San Francisco and felt both jealous and disdainful. It seemed too easy.

I clattered down the cement steps so fast I tripped, but nobody saw. My black jeans absorbed the blood from my knee politely.

They drove me around to chain restaurants and donut shops and the 7-Eleven where they had spent their Saturdays pouring vodka into partially consumed Snapples. The streets were so wide they felt like freeways. The conversation kept returning to whether

Joe should do a set at some open mic (Zoe was anti, not wanting to see the crowd of high school friends that would be there; I was pro, with the motive of seeing Joe sing "Somebody Said" for an audience). In a booth at Macaroni Grill, Zoe told Joe about my column.

"My favorite part was when you said you can't mosh because your boobs are too big," she said, spooling spaghetti around a fork. "I'm hoping you do more of that stuff—that's what zine culture is all about." She had a way of going concave when she talked, her shoulders leaning into her words to give them more force, her sternum receding. "Telling our own stories. Things people can't know unless they're in your life, in your body."

Joe nodded. "I definitely have never thought about how it would feel to mosh with boobs."

"Me neither!" Zoe said, laughing.

"Boobs hurt," I said. We were all talking loudly over the noise in the place, which was packed with a mix of families and middle-aged couples in their date-night finest. "Why does nobody ever talk about this? I have been made aware of the pain a man feels when he's kicked in the nuts since I was probably seven."

A teenage-boy waiter arrived to deliver our second round of specialty cocktails, which were startlingly bright, each a different primary color (mine was red and tasted like Robitussin).

"Exactly!" Zoe said. She felt herself up, causing the waiter, who was clearing our first round, to blush into his acne. "Even mine hurt right now, but that's because of where I am in my cycle."

"Fat week?" I said, and Zoe nodded. "I'm in skinny week."

" 'Fat week'?" Joe said.

The waiter paused as if waiting for an answer, then scampered off.

"We get all bloated and our boobs swell," she explained, then turned back to me. "Although I'm increasingly taking issue with the way we refer to the miracle of ovulation through a male gaze. You know every time you talk about your body like that, you're playing into the capitalist patriarchy's hands, right?"

My brain reeled. This kind of question would become standard a couple decades later, when the world caught up to Zoe Gutierrez, but it was brand-new to me then. Even the "fat week/skinny week" terminology had been new to me, picked up from Megan just days earlier; I was showing off my college-girl talk. The truth was I rarely thought about my body at all, let alone spoke about it. I saw Joe's eyes flick up from his plate to my chest, so quickly he thought he got away with it.

"To be fair," I said, straightening, "why do you think our boobs swell while we're ovulating? All of human physiology is built for the male gaze."

Zoe pretended to choke on her pasta. "Jesus, what are you saying?"

"I'm saying I like to argue when I drink," I said.

"Are you a constitutional originalist too?"

"I'm a constitutional McCartneyist."

Joe leaned in. "As in, Paul over John?"

I made a face. "I hate being asked to choose, like they're New Kids on the Block or something. Talk about playing into capitalism. That attitude sells merch, but it has nothing to do with music. They're both geniuses who made each other better in ways we'll never know—"

"But you just said McCartney's in your *constitution*," he said.

"I think I said I would interpret the constitution through the lens of McCartney."

We watched each other enjoy the absurdity of this idea.

"If we're back on music," Zoe said, pushing aside her plate, "I have to say, No Doubt still sucks. I'm sorry, but I listened to that 'Total Hate' song and it made me throw up in my mouth."

"That's cool," I said. "Do you think that's because you have no taste, or . . . ?"

Joe whooped.

"Or maybe because that song is fun, and you take yourself too seriously?" I said. "Just spitballing here."

Zoe sat back, her eyes narrowing under her painted black lids. "You are truly annoying, Percy."

"I know," I said. I took a slurp of my cocktail. "Don't worry, I hate myself."

"I don't hate you," she said.

"Me neither," Joe said. "I love you, actually."

"I'm just annoyed by you sometimes," Zoe finished, shooting Joe a look I couldn't decipher. "There's a difference."

"I'm mostly annoying when I talk about music," I said, shrugging. I was drunker than the two of them, who'd been trading off driving duties. "But that's also when I'm at my best, so."

Zoe tilted her head at this, then surprised me with a considered nod. "Bit of a dilemma," she said. She held my gaze for a long second and then laughed.

I thought about saying I love you too Joe—the words were ready and waiting, banging on the roof of my mouth to get out; I would say them in a jokey tone, just like he had, no big deal—but I was too scared of ruining what was happening. I couldn't believe I hadn't ruined it already, that they were both still smiling at me, their faces warm, open, wanting more.

We ended up at the open mic. It was a sprawling bar pretending to be a dive, wood-framed velvet paintings tacked on the wall at intentionally disheveled angles. There seemed to be an informal reunion of old friends in town for the holiday. Joe was swallowed by tall-people arms, and Zoe pulled me into an alcove by the bathroom with one round table and a lone chair.

She sat on the table and pointed at the chair. "Sit with me."

"Why?" I peered out at the crowd. He seemed more comfortable around these people than he did at Berkeley. I wanted to be out there, observing him in his habitat. But I sat in the chair.

"Everyone loves him, but he doesn't love them back. He just pretends to. Lately I can't stomach it."

"He was popular in high school, huh?" I said. "It's actually impossible for me to imagine what that would be like."

She swung her feet a few times, boots kicking the wall behind us, then looked down the length of her nose at me. "You can have him if you want."

I swallowed. A hot clang in my groin.

"I'm serious," she said. "Not now, but when we break up."

I didn't know where to start. What? Why? When? "How do you know he wants me?" I finally asked.

She rolled her eyes. "Come on," she said. "You're his musical soulmate, and you're cute. Dudes aren't that complicated."

I peered into the main room, where someone's set was ending to distracted applause. Joe was standing against the back wall with his acoustic strapped on, waiting. I felt the urge to run to him, to seize my chance—like it would be too late once all these people had seen him sing.

Zoe was watching me with a knowing look. "Don't be intimidated," she said. "His bar is pretty low after five years dating a dyke."

I stood. What had she said?

"Sit down," she said. "This is why I hate telling girls, they always think I want to make out. Do you want to make out with every guy you know?"

I became unbearably thirsty, my mouth gluey with the residue of suburban drinks. Joe was stepping up to the mic. "Why haven't you told him?"

She sighed. "I promised him I'd never leave him. I know what that sounds like, but . . . you'll see, if you stick around long enough. You'll get to know him."

"I'm sure he doesn't appreciate being lied to, though?"

"I'm not lying," she said hotly. "I've been on my own journey too, dude. Last year I told him I was bi, to which he was like, 'Cool, whatever.' Then in the summer I basically told him his dick makes my skin crawl, and he was like, 'Okay, let's snuggle.'"

A weird burp of a laugh escaped my mouth.

"Recently, finally, the *Ring Finger* girls started talking and it got back to him, which was . . . clarifying, I guess."

Somebody said you said it was over. "So he does know," I said, understanding.

"It's just a matter of sawing off the limb. I said we'd wait until he was ready—first it was going to be after Thanksgiving, now we're saying after winter break. You know his dad is a shit show, right? Real classic alcoholic. Joey spends holidays at my house, most weekends too. I can't keep doing that once we break up. I've been very clear about that. But it's hard." She leaned back against the wall, looking suddenly tired. "It's like I'm orphaning him."

All this information was making me claustrophobic. "I'm getting water," I said, and left the alcove.

Joe was on a small stage in the corner of the main room, midway through a gorgeous song that I thought for a staggering moment was an original, until I overheard someone identify it for a friend as "Strangers" by the Kinks. I stood by the water station and watched. His voice sounded a bit timid, but still managed to rain all over the place, clean and cool. He had given up trying to extend the mic higher and resorted to stooping. People were listening more than they'd listened to the last singer, although that wasn't saying much.

Zoe came up beside me and tucked my hair behind my ear so she could speak directly into it: "You've been good for him," she said, as he transitioned into the opening to "Somebody Said." "Thank you."

This bothered me, like I was a stuffed animal handed to a child in crisis. "I mean, I also helped him write this song," I said. "Maybe thank me for that."

"Oh fuck off, Percy," she said, and refilled my water glass for me.

We went back to Zoe's parents' garage with a six-pack and Luke Skinner, a long-haired dude in a Metallica shirt. He seemed to be a vague acquaintance, judging by the fact that they called him only by his full name, but he'd made an impression on Joe that night when he'd bragged about spending eight hours a day practicing guitar while Joe wasted his life at college. Zoe and I played ping-pong while Joe sat on an old blanket-covered couch and watched Luke Skinner perform what I realized was an audition, strumming capably on an unplugged Telecaster. When he ripped into the lead riff from the Pixies' "Here Comes Your Man" and maintained it for a full song length without rushing or fumbling, Joe turned to look at me over the back of the couch. I nodded.

Luke Skinner tried to turn the night into an inaugural jam with his new bandmate, but Zoe wasn't having it and sent him home on Joe's old skateboard. We watched him from the open garage as he sailed down the hill, wind lifting his hair above the guitar on his back. Joe's eyes were bright.

By this point I had missed the last train, so we all slept together in Zoe's childhood bedroom. Without much discussion I took the floor and the two of them shared the bed. But when I woke up, I found I had been moved to the bed with Zoe, and Joe was in my spot on the floor, apparently attacked by chivalry in the middle of the night. He was stretched out on his back in a holey undershirt and boxers, his mouth partly open. The boxers had tiny Christmas trees on them.

I made my way to the bathroom and rummaged through a medicine cabinet for Advil. Through the thin wood-paneled door I could hear CNN—hanging chads, Broward County—and Zoe's parents making coffee. Her mom was Jewish, but her dad was Mexican, and I had spotted a decorative crucifix in the living room. The whole house teemed with layered, nonsensical clutter; in a basket on the bathroom counter, for example, I could see a pamphlet about state parks, a small bag of safety pins, and an old five-by-seven photograph, unframed and creased in the middle. It comforted me, this mess. It made the house feel like a proper family lived here, one with better things to do than clean.

"Joey likes it black now," I heard Zoe's dad say through the bathroom door.

"Since when?" came the mom's reply. "He used half-and-half last time. I'll run to the store."

I plucked the photo out of the basket. A younger Joe and Zoe stood in front of the mantel holding up their Christmas stockings, still full—lottery scratchers stuck out of the tops of each, a rolled-up poster in Joe's. Zoe was wearing a *Nevermind* T-shirt and plaid pajama bottoms, and hadn't yet come into her punk look; her hair hung straight and black to her collarbones. Joe was smiling with a teenager's self-awareness, eyes mid-blink, a zit on his chin so big I could feel the ache of it. I was starting to piece together the timeline: after his mom's death, Joe had survived for a year while his dad spiraled; then he'd gotten together with Zoe and become, effectively, a Gutierrez. An uninformed observer of the photograph would've thought they were siblings.

I slid the picture back into the basket and washed my face, then stared at myself in the mirror. I was cute, Zoe had said. Was it true? I wasn't completely oblivious, like that girl you see in movies who inexplicably perceives herself to be a bridge-dwelling troll when actually she's Molly Ringwald—I knew I was neither, and probably closer to Molly than the troll. But I had factors working against me when it came to guys: I was obnoxious, I was inexperienced, I didn't play the game. And I'd never zeroed in on any one style, as Zoe had done so well in the years since this photograph, which made me feel recessive in the context of my peers, a vague smear of a girl. But maybe Joe saw me clearly, the way some people can look at an abstract painting and instantly discern the figure. Maybe it was actually going to happen for me. I shuddered with happiness and a splitting headache.

Funny Strange

The rest of the semester passed slowly, but it was a good slow—it was the way I suspected time was always intended to pass. It feels like a calendar error, when I think about it now, that there were only a few weeks between that night in the suburbs and the end of that year. Most weeknights, Zoe and I met at one of a handful of local coffee shops named after Italian cities, studying and talking and eating stale muffins for dinner, while Joe did the grunt work of building a band: teaching his songs to Luke Skinner, posting flyers for drummers and bassists in Amoeba with his number on tear-away strips, auditioning all the randoms who called, securing a shared practice space in Oakland. Around ten or eleven he'd meet up with us and download on the latest: who was sounding good, who was sounding bad, when they might be ready for shows.

I waitressed on Friday nights and Sunday brunches, collecting my tips in an envelope I kept under my mattress; I usually had enough to cover rent by the middle of the month. Joe worked at a frozen yogurt shop for minimum wage until I got him a job at the diner by lying to my boss about his experience, then covering for his mistakes once he started. Zoe often came in for the last hour of our shifts, drinking coffee and studying at the counter while we balanced the register. And then we went out.

It's hard to say where we went. My memories are vague on context, usually in transit or sitting on stoops, occasionally at shows or poetry slams or parties full of people we ignored. Sometimes eating fries and veggie burgers (I had eased into their vegetarianism without fanfare) at Irish bars. There were other people around—the *Ring Finger* girls, Joe's roommates, Megan—but we had the most fun, the easiest time, as a threesome.

We each had our roles. Joe the engine, me the contrarian. Zoe the grounded one, actually well-rounded, though given to bursts of irritation with us both. She was eager to moderate when the conversation became too musical, probably to exert some control in an area where she had less to contribute, and liked to give us conversational assignments.

For example, one late weekend night while waiting in the bathroom line at a co-op party, Joe and I were talking about the title of the new Microphones album (*It Was Hot, We Stayed in the Water*) when Zoe barked, "Favorite album title."

"*Genocide and Juice,*" Joe said soberly.

I went for humor to balance him out. "*CrazySexyCool,* TLC," I said. "Left Eye was crazy, T-something was sexy, Chilli was cool. Plus it was one word, you guys. But with capitals."

Zoe laughed and gave Joe the point, poking her thumb in his direction. "Chilli was sexy. *Worst* album title."

I clapped with excitement. "*Songs in the Key of Life,* Stevie Wonder!"

"Oh my god," Joe said. "I've never thought about how stupid that is."

Zoe made a face. "That's just because you guys are white. White people can't handle things being obvious."

"What are you talking about, we're the most obvious," I said. "We invented country music."

"Did we, though?"

I paused. "Probably not."

"Even if we did, it wasn't white university students," Zoe said, nodding down the hall at a circle of hacky sackers. "It was white people who were impoverished. It takes privilege to think some-thing's cheesy."

"Here we go," I said. "The millionaire who said imagine no pos-sessions."

Joe gave me a look that said he knew this was an Elvis Costello reference and we would discuss it later, but Zoe was pissed. "I'm not a millionaire!" she said.

"You're the only one here whose bedroom has a door on it."

"You guys will never stop punishing me for that door."

"Shut up!" Joe said, pulling his hair. "How am I supposed to think when you're charging everything with cultural context?"

"Speaking of TLC," I said, pivoting to distraction tactics. "Did you know they got the idea for 'Waterfalls' from a Paul McCartney deep cut?"

"Yes," Joe said. "I mean no, but stop talking. Okay. Okay. Thank you for that reference. Ringo Starr did a solo album called *Time Takes Time*."

I had to cross my legs to stop from peeing myself.

I know it all sounds familiar: record-store nerds and their dumb games, one-upping each other to pass the time. But it felt different to me. The goal was stream-of-consciousness riffing; any evidence of posturing or preparing was a greater sin than losing. Losing was fine, actually. Lame references were fine. That we did not process music entirely through a lens of coolness felt radical to me at the time.

Here's a better example: instead of patting each other on the back for hating "Let It Be," as they did at Amoeba, we tried to understand how "Something" managed to sound so magical despite being one of the least melodic songs on *Abbey Road*. Zoe said it was the honesty of the lyrics ("How many love songs admit that they don't know whether their love will grow, that they don't even know what it is they love about the person? It's fundamentally anti-establishment"); Joe said it was the major sevenths and ambiguous key, which matched the blurry experience of Harrison's love.

Joe and I were always working on his music, though we never

pulled another all-nighter; the songs were just always there between us, like a balloon we'd been tasked to keep afloat. On my way to work I would pass his house and leave lyric revisions taped to his door: *Don't switch tenses in the second verse, it's distracting/serves no purpose.* He attached MP3s to unrelated emails: *My friend is working the door for the Aislers Set tomorrow so we can get in free. Hey am i ripping something off with this melody?* He picked up every guitar he ever saw to play me something, at parties or thrift stores or (once, drunk) from the hands of a busker on Telegraph Avenue. If Zoe was around she would usually wander off, though sometimes I saw her watching us carefully.

I relished my role as his musical sidekick. It gave me great power without risk or accountability. I'd spout my opinions, which came easily to me, then bask in the glow of creative satisfaction.

But sometimes I took it too far. Maybe it went to my head. About a song itself, I could say anything—I could say it was derivative junk; he'd just toss it out and return days later with something new. (He was enormously prolific those first few months of our friendship; he must've written a song a week.) But sometimes my pushback slid outside of the song and onto his broader tendencies as an artist, and that was when things got sticky.

The worst was when he first showed me a song called "Funny Strange," an up-tempo jam about the apocalypse that would eventually become the title track of his band's album. We were in his house, leaning back on his futon, our feet on the coffee table between scattered beer cans and half-empty chip bags. Zoe had left early to finish a paper and he'd played the rough recording for me at max volume. It had an obvious, easy hook: "What was funny haha / Became funny stra-a-a-ange"—then he half spoke the final line with a maximum of mumblecore charm: "How long till we're laughing in our graves?" That chorus worked brilliantly, and I told him so. But I also told him that the verses, a metered list of environmental horrors, reminded me of "We Didn't Start the Fire"—a reference that, understandably, made him bristle.

And then I pushed it further:

"You always do this, when you have a great hook," I said. "You phone the rest in." I could feel the momentum of the idea forming in my head, barreling toward expression without my permission. "And if you have no hook, it's the opposite—you labor over the thing, strangle it half to death. It's always one or the other."

He stared at me, his face slowly reddening until he spat out, "And what do *you* do, when you write a great hook?" Then he stood up and left his own house, slamming the door behind him.

It was a shiv stuck in the worst place, but of course I'd asked for it. "Fuck your feelings!" I shouted at the door.

I cleaned up the beer cans just for the feeling of doing something right. After throwing them in the garbage I lingered in the kitchen awhile, imagining what it would be like to be him, shuffling around this giant house of dudes. When did the hooks come to him—as he was making coffee, going about his morning routine? I lifted the glass coffeepot, stained brown in its lower half, imagining being struck by a bolt of inspiration. When a floorboard creaked upstairs I let myself out.

I slept zero hours that night, as always happened when we had these fights. But I never apologized. By the second day my regret was always tangled up with some weird responsibility, some sense that I was playing the role he wanted me to play. We would avoid each other for however long it took for him to complete the song—usually a couple of days; he would skip class, according to Zoe, heave all his attention on to the song. Then he'd deliver his revision, showing up on my doorstep with a guitar or, in the case of "Funny Strange," leaving a disc in my mailbox. The new "Funny Strange" was infinitely, undeniably superior, the verses weirder and stumbling, more Dylan than Billy Joel. I responded with effusive praise, and our trio reunited.

But it would be a lie to say these incidents didn't leave their mark. Each one seemed to deepen a dark, murky well that sat just below the surface of our friendship. Maybe that well was normal, though,

I remember thinking. Maybe it was just the complexity of really, finally knowing someone.

One thing he never asked me about was the name of his band. He mentioned it in passing, a done deal: their newly assembled foursome, comprising all dudes, would be called Caroline. I recoiled, confused.

"*Caroline?* What kind of a band name is that? Why can't you be Joe Morrow? They're just a backing band anyway."

He shot me a look and I never mentioned it again. Of course, in this era of indie rock, it was zeitgeisty to hide behind a band; leading with yourself was for pop stars and rappers. And Zoe told me later what I probably should've figured out: Caroline was his mom's name, and this was not a subject where anyone's opinion meant anything, not even mine.

Weird Divide

The three of us planned our respective Christmas visits to be as brief as possible—I was flying home for just three and a half days, a decision my mom found so irrational she made me buy the ticket myself—which left us a solid week after finals to roam around Berkeley, unfettered by schedules. We traveled as a unit with CD wallets in tow, cycling through our roommate-free apartments, sleeping in all the beds. We piled dishes in all three of our sinks to be dealt with on December 23rd, before my ten p.m. red-eye that had come to represent the end of our year. It felt ages away, even as the days passed.

There was an unspoken edict that week to avoid TV, email, anything that felt dry and normal. Often this translated to doing things outside that would be more comfortable indoors. Comfort was low priority. There were also a few spoken rules: share everything; no talk of school or next semester; no working on music. This last one was Zoe's decree, and it gave Joe the affect of a businessman on holiday, restless at first and then deeply, increasingly relaxed.

One night we cooked an actual dinner and drank no alcohol, the novelty of which was its own thrill, and mapped out a hike for the next day in Tilden Park. In the morning we took a bus north and hiked up to a clearing where trees rolled in peaks and valleys all the way to the horizon. I felt like I was in the Alps. Nothing like this existed anywhere near Indiana. As it became clear that Joe and Zoe were used to seeing comparable or even more impressive vistas, I kept my amazement in check.

We went to bars, of course, empty except for grad students and, one time, my American Literature 1900–1945 professor, who left her table of women in gem tones to come tell me how much she'd enjoyed my final paper on *Their Eyes Were Watching God*. I asked how she'd known it was mine—there were probably a hundred kids in that class—and she said she'd had the TA point me out. I thanked her awkwardly and turned back to Joe and Zoe, who seemed stunned by the event; it took two pints of beer and a round at the jukebox before they could talk about anything else.

But the day I remember best began with eating sandwiches in the backyard of Joe's house. We brought out a boom box and the big black stack of our CD wallets. There was no furniture back there, just a rusted-out foosball table in a tangle of extremely overgrown grass. Joe put the boom box on the foosball table, pressed play, and sat ceremoniously in the grass, cross-legged. The sight of him with the grass fanning out around him was bizarre—"Lilliputian," I'd said, then had to explain Jonathan Swift to them—but we joined him, of course, a triangle of humans in a mess of nature.

We ate our peanut butter and jellies and passed around a carton of milk. Damp earthiness seeped through my jeans. There was an unusual warmth to the sun that day. I leaned back on my hands when I was done with my sandwich and looked at Joe's house, a brown-shingled beauty that appeared, from this angle, like it might topple any minute. I loved these Craftsman homes of Berkeley, especially the undisturbed, unkempt ones. They were soulful and comfortable and had all the amenities that actually make people happy, like porches and window seats, and none of the things we believed to make us happy, like open-floor plans and living rooms optimized for Super Bowl viewing. They were built for reading and close conversation. Berkeley felt like a glitch in the modern machine, back then, an alternate universe for the chosen few. Maybe this is how everyone feels about their college towns.

"Somebody play the happiest song," Zoe said.

I scrambled to my feet before Joe could beat me. I had the perfect track, from a compilation I'd found at Amoeba of '60s sunshine pop, called "To Claudia on Thursday," with a stony lyric about enjoying the moment. Joe started freaking out at how good it was. We all took off our shoes, working our toes into the matted grass. Zoe found a live worm wriggling in a broken earthenware ashtray.

"So it's a song about having fun," Zoe said from her grass-hole as the outro arrived. "Feeling present, hippie shit. Is that happiness?"

"Not really," Joe said.

"Yes," I said at the same time. I cleared my throat. "Honestly I think happiness and fun are kinda the same thing, at this point in my life."

Joe looked betrayed. "How can you say that?"

"Because having fun is new to me. You guys couldn't understand, you've been having fun your whole lives."

This was embarrassing to say out loud but neither of them reacted. I hadn't told them certain things about myself, and they seemed to have filled in these blank spaces with lighter brushstrokes. For example, they knew I'd dated that Neil guy from Amoeba, so they assumed we'd had a normal sex life; they didn't know Neil had left me a semi-virgin, that the sex had been so painful there was probably something anatomically wrong with me. They knew I'd lived in the dorms, but they didn't know I'd been spectacularly unsuited to communal living, that I'd hauled myself around those brutalist buildings in a high-functioning depression before finding my way to Megan. They knew she and I were close, but they didn't know our relationship had always felt a bit stiff, like a pair of jeans you can't wait to take off when you get home. They didn't know they were the best friends I'd ever had. How can you tell that to people you've known only a few months without sounding pathetic?

"Peace, maybe," Joe said, as a compromise. "The word 'fun' just sounds so trivial."

"I disagree," I said. "We're having fun now, and it feels profound."

"That's because this is happiness," he said. "Not just fun."

"It's just semantics," Zoe said. The *Ring Finger* girls said this all the time: "It's semantics." It annoyed me. She stood up and began flipping through the CD wallet for her turn. I tried to think of times in my life when I'd been genuinely happy in a way that didn't involve fun.

"What about when you were accepted to college?" Joe said—not the first time he'd seemed to read my mind. "What about that professor coming up to our table in a bar and basically calling you her favorite?"

"Okay, yes," I said. "Those were happy moments. But there's a dark side to that kind of happiness. There's a pressure. They feel like the universe saying, 'Great job, now don't fuck this up!' It's not as *pure* as the happiness you feel when you're having fun."

Joe didn't want to agree. "But it's also not as meaningful, right?"

"I don't know," I said. It may have been the first time I'd said those words at Berkeley. I liked how it felt.

Zoe played "I Can See Clearly Now," the version by Jimmy Cliff. Joe and I vocalized a simultaneous ecstasy at the first notes of bass.

"This one is earned happiness," Joe said during the bridge.

Zoe nodded. "And clarity. You can feel how hard he worked to get here. Like, *finally,* some bloody clarity."

I looked at Joe. He was looking at Zoe. Zoe was looking at her hands.

Joe announced his choice before he started playing it: "Everyday" by Buddy Holly. I wondered aloud if it meant something that all three of us had chosen songs from before we were born, and Zoe said happiness was better before Reagan and Thatcher.

I hadn't heard the Buddy Holly song since my parents' oldies radio and I couldn't believe how amazing it sounded. The production was startlingly minimal, fresh; some sort of glockenspiel sounded through the boom box speakers like it was right there in the yard.

"This one is optimism," I said.

"Right," Joe said. "The happiness of knowing that happiness is coming." He glanced at me briefly, then looked down into the grass, suppressing a smile. I felt an eruption of joy in my chest spreading outward so fast it made me dizzy.

We kept going all afternoon, moving up through the decades one by one, building a taxonomy of happiness. The carton of milk lost its nostalgic appeal during Lou Reed's "Perfect Day," when we switched to beer. Zoe got restless in the '80s and announced she was going home to shower. I remember protesting mightily, somewhat performatively, at this separation—the three of us hadn't been apart in several days at this point—until she promised with a laugh to be back before dark.

The '90s were tricky, but I finally found "No Diggity" ("the happiness of knowing exactly what you want," I said); Joe mined a mini-wallet he kept entirely for the Magnetic Fields, landing on the synthpop ditty "You and Me and the Moon" ("pure, sweet, simple romance").

For 2000, our brand-new decade, we had only a handful of CDs. It was getting dark—Zoe must have forgotten how early that happened now—and cold in that California way that wouldn't have been cold if you had proper clothing, but was, because you never did. We moved the boom box to the front porch, where at least we had overhead light and a wide wooden ledge to sit on. Joe brought out a scratchy wool blanket and spread it over our legs.

After much thought, I cued up "Last Days of Disco" from the new Yo La Tengo, a moody, looking-back ballad. Joe was lighting a cigarette as the song began, and he turned, mid-inhale, to look at me. I nodded, and he nodded with me.

"Lost happiness," I said.

He sent out a long stream of smoke, still nodding, and held the cigarette up to share. I took it for the intimacy, for the moment when my fingers ran up along the backs of his. He turned up the volume until it felt like the whole porch was swallowed in the atmosphere of the song, teetering amid the shuffling brush-drumming and bending guitar notes. The lyrics were about music's almost supernatural power to make you feel, but only at the whims of memory and experience: a song never made the narrator happy until he danced to it with her, and now when he hears it, much later, it makes him lonely. I had the sensation of my own memory packaging up this moment, absorbing and capturing its every element: the cold smoky air, the side of his leg against mine, the feel of his knuckles under my fingertips.

For his turn, he played "Gravity Rides Everything" by Modest Mouse. I was instantly confused, but I tried to listen carefully, determined not to ruin the moment. I stared into the blanket on our lap. Certainly the song had a positive *feel* to it.

"The happiness of knowing things will fall into place," he said during the second verse. "Right?"

The shared cigarette had ended. I shook out the last of the beer from my can into my mouth. Joe was watching me, waiting. "2000 is hard," I said.

He swore under his breath and returned the track to the beginning, then leaned forward with his elbows on his knees, listening.

"He's playing with you, when he says things will fall into place," I explained. "He means because of gravity, because of time. Flesh sags. We fall into the earth."

Joe straightened up abruptly, clapped his knees on his hands. "Why you gotta be so *sure* all the time, Percy?" he said.

"But it's better than floating away, he says!" I could see Zoe coming down the sidewalk. "He sees the beauty in it too! All things must pass!"

Zoe climbed the stoop and sat down next to us, her hair damp. "That's not exactly happiness, though. More like acceptance."

"My failure in this moment has been established," Joe said, stopping the song.

"Let's go," Zoe said. "Ethiopian tonight, I got a coupon."

Late that night I caught him breaking the rules. I'd gotten up to go to the bathroom and heard acoustic strumming coming from outside. He was sitting on the porch ledge in his boxers and peacoat, no shirt. The blanket from earlier was over his legs, although most of it had fallen off, and his marbled notebook lay open beside him. He appeared to be reworking the verses of "Funny Strange."

"I'm telling," I said from the doorway.

He looked up. "Why didn't you tell me the new verse sounds exactly like 'So It Goes' by Nick Lowe?"

I stepped outside and closed the door, shivering through my pajamas, and tried to remember the song. "Okay, I see what you mean—that sort of lagging, talky, descending melody—"

"It's pretty obvious, Perce," he said.

"Are you mad at me?"

"No," he said shortly. He stared at the page, leaned over his guitar to cross something out. "It hit me as I was falling asleep," he mumbled. "Just wish I'd known before I spent forty-seven hours getting that recording exactly right."

"Nick Lowe got a lot of that from 'Reelin' in the Years' anyway," I said. I ran the verses in my head, hugging myself for warmth. "And 'The Boys Are Back in Town,' isn't that similar?" I remembered, triumphant.

He scoffed. But I could tell he was thinking about it.

"None of those people got sued! Now come back inside before Zoe discovers this flagrant disrespect for the rules."

He ignored me and started humming a slightly tweaked melodic line, maneuvering it upward in the middle.

I watched him for a minute. I was pretty proud of myself for these two perfect references, but they had apparently won me no gold stars. "Sorry I let you down," I said petulantly.

"Shut up," he said, with a hard, dissonant strum, and then sat his guitar to the side and reached for the boom box. "I thought of a better song for 2000."

I shivered, and he pulled up the blanket, creating a space beside him on the ledge. I sat in spite of the angry strum still ringing in my head. The side of his leg radiated warmth under the blanket.

"It's called 'Weird Divide,' " he said, dropping a burned disc into the tray. "By the Shins. Got this EP at their show for five dollars."

A voice I'd never heard before began singing us a sweet, languid melody. It sounded a bit like a Beach Boys song, except new, brand-new, I'd never heard anything so new. Another looking-back song, this time a guy recalling a series of late-night strolls with a girl in his youth. The lyrics were blurred by reverb, but I caught the title line: "Far below a furry moon, our purposes crossed / The weird divide between our kinds."

Then it was over: a wispy poof of a song, under two minutes. He pressed stop. I almost asked what happened to the rest of it, but I forced my mouth shut.

He leaned back against a wide, wooden pillar. "Zoe told me she told you," he said, so quietly I almost didn't hear. I twisted to look at him. He was staring above my head, at the porch light. "Do you think we're being ridiculous?"

"No," I said, then realized I needed to say more, to explain why not. As if I knew anything. "I think . . ." I cast my mind over the song we'd just heard, then over all the songs of the day, but the only line I could find was by Stevie Nicks, and so obvious I almost didn't use it. "I think you've been afraid of changing because you've built your life around her."

His gaze dropped back onto me.

"And same with her," I added.

He squeezed his eyes shut suddenly, hard, as if experiencing some sharp pain. His lashes wettened.

"It'll be okay," I said quickly. "Time makes you bolder."

He opened his eyes, and there it was: my gold star. It was beaming out of him, the relief, the gratitude, a wash of wonder—aimed not just at Stevie for writing these lines that so gracefully justified and normalized his inertia, but also at me, for plucking them out of my brain and tossing them to him like a life raft.

"Anyway, 'Weird Divide' is perfect," I said. "The happiness of connection, right?"

He smiled. "Right."

He played it again and we sat listening together. During the second verse he leaned forward and the entire sides of our bodies were touching—thighs, hips, my left elbow resting in the curve of his forearm. Then the song ended and the moment became instantly illicit, embarrassing: we had passed back over the divide. He jerked away.

That's why the song was so short, I decided—because connection, like memories, came in the briefest of flashes.

He stood and picked up his guitar. I felt a bizarre urge to yank it from his hands and gently toss it over the edge of the porch, into the weeds below. But I just followed him silently back into the house. He disappeared up the staircase to the room he was sharing with Zoe and I crawled into his roommate's bed downstairs, under a fraying quilt that smelled of mothballs.

I replayed the day in my mind as I fell asleep, the dreamy serenity of that last song swirling in my veins. How very weird it was, the divide between Joe and me—how spiky one moment and swampy the next, then poof, just a calm, clear lake. I wondered if that was what made us feel so close sometimes. If the weirder the divide, the sweeter it was to cross.

Just Like a Woman

The split finally happened in spring: a clean break, they called it, which meant the end of our trio. Exactly a week later, it was Zoe and I who kissed.

I'd been giving them space, unsure how to help and frankly obsessed with the idea of what it all meant for me, when she invited me to study in a park. I was so relieved to hear from her, I exhaled loudly into the phone. We spread blankets on the grass and lay on our stomachs propped up on elbows. It was a warm day, bees buzzing around the open textbooks we were ignoring.

Zoe wanted info. "Does he seem okay? Is he smoking during the day? I don't want him to become like a real smoker. What's he doing this summer? Don't let him go home to his dad's."

"I don't know," I said. "He's always at band practice." I didn't mention that I hadn't even heard from him since the breakup. That every day I had awoken to a blast of possibility—this might be the day!—and fallen asleep disappointed. "You're coming to his show next week, right?"

She shook her head. "If we keep hanging out, it will be like we never broke up. That's all we ever did together anyway. It was codependent and weird and it kept me from becoming myself, you know this, I've told you this."

"But it's his first show!"

She shook her head again, one sharp, decisive swoop. "What about you guys? Has anything happened yet?"

"No."

She looked relieved, but she said, "Chickenshit, the both of you."

I wanted to ask her what she knew—what he'd said about me when I wasn't there—but I did the right thing for once and said, "What about you, Zo? How are you feeling?"

The question seemed to surprise her, and then her chin wobbled and she started crying a little. "Excited," she said. "But also scared. I know my parents will take it okay, but I haven't worked up the nerve to tell them yet. My dad's got Catholic baggage. Also I just—I don't know how to be gay! I know how to be Joey and Zoe who both like Bowie, and I know how to be a good student. That's it. That's all I know."

I shifted my elbow so it was touching hers. "Maybe focus on being a good student, then, for a while. Just until you're not so scared. We can be good students together."

She nodded, wiping her makeup-streaked eyes. The sight of her made me think, for the first time in years, of Dylan's "Just Like a Woman": for all her smarts and self-possession, here she was, breaking like a little girl.

"I know it's selfish," she said quietly. "But I have this fear I won't see you anymore when you start dating Joe."

"When?" I blurted, laughing nervously. "If that happens, of course we'd still see each other."

"Right," she said. "That's what girls always say. What about your roommate? Didn't you used to be close before she started dating that frat boy?"

I felt a pang of guilt at the mention of Megan, who had become a distant acquaintance with whom I still shared a home. "You guys came between me and Megan more than what's-his-name."

She looked unconvinced. "I know Joey—he'll be all in. He was like that with me. Remember this is a boy with a giant hole in his life."

She said it like a warning, but it didn't scare me; I wanted to be all in too. Instead of telling her this I hugged her, which was awkward since we were lying on our stomachs. We ended up sort of rolling around and laughing at ourselves, and then she kissed me. I decided to go with it; I knew it was safe, unserious. She tasted like stale cloves and Jamba Juice. Almost immediately, her hand was up my T-shirt, and she pulled back to ask, "Can I?"

I nodded, and her hand slipped under my bra, traveling over my breasts like a spider—clutching, jiggling one breast, then moving to the other. I rolled onto my back to make it easier for her.

A young family nearby packed up their picnic and left. Zoe had stopped bothering with the kissing now and was just staring at my shirt, at the movements she was creating with her hand.

"You're welcome," I finally said.

She looked up at me. "Sorry. These are my first boobs. Can I take your shirt off?"

"No! Zoe! We're in a park!"

"But you're never going to let me do this again, I can tell!"

I laughed and rolled over onto my stomach, forcing the retreat of her hand. My breasts, relieved, settled back into my bra. "That's true," I said, and picked up my textbook. "But I'm still your girl."

Black streaks still on her face, I saw a tiny smile. She opened her book, then looked back at me. "Hey, can I ask you something?" Her voice dropped to a hush: "What do girls like?"

I smiled. "Are you not a girl, Zo?"

"I'm a sample size of one. With the body of a little boy, let's face it."

I looked out at the park and tried to think. What did I like? I liked talking about music in bars. I liked any contact between my body and Joe's. A hippie couple was walking through the park, the guy's arm slung around the girl's shoulders, her fingers entwined in his dangling hand. She wore a lazy expression and sandals that consisted only of a thin leather sole and a loop around her big toe. She looked like she knew what she liked.

"I don't really know, if I'm being honest," I said. "You playing with my boobs like a kid discovering Jell-O didn't do much for me, I can tell you that."

"Damn. It did for me."

The hippie guy had a guitar on his back, swaying with his long blond dreads. "What does Joe like?"

Zoe was watching the couple too. She shrugged. "I don't know either. Same stuff they all like, I guess—touch it, suck it, worship it. What's that English-major word for the part being the whole?"

" 'Synecdoche'?"

"Men are walking synecdoches. Sorry I can't be of more help."

I smiled and held her hand. "Me too."

When I got home that evening I couldn't find my *Blonde on Blonde* CD, so I looked the song up on Napster and was surprised to find a version by Nina Simone. A woman singing "Just Like a Woman"? I downloaded both versions and then brought my laptop to my bed. I played Dylan first, then Nina.

I knew little of feminism at the time, beyond what Zoe interjected into unrelated conversations. I had been introduced to the concept as a teenager by late-night talk-show hosts who couldn't say the word without rolling their eyes, and man did I love those dudes. It's not ideal for a young girl to discover Letterman before the patriarchy, but that was the order of things for me. Dylan had loomed large over my adolescence too, and introduced me to certain systems of oppression—court-ordered racism in "The Lonesome Death of Hattie Carroll," communist fearmongering in "I Shall Be Free No. 10"—but never, of course, gender. I wasn't particularly curious about the women of *Blonde on Blonde*, about *their* stories; I viewed them only through Dylan's filter, sad-eyed and bony-faced in ribbons and silly hats.

Nina Simone changed that. It took me hours that night to peel back the layers of her song—years, even; I still have new thoughts about it. The wounded bitchiness of Dylan's version was quickly, finally, laid plain for me to see. Then the power of a woman reclaiming it. (Later: the power of it being a Black woman, and this particular Black woman—brilliant, bipolar, so incredibly singular.) But mostly what hit me that night was the deep womanly kindness of it. She spends most of the song observing another woman's flaws and pretenses without any of Dylan's judgment, and then, switching to first person in the final chorus, she finds it all in herself—the taking, the breaking. And the acceptance of her own frailty becomes the thing that makes her just like a woman, the thing Dylan couldn't do.

I loved this idea, but I didn't know where to put it. I didn't know how to use it. It felt bigger than a *Ring Finger* column, but I wrote it in my binder anyway: "Simone's acceptance of her own frailty is what makes her just like a woman." As I fell asleep that night I could see both of their faces—Nina's and Zoe's—hovering in the darkness of my almost-sleep. I wished we knew how to help each other.

Never Is a Promise

When I finally saw Joe it was at his debut gig, in the basement of a popular bar close to campus. He killed. Granted, he'd stacked the audience with friends from home, girls with blown-out hair and back-slapping dudes—he was the Beatles to them—plus his many roommates and every college classmate he'd ever chatted up. It was enough to fill the space with a great, buzzy energy. The drummer and bassist had been chosen for their devotion to the cause more than their skills, but they kept a steady beat, and Luke Skinner's guitar sounded great, at least until he turned his amp up too loud halfway through the set. Joe's singing had improved too, though it still lacked the round confidence of when he sang alone to me.

I watched from the back like Oz behind the curtain. Nobody knew me. Nobody knew that lyric had been my idea. How lucky he was to take these songs public, to stand up there in the glow of their magic.

He closed with "Funny Strange" in its new form, easily nailing the new lyrics' complicated, behind-the-beat phrasing. The crowd became destabilized by multiple discrete pockets of dancing girls; the guys either filtered to the back or began nodding vigorously, pumping their fists. I could barely see him now, there were so many hands in the air. "Thanks for coming out," he said into the mic after the song's crashing end, and yanked the plug from his guitar.

Immediately he was enveloped by hugs. I waited uncertainly for a while, holding my plastic cup of beer. Maybe it was five minutes, maybe fifteen. When my cup was empty I walked home alone.

It's fine, I said to myself, over and over. This is fine. My friend played a show and it went well. I opened the door to my apartment: no Megan. I crawled into my bed fully clothed and turned on the TV. This was normal. He was my friend; I had helped him. I thought about calling Zoe, telling her how it went, but that felt wrong. Everything felt wrong.

Then the doorbell rang and he burst through the door, sweeping me into a hug, whirling us in a circle, shouting thank-yous into my hair: "We did it, we did it, thank you thank you thank you." I responded with uncontrollable giggles, all my nerves releasing in tiny pockets of air.

When the whirling stopped it seemed strange that we were still in my hallway, that we hadn't been transported to another, more colorful dimension. He leaned against the back of my front door, still holding me. I wanted to lift his T-shirt and crawl up in there. I looked at his face. The smile was gone; he looked like I felt now, serious and charged. His forearms rested on my shoulders now, loosely. I saw an opening to pull his hips in until they touched mine—it was such an easy move, I'd seen it in movies, it was right there. I summoned every scrap of courage from every cell of my body and then I did it: I hooked my fingers in his belt loops and tugged.

A tortured sound came from deep in his throat.

"What?" I said, panicking. Too aggressive. The wrong move. Oh god. Humiliation inflamed me, burning the entire organ of my skin. Why didn't I just lean in for a kiss like a normal person?

"They're waiting for me at the bar," he said. "I just came here to thank you."

I flinched. It felt like a violence. "Too soon?" I said, in a voice that didn't sound like mine.

He shook his head. "It's not that."

Another flinch, this one worse. "So . . . never?"

"I can see it all like a movie in my head." He looked like he was trying to back up, but he had nowhere to go, so his body inched up against the door. "We'll be happy for a month, or a year, and then we'll break up and it's just—you're too—oh god, this sounds terrible, but you're too important. You know? Like you said when I asked why you don't write songs—remember?"

"But that's me," I said, genuinely confused. "You're not a person who's afraid of trying."

"Maybe I am," he said, inching up again. "About this, anyway. Sex is weird and embarrassing, and you're . . . you're my critic."

This echoed in my brain, louder and louder. I began to feel sick. I stared into the blackness of his T-shirt, the fraying collar, refusing to cry. I hadn't fully admitted it to myself, I realized, how badly I wanted him.

"And I love your criticism!" he said. "I can't lose that. I *can't.*"

I looked up at him sharply. "Buddy, I can stop helping you with your songs any time I want."

"No, you can't." A coolness entered his eyes, and his body seemed to settle, his heels planting. "You love it too much. You've never had this much fun in your life."

"Neither have you."

We stared at each other a minute, breathing audibly, his nostrils flaring slightly on each inhale. Then he looked away. "Maybe you're not my type," he said limply. He focused on his left forearm, which still rested on my shoulder. "I can see how I might've implied otherwise, fall semester. Once the album started coming together I got my head on straight."

A garish visual appeared in my head of me and Zoe in a split-screen juxtaposition, like they do to celebrities in *People* magazine: her straight, muscular body and bright black makeup facing off against my curves, my mousy hair, my heavy stare. The sight was so painful I heard myself utter a small cry, and began squeezing my head with both hands.

"I'm sorry," he said.

I released my head and held up a warning finger. "Look," I said.

"I want you to know I'm not waiting around for you to change your mind. What you're saying, right now, is never—you and I are never going to happen. And never is a promise."

This was a Fiona Apple song I had loved in high school. I intended it as a negotiating tactic—fishing for a shrug, a foot wedged in a closing door, a never say never. What I got instead was a look of recognition, and a slow, serious nod. "And I can't afford to lie," he said, finishing the lyric.

It made me livid. "Why the fuck are your fucking hands still on me, then?"

He sprang off and pushed past me down the hall, into the kitchen and into the living room, then back into the kitchen. I stalked after him and watched him fumble in my fridge until he produced two bottles of different brands. He placed them across from each other on the kitchen table, then went into the living room and started digging through my CDs.

I sat and opened one of the beers, still adrenal. "I don't have it," I called through the open kitchen door.

"I've seen it here," he insisted. He moved to the stacks on the bay window seat, where we kept leftovers from parties and never-returned loaners, and finally held it up. Fiona Apple's whitewashed face bobbed at the end of his arm. He started "Never Is a Promise" and walked back to sit with me at the table.

The thing about Fiona is she fully commits. She's not worried about sounding maudlin; she is always 100 percent inside of her emotions. Her songs can sometimes be a little tuneless as a result, weighed down by the heaviness of being Fiona Apple, but not this one. The melody moves with her emotions: low and limited when she's pissed, climbing intervals with the release of her epiphany. Fiona would never do what you're doing, I wanted to say to Joe, sitting at that tiny table, both of us peeling the labels from our bottles. Fiona would fuck me.

"Well, that was depressing," I said when it was over. I didn't mean this strictly as a complaint—the song had scratched the exact right awful itch, elevated my sadness to the cinematic, if only briefly. But it landed like a cheap shot, and I let it.

He looked miserable. I felt a flash of guilt for ruining his big night—but no, he had ruined it! He had ruined it! What a night it could've been, we would've stayed up till dawn again, we would've worked on his songs in fits of postcoital inspiration!

"Why are you even still here?" I said. "They're *waiting* for you."

His expression hardened at my tone. "Look, I don't get red A-pluses in the corners of my papers. I don't get proud parents. This is all I get."

"Well, they adore you." I gestured to the door. "Go forth and receive."

He stood. "You should be with someone better anyway. Someone who doesn't rhyme 'bad' with 'sad.' "

A line I had mocked—gently teased, really—in the original "Funny Strange." "Good point," I said, standing, pushing in my chair. "Or 'frosty' and 'costly,' while we're at it."

I saw him wince as he turned away. This was from the final version of the song, an awkward, forced line I had never mentioned because the rest of it was so good and I felt I'd used up my critiquing chips.

I followed him to the door. He turned back at the last minute, in the same place where I had made my big move, his expression suddenly open. "Perce? Is this going to ruin everything anyway? Because if everything is ruined anyway, we might as well just go for it." He put a hand on his belt buckle. "Seriously."

It made my skin prick with horror, the idea of losing what we had together, whatever it was. "No," I said quickly. "You're a jerk for saying it, but you were right: I'm having too much fun."

"Oh thank God," he said, sighing. He leaned back against the door again and ran a hand through his hair. "It's a bit of a relief to have it off the menu, honestly."

I nodded numbly. "Eighty-six the sex."

"Hah—yeah! We've still got the collaboration, the conversation, right?"

I couldn't stop myself from frowning. "So which am I, your collaborator or your critic?"

He ignored this, keeping the tone upbeat. "My point is, sex is just one thing on the menu. It's not even the best one!"

I hesitated. This had been true in my experience so far. But the sex we'd been about to have, in my head, was better than any collaboration in history, better than Lennon and McCartney going eyeball-to-eyeball in Hamburg. I reached around him to turn the doorknob, put my hand on his chest, and shoved him out.

I met Zoe at Cafe Milano the next morning and she made me tell the story twice. I ordered a coffee and a low-fat cranberry muffin but couldn't consume more than a few sips of the coffee. The muffin smelled like cough syrup.

After the second retelling she went concave, hugging herself. She wasn't drinking her coffee either.

The first thing she said was "Not his type, my ass. He can't keep his eyes off you. And we've had multiple conversations about how gorgeous you are."

This made me feel better, though I wasn't convinced. It seemed to me the truth was probably somewhere in the middle, and the middle hurt just as much as the idea of him being completely repulsed by me.

"I'm not buying the excuse about protecting the music either," Zoe said. " 'Too important'? Joe's a weirdo, and he's very driven with his music, but he's still a red-blooded college boy."

"Seriously," I said. "We were *this close* to kissing—in my apartment, alone—and he's thinking about his *songs*?"

Even though I was agreeing with her, my insistence seemed to make her reconsider. "Well, he is always thinking about those damn songs."

"He mentioned me making fun of his rhymes too."

"What's weird is he's never been the type to care what people think, until he met you." Then she nodded suddenly, firmly. "That's the problem: his ego can't handle you. It can handle you creatively, although just barely—he knows he needs you—but it can't handle you in the bedroom. What a spineless little boy."

I saw it clearly, finally, a Venn diagram diverging in my head. He needed me to be his critic. But a critic will never be girlfriend material.

I moaned. "Why am I like this, Zo? I have nothing but respect for his songwriting—and admiration, and *envy,* honestly—why can't I just tell him that?"

"Stop it," she said firmly. "He begs you for your criticism."

I slumped over my muffin.

Zoe looked over my shoulder so intently, I thought for a second he might be standing behind me. "He's a bit weird about promises, you should know." Then she told me that when his mom was first diagnosed with cancer, his dad had promised him she wouldn't die. And when she did, of course, little Joey was furious. "He felt like he would've spent the summer differently if he'd known, spent more time with her or whatever. He's taken promises super seriously ever since."

My eyes stung, as always when I imagined Joe that summer. "Cool," I said, blinking hard. "So by trying to find an opening, I actually slammed the door completely shut." I sat back in the rickety café chair, astonished by my stupidity. "Why do I push so hard?"

"That is not what I said," she said. "It's really grossing me out how you keep blaming yourself."

Then a new thought occurred to me: if the promise had been my idea, it had less power than Zoe seemed to think. I could wait it out. I could be less critical in the meantime. More patient.

"This is classic Joey," Zoe was saying. "Obfuscating everything so there's nothing left to do but blame yourself. It's borderline Republican, honestly. Global warming is all our fault, we didn't recycle enough!" She was getting breathless, her chest puffing, teeth on edge. "God, this is making me so glad Joey Morrow is finally out of my life. He can be a real manipulative son of a bitch."

"Don't call him that," I said sharply. And then I doubled down: "Don't call *her* that."

I held her gaze as her face registered surprise, then hurt, then a sputtering pissiness. "It's something people say, Percy. Are you serious right now?"

I didn't know who I was defending. Maybe Joe, maybe his dead mom, maybe just my right to hate myself, which I'd been doing since long before I met either of them. My chin inched upward of its own accord; a defiant muscle twitched in my jaw. I felt a small, pathetic relief of having exited a crossroads, having chosen a path—not the one I'd wanted, but at least Joe was on it.

"Fuck you, Percy," Zoe said, and sent her café chair skidding.

After the Gold Rush

On September 11 my dad called early—"Do you have a TV? Your mother isn't sure you have a TV," he said over and over, as I switched on Megan's old, hulking TV in the dark of dawn. The towers were coming down in slow motion, the chyrons stacked and screaming. "Columnated ruins domino," I whispered at the screen, terrified. My dad hung up to call my brother, and Megan left for her parents' house, leaving me alone with the TV. When Joe knocked on my door, I collapsed with relief in his arms.

He sat down on my bed and didn't leave. I tried to go to class but there was a cancellation note taped to the door, and when I got home Joe was still in my room, cleaning up. He'd moved all the CDs out of the bay window seat and covered it with pillows so we could watch the news from there instead of the bed.

For dinner we shared a bottle of Trader Joe's wine and ate beans from the can with tortilla chips, and then we lay down in my bed together at some crazy early hour, eight or nine o'clock. My head was in the crook of his arm, but we faced the ceiling, not each other. We had seen each other often at work that summer, had nursed a shared obsession with the Shins' finally released full album, *Oh, Inverted World,* over countless beers and Sundays on his porch—but we hadn't been this physically close since the night after his first show. His warm skin and wiry muscles filled me with a yearning that felt somehow comfortable; I'd gotten used to the yearning, I supposed.

"Do you see yourself having kids one day?" he asked, voice barely above a whisper.

"Maybe. Obviously not any time soon."

"I've always thought I'd be a dad. A good one, you know? Really do it right. But days like this . . ."

"Yeah. Morally speaking, it's an increasingly dubious choice."

"Exactly." I felt his chest rise and fall. "You know they're going to turn this into votes," he said. "I have paid just enough attention in my poli-sci classes to know this for sure. They're going to turn this into the worst kind of votes."

Nobody was saying things like this yet, at least not that I'd heard. It made me feel scared. "Do you regret voting for Nader? I mean, I know it wouldn't have made a difference, but—"

"I didn't vote for Nader," he said.

"Really?" A year earlier, the wisdom in our circles had been that four years of Bush would be better than Gore; we'd do our time, and then the pendulum would swing back to a true left.

"Didn't feel right. Never told Zoe."

I thought about this a long time. Joe in the polling booth, hand veering at the last minute, following his gut. I had an election night secret too—I'd been turned away because I was registered under my old dorm address, hadn't voted at all—but I didn't confess. I was too tired, too comfortable. We fell asleep like that, on our backs, his bicep my pillow.

The next day we had proper cancellation emails for our classes, but stores and restaurants were open again. We went out to get coffee and croissants and brought them back to our bunker. My dad kept calling; he was talking about the topography of Afghanistan and had started watching Fox News because the coverage seemed more honest.

"I think my dad is turning Republican," I told Joe in the early afternoon, when we decided it was time to start drinking. I had made us a pitcher of margaritas from a mix.

"Told you," he said. "Votes." He had left a message for his dad telling him to call my number, but hadn't heard back. It was clearly bothering him.

Zoe came over briefly, all lit up with anti-war energy. She had gone to Joe's to check on him—they were in a distant sort of touch, downgraded from siblings to cousins—then figured he was with me. It was my closest interaction with her since the fight in Cafe Milano; I had been submitting her my music column via email. The next *Ring Finger* would be an all-pacifist edition, she told me, doing a shot of tequila. "You can go hard-core folk, I don't care. Fucking Pete Seeger it." She wanted to organize a protest in the plaza, but it wasn't yet clear what we would protest; the news kept predicting different plans for retaliation. I thought it would feel good to have the three of us together again, but there was a bitter edge to everything she said, and Joe hurried her to leave.

"Better just us," he said quietly once she was gone, and shut the metal blinds in the bay window. Thin stripes of bright sunlight fought through, painting the floor. He sat down in the window and looked at me with a tired smile.

I sat next to him. The news was on but muted. We were listening to Neil Young. Joe had tried to show me some music he was working on earlier, but neither of us was in the mood. Since our "Never Is a Promise" night, I'd become more careful with my critiques, kinder and more likely to swallow complaints; and he had dramatically slowed down his output, producing new fragments for me on a monthly basis instead of the near-daily clip he'd maintained the previous year. I wasn't sure if these events were related—if my gentler approach had curbed his productivity—or if he was just focused on the live act now that the album was finished. In the old days I would've asked Zoe.

"Do you miss her?" I asked.

"It's weird what I miss," he said. "I miss her parents. I miss Sunday dinners at her house so bad it hurts."

I took his hand.

"Thanks," he said with an embarrassed smile. "Times like this kinda freak me out. Upheaval or whatever."

I squeezed his hand.

"And I'm probably going to fail out of school this year," he said. "So there's that aspect of missing her."

"What are you talking about?"

He sighed. "I can't pass a test without Zoe. For multiple-choice tests, she would tuck her hair behind her left ear for A, right ear for B, cross feet left for C, cross feet right for D. And she basically wrote my papers for me."

I must've looked shocked because he rolled his eyes.

"Come on, Percy. Like I'd be able to write and record all these songs, and work, and practice, if I was a real student. It's over now anyway—she won't help me in class, she just says hi and then goes and sits across the room. Which is fine, I understand. This whole charade was for her anyway. But it's just hitting me now, that it's really over."

I still couldn't believe it. "But Zoe's so . . . principled."

"Ah, but see, the system is rigged against me," he said, raising a knowing eyebrow. "Poor blue-collar boy with a dead mom and a drunk dad, education wasn't valued in my home . . . How could I ever succeed in this world? She was correcting an imbalance."

I nodded. I could hear her saying it.

"But I suck at school," he said. "And I'll suck at any job this education gets me."

"That's not true."

"I think it is," he said. "I went along with it because I loved her, but now it all seems ridiculous. I've always known what I have to do. I have to make a living from music."

"That's incredibly difficult, Joe," I said, as gently as possible. "Increasingly difficult."

"I know." He looked down at our interlaced fingers. "That's why we gotta make it good."

This carried an implication of pressure, of responsibility, as if his songs were mine too. But they weren't mine. Were they? Over the summer he'd self-released a thousand copies of *Funny Strange,* and the songs were all credited to him, "with special thanks to Percy Marks." I didn't love that phrase. There were a few close calls on the album, two or three lines that were entirely mine, one melody I'd hummed out for him that ended up being a song's secondary hook. He'd asked me once if I wanted co-writing credit, but it was early on, and I'd demurred. Still. "Special thanks to Percy Marks": it hit me in my gut, every time.

"I can copyedit your papers," I offered. "Fix your comma splices."

"What the hell is a comma splice?"

"Exactly."

"Have you been judging my commas all this time, in emails and stuff?"

"No," I said, but he looked away, wounded. Of course I'd judged his commas; his commas were like gnats that crawled onto the screen and settled in random corners of his sentences. But I had surprised myself from the very beginning by not caring. What had all my proficiency with the English language gotten me? Joe could play guitar. He could *sing.* I would trade every last drop of my innate understanding of punctuation for a voice like Joe's.

"After the Gold Rush" began to play, and of all the songs about the end of the world, it was the perfect one for the moment, so imagistic and unsettling. I knew we were both thinking it, how the title could've been on the news that day: we had pillaged the earth for its riches, stoked violence for its oil, and now it had come to this. But my favorite lyrics were the personal ones, the way the narrator lies in a basement watching an entire ecosystem collapse while having the vague, weary thoughts of everyday life. Thinking about what a friend had said.

"Hey," I said during the flügelhorn solo. "Remember that night you came over here, after your first show?"

He took a breath, not quite a sigh. "Of course I do. The night we made the promise."

I untangled my hand from his because it was starting to sweat. "The promise, right," I said. "Kinda silly, isn't it?"

"I don't think so," he said quietly.

A red banner at the bottom of the TV screen read: CALLER FROM HIJACKED PLANE: "I'M GOING TO DIE." He took my hand again and scooted his body closer so our thighs were pressing. It wasn't enough. I felt a bottomless thirst for closeness. The song ended and he started it again.

"So what are the parameters of the promise?" I said. "I mean, we're holding hands right now, so I guess that's in bounds. What exactly did we promise not to do?"

He turned toward me. His eyes moved over my face. "Kiss, I guess," he said.

"On the lips? Be specific."

He nodded.

I straightened up and kissed him slowly on the cheek. The feel of it surprised me—tiny pricks of stubble, a cheekbone close beneath the surface. A man, not a boy. When I drew back his eyes were closed.

"So that was in bounds?" I asked.

He nodded.

I stood up. I walked around the length of his legs—they were pointed straight out, bare feet crossed at the heels—and then stepped back over so I was straddling him.

"Percy." He looked up at me.

"What. I'm just trying to get a good angle." I held his face and kissed the other cheek.

He tilted slightly toward me. His lips parted, and we were breathing in perfect unison, and then he said, "You're ruining this song."

I dropped my hands, mortified. He wouldn't look at me. My legs were frozen in place, trapping us both in the moment, refusing to admit it had happened.

The phone rang, then rang again. "It might be my dad," he said. I let him go.

Let Down

For the first time in two years, I went to Amoeba on a weekday. A Thursday, September 13, 2001. Neil was behind the buyer's counter: a promotion.

"Percy," he said. My name seemed to erupt from his mouth. "Whoa."

"I know."

"End-times got you thinking?"

"I guess. You're buying now?"

He rolled his eyes, perhaps mature enough to realize that being a buyer at Amoeba was not a position of awe-inspiring power.

I tried to think of what to say. Let's finish, is what I wanted to say. Let's just finish already. Planes are flying into buildings and Joe doesn't want me—let's finish. Instead I said, "You want to get a drink when you're off?"

His heavy eyelids lifted. "I've got plans," he said. "Hip-hop show in the city." He leaned against the back counter to make room for another employee to pass, one of the elders with '80s metal hair. The store was eerily quiet, no music playing; you could hear the employees' Converse shuffling over the dusty floor as they wandered, straightening displays. "You could come with?"

"Sure," I said. His sideburns had lengthened, flaring into the hollows of his cheeks. I observed that I felt no attraction to him. But that was okay. My theory, which had arrived in full that morning as if implanted in my brain during sleep, was this: in order to close this anxious semi-virginal chapter of my life and become a fully formed adult with the capacity to find her own purpose, I needed to complete the act with the same wrong guy. I didn't have time to start from scratch finding the right guy—I was practically about to graduate from college, for God's sake—and I certainly couldn't risk a fresh new humiliation with a *different* wrong guy. I knew Neil, at least. I knew how to avoid him. And I knew how the sex would go, at least up until the very end.

I spent the afternoon grooming and plucking, as I'd done the first time, then assembled an outfit I now remember as try-hard and culturally appropriative, hoop earrings and all—I never knew what the hell I was doing with clothes. He picked me up from my apartment in his same old maroon Honda Civic. I wedged into the back seat between two friendly dudes, and we drove over the bridge to a dark, clubby venue across the street from a floodlit grocery store.

The show was good, a trio of young, energetic rappers stalking a small area of concrete just a few feet from us. They would later add a female vocalist with a six-pack and climb the Top 40 with some of the worst songs ever written, but that was years away. Neil brought me a Long Island iced tea, a whole pint glass of liquor that I assumed was beer until I took a gulp and nearly choked.

"Isn't that your drink?" Neil shouted in my ear.

I'd forgotten: for a brief time, when I was first learning to socialize, I had appreciated the efficiency of the Long Island iced tea. One and done, I used to say. "I've grown up," I shouted back. The next two drinks he brought me were clear and short, but strong.

On the drive home, it was just us, so it seemed I had sent the signals I had wanted to send. He put on a Pavement tape, remembering it correctly as our only musical common ground. He went too fast over the Bay Bridge and excitement mingled with my nerves.

"You know the last time we spoke?" I said, grabbing the handle above the door. "I think it was some awkward exchange about a condom."

Streetlights through the window lit his face in bursts, one after the other. He changed lanes without a turn signal. "No, I think it was me yelling down my stairwell after you—'Come back! What the hell?'"

"Oh god. I'm so sorry."

He shrugged. "I didn't sweat it. You were a freshman."

"Sophomore."

"Still. You're a senior now?"

"Yeah."

He made a gesture like this proved his point, and we didn't say anything else. That he didn't seem to want any more information about that night seemed odd to me, but Neil had always been odd. He merged onto the 80 and the car sailed north toward Berkeley. An IKEA sign visible from the highway teetered and spun; I was drunk, which I noted with satisfaction.

Both our roommates had people over so we did it in his car. He had a condom in the glove compartment, wedged between tiny tubs of old-school Blistex, which explained a lot about the way he always smelled, cool and medicinal. He cranked the driver's seat backward and I got on top of him. It hurt just as bad as the first time we'd tried, but I forced myself to get through it. I imagined the pain obliterating my past, each thrust sending a black ink splotch over another memory, another childhood fantasy. When this is over, I thought, I'll be wiser. When this is over I'll be harder.

But it kept hurting afterward, after he pulled up at my house and said, "Maybe I'll see you next global catastrophe!" and I stumbled up the stairs into my house, where I immediately decided I did not want to be. I tried to take my Discman for a bowlegged walk, but made it only two blocks before I lay down on the sloping lawn of a fraternity house, sore and nauseated. I rolled onto my side and hugged my knees.

OK Computer was the CD in my Discman, a time capsule from a year earlier. I had been in a Radiohead phase under the influence of the Rasputin staff, a portion of which was so obsessed with the band as to be incapable of discussing anything without steering the conversation back to their albums. Had I really not played *OK Computer*, or even used my Discman, all year? I realized it was true: I almost always listened to music with Joe now, or on my boom box while I studied, letting it fill all my space. It felt good to hear songs so privately again. I let myself be cocooned in *OK Computer*. Nobody paid me any mind when I threw up a little, sending a stream of Long Island iced tea trickling down to the sidewalk. Briefly I dozed off and had an insanely unsubtle dream in which my vagina split open as I walked, causing a whole bloody spectacle on Telegraph Avenue, children screaming, men fleeing.

I awoke to the album's fifth track, "Let Down," which sounded so perfect I played it again. Louder this time, so loud it hurt. I had a sensation of the song coming from inside me, the wailing weirdly my own. With complete certainty I decided the song was a retelling of Kafka's *The Metamorphosis,* which I had just read for class—all that imagery of transformation, bugs on the ground, hysterical and useless, growing wings. Wings are typically a coming-of-age metaphor, I knew—they signified freedom, the ability to finally explore beyond yourself. But wings could also be useless. Wings could make you a grotesque.

I played the song again and it gave me the strength to stand and start walking home. I felt the pain subsiding the deeper I went into the song, the more dark layers I heard. I thought about how it must feel to be Thom Yorke, to have created such a perfect exorcism of one's own misery, to be able to perform it whenever he wanted. Of course, Kafka had done it too, with mere words on a page, and even though that made the work less powerful—I'm sorry but it did, it just did—it was still something. I turned the volume down. I could put words on a page. Maybe I could learn to do it better. Maybe now that I'd been split open, made wiser, my words on a page could get closer to music.

NEW YORK

Bag Lady

I fell in love with Erykah Badu's "Bag Lady" in the fall of 2002 at a Columbia University literary reading, where someone had chosen an assortment of neo-soul to accompany the cheese and crackers and wine in plastic cups. It was a Wednesday night, twenty minutes past the stated start time, and nobody was reading yet. We were supposed to be mingling but I didn't come to these things to be social; the lights were too bright. I came to get out of my apartment and maybe hear an idea, some nugget or way of turning a phrase, that I could bring back home and fold into my own work.

When I heard Badu's voice, I brought my wine to the window and looked out at another stately building like the one we were in. Even from a foot away I could feel the coolness of the windowpane, refreshing in the overheated room. My hair, reflected in the glass, looked messy. I took a sip of wine and let it lie on my tongue as the background vocals advised me to "pack light"—to let go of anger, resentment, all the emotional junk we drag around.

Had I packed light, coming to New York? I believed I had. I was fresh out of undergrad and starting over, alone again; there were days I didn't use my vocal cords. But now I could see the beauty in that.

The song's sinewy guitar sample rose above the small talk. I finished my wine and grabbed another. When I returned to my window a girl from my nonfiction workshop was there, waiting for me, it seemed: the former model who wrote about fashion.

"Oh, hi, Nomi."

She smiled warmly. "I love how you're just standing here dancing in the corner of this stuffy-ass reading."

I felt my cheeks go hot. "No. Was I?"

"There was discernible swaying."

I grimaced, but she was still smiling. Nomi wrote well-researched pieces about clothes that I found a little boring. She seemed friendly and good-natured—odd for a writer, not to mention a model—but her comments in my margins bordered on cruel: "Why are you so obsessed with this sentence structure?" "This made me laugh, not in a good way." I liked her.

"I was just marveling at how *light* this song is," I said. "The sound of it. Weighed down by nothing, you know?"

Nomi listened for a minute and nodded. "The song makes you feel the way she wishes you'd make yourself feel."

"Yes!"

She leaned a hip against the window frame. By her own description, in a piece she'd submitted to workshop, she was "Black with a Chinese grandma"; she'd been discovered as a child in a mall while buying back-to-school clothes with her mom, a scene so classically '80s it would sound made up if it weren't for her body. Nomi's body was like the guitar sample in "Bag Lady": a clean, elegant line that went on and on. I attempted to smooth my hair in the window.

"You hear about those two?" she said, nodding at two poets laughing conspiratorially.

"Yeah."

"I wasn't expecting it to be such a meat market here," she said. "So not what I signed up for."

"Me neither," I said forcefully, surprising myself.

"Oh yeah? Why not? You're young. You got someone?"

"Nope," I said. "Just, you know. Packing light."

She clinked her plastic cup against mine. Her fingernails were free of polish but had clearly been groomed and shaped by a professional. Mine were chewed and sprouting hangnails.

My cell phone vibrated in my bag and I reacted swiftly, holding it up to the light to see the name in green-gray pixels: JOE. I answered in a whisper and told him I'd call him back in an hour.

Nomi wore a smug look on her face.

I shook my head and laughed, though it sounded forced, and pressed the end button repeatedly. "No, he's just my best friend. My songwriting partner, actually."

She raised her eyebrows.

"I mean, collaborator," I amended. What was I saying? Words were running out of my mouth.

"That's cool," she said, and looked out at our classmates. "Writers are not natural collaborators. Which makes writers' workshops an odd experiment, don't you think? Maybe that's why everyone's making out. We don't know how else to help each other."

I laughed nervously. The song had ended, but I was still thinking about it. "Sometimes I wish writing had more opportunity for collaboration," I said.

"Not me. The solitude is my favorite part about writing."

"Actually . . ."

"What?"

I was thinking that my attempts at collaboration were all tied up with my baggage. *Funny Strange* had been picked up by a respectable indie label and I'd bought it eagerly at the Virgin Megastore, but its songs came loaded with so many memories, I could hardly listen to it. And my old *Ring Finger* writings just made me think of Zoe, of the times I'd seen her on campus senior year and the awkward nods we'd exchanged. When the zine went defunct after graduation, I'd packed all my issues into an accordion folder and sent them to Indiana.

"I was just thinking about the Erykah Badu song," I said. "It could be about being a solo artist, in a way. Shedding that baggage of needing other people."

"I love that idea. But doesn't she make it all about finding a guy, in the end?"

I had to confirm this later, finding the song online that night in my sparsely furnished room. Nomi was right. The problem with your baggage, the song seemed to say, is that no man will want you. It wasn't Erykah's fault—this was normal for the time, the clear undercurrent of every empowerment message in the mainstream. I found it deeply disappointing even as I related to an awful seed of truth inside it: that all my attempts to grow, to find creative independence and purpose, were at least partly in service of becoming more lovable.

Screw that, I thought, closing my laptop. I was a New Yorker now.

NYC

Turn On the Bright Lights by Interpol was the official album of the Lion's Head Tavern on 109th and Amsterdam. By the midpoint of that first semester, I was spending several nights a week there, and had identified the fiction writers as my preferred pool of casual acquaintances. My nonfiction brethren were a tougher bunch—the memoirists no fun, the journalists too busy—and only a couple ever came to the Lion's Head: Nomi, though she always left early to get back to Brooklyn, and a food writer who brought lime wedges to the bar to make the PBR more palatable. We liked the Lion's Head because PBRs were a buck fifty, two with tip. Most of us had taken out federal loans to get our MFAs, and the idea of ever having money for nice things was as irretrievably lost to us as our innocence.

One of the fiction writers, a guy named Harrison who had dozens of small, unrelated tattoos on his arms, had somehow gotten *Turn On the Bright Lights* on the Lion's Head jukebox. He was rumored to have purchased this favor by going down on a bearded bar manager in the stock room, but you couldn't believe everything those fiction kids said. God I loved that album. Everyone did that year. Either you'd never heard of it or you loved it. We'd all bought tickets to the show and set list predictions were a legitimate topic of conversation.

One night just after the weather turned from cool to heinous cold, I sat at a long table full of a dozen or so fiction writers, listening to the whole album track by track. When "NYC" came on, I muttered something about it being the least derivative song of theirs, the most unique to our own time and place, which was met with agreement, even though it seems insane to me now that anything on that album could evoke any time or place but 2002 New York.

"You're the music writer," someone said, just as the outro was peaking.

The fiction writer at my left had been replaced by a guy from my workshop. I waited until the song ended, then nodded. "You're the food writer."

He took his baggie of lime wedges out of his pocket. "Guilty as charged."

I shifted my body slightly away from him. But the people on my right had started talking about Faulkner.

Now he was shaking out a red powder onto the rim of his beer. "Chili," he said, noticing me watching. "It's meant to be done with Mexican beer. But the way beer is mass-produced these days, there's very little difference between a Pabst and a Tecate, other than branding. Even a Singha is pretty similar."

"Doesn't the branding matter, though, a little?" I asked. "I bet that would taste better if it were a Tecate and you were in a Mexican restaurant."

"Probably," he said. "But it's better than drinking straight Pabst." He handed me the can, pushing up his glasses while he waited.

I took a swig. "Yeah, that's delicious."

"Sorry I said 'guilty as charged,'" he said as he took the beer back. "I've never said that before, and I shan't be doing it again."

I laughed. He'd said "shan't" ironically, I was pretty sure. His affect was such that it was hard to tell.

"Tell me," he said. "Why does everyone love this band so much? I'd never heard of them until I got here."

"Nobody had," I said. "This is their debut, and it came out right when we all arrived."

"Ah. Does that make it particularly meaningful to you?"

"Meaningful": what a word. The truth was, New York and *Turn On the Bright Lights* were so deeply connected to me that I could not form an opinion about one without forcing it to be true of the other. The album's sound was dark but shiny, like Times Square. Living in New York made you feel heavy and lonely but full of promise, like listening to those songs. You get the idea. There were times I felt fully inside of both the city and the album, peering out at the world through gorgeous layers of light and sound; and there were times that I felt outside of both, an audience to two great spectacles. Did I really relate to the tortured drama of these songs, so affected, so male? When I walked these famous streets did I really belong, or was I an accidental extra in someone's short film? 9/11 was still fresh enough that people talked about where they'd been that day, their hundred-block walks; I felt almost ashamed of my cozy day in Berkeley with Joe.

"Yeah, it makes it super meaningful," I said.

"So should I buy the CD, then?" the food writer asked.

I looked at him. He always had the same frank, relaxed expression on his face. I felt a refreshing sense of not needing to impress him. "Viraj, right?"

"Raj." He shrugged. "Or Viraj. I tried to go back to that for a while, but there's an element of laziness, of not actually caring very much what people call me, so I just—Raj. Sorry."

"What kind of music do you like, Raj?"

"Mostly old stuff, if I'm being honest," he said. "Sam Cooke, Carole King. My parents assimilated me and my sister by shopping the dollar bin at the record store."

I laughed. "Carole King's *Tapestry* is the best record that is *always* in the dollar bin."

"We had three copies. My mom kept forgetting she'd already bought it."

"When I worked at record stores we kept dozens in stock, and they'd always sell. Maybe it was all immigrant moms thinking, 'Oh, look at this nice white lady, she will teach us America.' "

He leaned back in his chair. I realized first that there would be no in-depth analysis of Carole King songs, and then, after a moment, that I had been glib and rude about something quite profound: a mother using music to help her son belong.

"Did it work?" I said. "Did *Tapestry* assimilate you?"

He laughed. "What do you think?"

"I think she should've sprung for a Run-DMC cassingle."

"Probably. But then I wouldn't have become who I am, which is a grown man who sings 'So Far Away' in the shower."

"Well, I've heard enough," I said. "Don't buy Interpol. You might like the new Neko Case?"

He retrieved a Moleskine from his pocket and made a note. He had a Band-Aid on one forefinger. "Thank you," he said, and used the Band-Aid finger to scratch his closely trimmed beard.

I missed Joe. It always came like this, a hard stab, dissipating slowly. I checked my phone.

Caroline, it turned out, was scheduled to be in town the night of the Interpol show. It would be the first time I'd seen Joe since they'd driven their swollen van out of Berkeley back in early June, halfway through finals week, nine credits short of his degree. Zoe had left shortly after for some save-the-world job in Africa without saying goodbye; I wouldn't even have known if I hadn't run into one of the *Ring Finger* girls while selling clothes at Buffalo Exchange, days before my own departure.

I followed Joe's tour through his mass email updates, which read like an enthusiastic travelogue—he was always falling in love with some small American city, encouraging everyone to pack up and move to Austin one day, Missoula the next—and through his phone calls, which struck a different tone. He called when he was lonely, once every week or two, late at night. He'd begin with gripes about sleeping arrangements and other realities of their underfunded tour, and then we'd transition into talking about the new Walkmen, the new Flaming Lips, the new Cat Power. We talked until we were murmuring sleepily, and then we fell asleep. He had started to feel almost like an imaginary friend; in the morning I couldn't remember how much of our conversation I'd dreamed. The idea of seeing him in person at a loud, raw rock show seemed exciting, like it would reactivate some portion of me I was starting to miss.

The night before the Interpol show I bought a pair of scissors at Duane Reade and cut bangs at my bathroom mirror, which sounds like the beginning of a cautionary tale, but was actually one of the most subtly powerful decisions of my life. For the first time since puberty, I felt like my face looked correct. A tentative happiness clicked into place as I inspected myself from every angle. I liked New York, I remember deciding in that moment. I liked working at home, then slipping out anonymously into a loud, churning world. It was just two different flavors of aloneness, but they complemented each other: when I had maxed out on solitude, the city made me feel observed and alive. I nodded firmly at my face in the mirror and went to bed.

In a prolonged trickle of communications, it had become clear that most of the classmates who'd said they'd gotten tickets had just *meant* to get tickets, and that the only ones attending the show would be me, Nomi, and Harrison. We met after lecture and walked to the subway as if we made perfect sense together. I was wearing clompy boots with black tights and no jacket because I didn't want to carry it throughout the show, a California logic that rendered me dangerously cold.

Harrison was from the Pacific Northwest and claimed to be friends with Modest Mouse. He had '90s heartthrob hair, floppy and sand colored, a prominent Adam's apple, and a pale blue handkerchief always hanging out his back pocket. I knew girls liked him, but he wasn't my type—or more accurately, I found his nervous tic of constantly pulling his shirt away from his neck to be uniquely repellent—and Nomi was out of his league, which gave an air of pointlessness to our trio. They were both older than me, like almost everyone in the program, hovering somewhere just under thirty. Nobody had told me you were supposed to go to grad school at thirty.

"My friend Joe is opening at Webster Hall tonight," I said. We were holding the same center pole, Nomi's elegant hand on top, my stubby one on the bottom, Harrison's tattooed knuckles in between (a punctuation mark on each finger). "He'll get to the Bowery as soon as he can."

"Is this the guy you write songs with?" Nomi asked.

I was hoping she'd forgotten. "I mean, yeah, I help him out," I said, which sounded crushingly lame. "Sometimes." As if that made it better.

"Don't you want to see his show?"

"He's playing in Brooklyn tomorrow, I can catch that one."

I thought Harrison was ignoring us until he said, stooping to look me in the eye, "Is he any good?"

"Extremely," I said, and looked up at him. "Is your fiction any good?"

Nomi laughed.

"Seriously though. You seem like the king of the fiction boys, but I'm just basing that on, like, the Lion's Head. Our view from the cheap seats in nonfiction isn't great."

Nomi nodded vigorously. "What's your vibe? Bukowski? Denis Johnson?"

He smiled and stuck two fingers in his T-shirt neckhole, gave it a quick tug.

"The Beats," I guessed. "Not Kerouac, too obvious, but—"

"Richard Brautigan," Nomi finished.

"Sure," I said. "Yes. Never actually read Richard Brautigan but I can tell by your confidence, Nomi, you have nailed it."

The train stopped and a big group shuffled out, creating room for Harrison to move off our pole. He leaned near the doors, folding his arms, watching us. When we didn't say anything else, he feigned surprise. "Are you done?"

Nomi groaned. "Oh no. He's about to tell us he writes true crime or something."

His eyebrows did a little dance. The train stopped again and he flattened to let more people off. Then he leaned toward us. "Love stories."

Nomi looked at me. "Bukowski," she said.

It was my first time at the Bowery Ballroom. We used the opening act to drink Jack and Cokes and find the bathroom, then Interpol took the stage and it was perfect. Almost disappointingly perfect, in that it was everything I'd expected it to be: the lights, the deafening volume, extended but otherwise note-for-note renditions of almost every song on the album. We lost Nomi a couple songs in; she liked standing near the back because her height blocked the view for other people, even though she wasn't much taller than Harrison. Joe did not appear in the crowd, nor on my cell phone screen.

"Don't opening acts usually end at the same time as each other?" I shouted at Harrison between songs, halfway into the set. We were so close to the stage now I could see sweat dripping from the guitarist's chin.

"What?"

"Just wondering where my friend is. Don't shows tend to have like, the same schedule?"

He shook his hair out of his eyes. "As soon as you told me this plan I thought no way that dude is coming."

The opening guitar chords of "NYC" started, quietly at first, then momentarily drowned out by cheers. Disappointment descended on me—I had so wanted to share this with Joe—but I forced it away. Maybe it made more sense to experience this song with a fellow New Yorker. I threw a look of anticipation Harrison's way and he caught it, returned it. And in that moment, I got what the girls saw in Harrison. I still couldn't have articulated it; I understood it only with my body. My shoulder seemed to move magnetically toward his arm as we swayed to the music, until finally it stuck there, my sweater against his leather jacket. A thick cloud of pot smoke wafted by and we both inhaled it.

The final crescendo built longer and louder than on the album, until it felt like we were endlessly suspended inside the song. Everyone onstage was singing. Everyone in the audience was singing. Our bodies were all touching by now, one giant organism, surging toward the stage. I closed my eyes.

One of the singing voices was quiet, a murmur in my ear: Harrison. He was behind me now. My eyes flew open as I realized the pressure I'd felt at the small of my back for the past few seconds was him, and now it wasn't just pressure but a repeated jabbing, in time with the song. An arm snaked around my collarbones. I tried to jerk away, but another arm braced across my pelvis, locking me in like one of those metal bars in a roller coaster car.

The singer sang the same line over and over, the album title line, "turn on the bright lights." The thrust moved lower, under my skirt. It was clear that he had removed himself entirely from his jeans. His kneecaps bent into the backs of my legs. A bright spotlight swept over us and I looked around wildly as if someone would see what was happening, but of course nobody was looking at us—they were looking at the band. I grabbed the waistband of my tights in case he tried to pull them down, but he didn't. He just went at it over the Lycra, faster now, no longer keeping time with the song. I widened my stance to create space and then I thought maybe I shouldn't, friction would make this over faster, but then he put two hands on the sides of my thighs and jammed my legs together so I didn't have to make that decision and then it stopped.

The song was over, a home chord sustained. He bit my ear lightly, licked the lobe. "You are amazing," he said. "Seriously, I fucking love you." Something like that. And then: "The way you were moving, I was like, okay, wow, why not." A chuckle.

The band started playing the lead single and the people around us freaked out, but he just kept hugging me from behind like a boyfriend at the big game. How had I been moving, exactly? At the reading, Nomi had said I was dancing when I thought I was standing still.

"Where's the . . . stuff?" I shouted. I couldn't think of what to call it, of the current parlance. I kept thinking of a Neutral Milk Hotel line about semen-capped mountaintops.

"Oh, babe, I wouldn't do that to you," he said.

I twisted around to see him, and felt a strange recognition upon seeing his face, like it had been someone else back there before. I looked at our feet, but it was too dark, and wet with spilled drinks anyway. I felt my inner thighs: my tights were dry.

His eyes flashed. "Don't worry about it." He extended the arm, an invitation. I remembered the handkerchief in his back pocket and thought I might throw up.

"Bathroom," I said, and began fighting my way through the bodies, prying apart tangled limbs. Finally the density loosened and I saw Nomi's head above the others.

"There you are," she said with a relieved smile. "It's a sausage fest up in here."

A lanky dude standing next to her slunk away. I took his place and faced the show, waiting for it to be over.

Afterward Nomi got on a train to Brooklyn and I had just started walking across town to the 1/9 line when Joe called.

"So sorry," he said. "We were the second opener, it turned out, and everything started late. Is Interpol done?"

"Yeah." I was walking fast, keeping warm. He was just a couple dozen blocks away but his voice sounded far.

"Sorry. I caught them in Philly anyway. Awesome, right?"

"Yeah."

"Okay, so where are you?"

"I'm walking to the subway. I decided I'd rather do a long walk than transfer at Union Square but I'm kind of regretting it now."

"What? How do I meet you? I'm in the Village."

I sighed. "This isn't Berkeley, Joe. It'll take some time for you to get down here and I'm not sitting in a bar waiting for you. I dressed like a damn teenager tonight."

I heard a long honk on his end, street noise. "Are you saying you don't want to meet up?"

"I can see you tomorrow, right?"

"Percy, I—I had planned on staying with you. Should I not have done that? Just for one night—we drive to Boston after the show tomorrow. I have music to show you, and hotels are crazy expensive here."

My head hurt. The final chord of "NYC" was like a razor blade embedded in my frontal cortex.

"I mean, whatever," he was saying. "The guys are staying in Brooklyn with someone I sorta know, I could crash there—"

"Joe, it's fine. I'm going to give you my address, okay? Just meet me there. Take the one or nine uptown to 116th."

By the time I got home my feet were numb from cold. I changed into pajamas and was soaking my feet in a shallow, scalding bath when the buzzer rang. I answered with my sweats rolled up above my knees.

The sight of him was an instant salve. "Perce," he said. He leaned down to hug me. Same old peacoat and worn-soft Levi's, same strong, warm arms. But his face looked stubbled and tired, and he smelled like showers were hard to come by.

He pulled back. "Wow, you look good," he said. "What's different?"

"Gee, thanks," I said. "Bangs. My room's this way."

His eyes widened when he saw the room. "Efficient."

"Fully furnished by Columbia. I use the kitchen to make coffee and sandwiches, otherwise I am right there, all the time." I pointed at the wooden desk where my laptop waited.

"There's a couch somewhere, though, right?"

I shook my head. "The living room has a door, so we sublet it to a med student. She's probably asleep."

He started to laugh. "Oh man, I'm sorry. I'll sleep on the floor."

I nodded. "Okay. Thanks. It's hard to explain but I feel this very strong need tonight for, like, space around my body." I tried to laugh, but that was taking the performance too far—it came out sounding comically fake.

He dropped his bag and stood quietly for a minute, shifting his weight onto one leg. "Did something happen, or something?"

I shook my head, but I felt my chin wobble. I knew I couldn't tell him. I hated it too much. I hated the way it made me look, and I hated what I knew he would say.

"Percy," he said. "What happened."

My face got hot. I was close to crying, and the only way out was anger. "I'm sorry, is this another promise you forced out of me? Am I required to tell you everything about my life?"

He took a step backward, stumbling over his backpack. "No—sorry."

I took a breath, then another, steering myself back to an equilibrium. "It's okay."

He nudged the backpack out of his way and looked at me. "That whole promise thing, I know it was only—what, two years ago?—but it's like remembering the thought process of a child."

I pressed my fingers against the razor blade inside my forehead. For fuck's sake, I thought—tonight? "I'm over it," I said. The dismissiveness in my voice surprised me, as if his rejection had been some minor blip in my life, and I could tell it surprised him too, because he was standing there with a frozen expression, like he wasn't sure whether to say the next thing he'd planned to say. "Let me get something to put down so you're not just sleeping on a hardwood floor," I said briskly, and left.

In the bathroom I locked the door and allowed myself to cry. It made me feel better. It was no big deal, I realized. I was lucky.

Nothing had actually happened, really, nothing with ramifications, nothing like other stories I'd heard. Just me and my tendency to incite terrible sexual experiences. At least I felt confident I would not be inciting another one here, tonight, in my depressing apartment. I swallowed four Advil and two melatonin, washed my face, and returned with two towels. Joe was looking through my CD piles.

"Your music is like an old friend," he said, opening up a jewel box.

"You have a Discman, right?" I shuffled down in bed and hugged a pillow. "Will you be okay? I'm sorry, I'm happy to see you, I've just got a headache. Catch up tomorrow?"

I rolled over without waiting for a response. I heard him leave the room, wander around the apartment. Some muffled talking from the kitchen, meeting one of the roommates. I wasn't sure which roommate. It didn't matter. They were strangers to me. I couldn't seem to relax the muscles in my face, around my brow and my mouth. I tried to picture my whole face melting which worked temporarily, but minutes later I could feel the muscles migrating into fighting position again, taut and aching.

I must've dozed off eventually because I awoke suddenly to the sound of "Let Down." It was so loud I sat up in bed, ready to yell at someone. But there was no music. Joe was asleep, fully clothed, splayed out like a crime-scene outline on my white bath towels. I was glad to see him and hated him for being there in absolutely equal measure.

Bay Window

The next morning brought a light, continuous snowfall. I stepped over Joe without waking him and took a long hot shower that restored me more than my sleep had. When Joe finally woke he sprang to the window like a boy on Christmas.

"Let's get out there!" he said, looking back at me with an open-mouthed smile.

I handed him the towel he'd just slept on. "I thought there was a mangy animal perched on your head and then I realized it's your hair, Joe. Take a shower."

He took the towel. "And she's back."

This was the perfect thing for him to say. It acknowledged my weirdness the night before while sealing it shut, closing it for discussion. I smiled gratefully as he loped out of my room to the bathroom, my towel on his shoulder.

Outside he was giddy, catching flakes on his tongue, taking pictures with a digital camera. We ate egg and cheeses at a deli on Broadway.

"I burned you some fragments," he said as he chewed. "Send me your thoughts?"

"Sure."

He took a sip of his coffee, pausing to appreciate the classic Greek design of the paper cup. He had shaved in my bathroom so I could see his cheekbones again, but there was something different about the way he set his jaw. The time we'd been apart, when he'd been traveling, experiencing America without me, seemed to sit between us on the table. Senior year we'd seen each other nearly every day—he'd helped himself to my fridge, and I to his—and now it had been six months since we'd even been in the same city.

His eyebrows jumped and he reached out, resting his hand on my forearm. "I know what we should do," he said. "Let's go to a Guitar Center, or whatever—anywhere I can play a piano."

"Why?"

"Wanna show you something. Brand-new, a piano song—I don't have much but I think you can help. Our last venue had this amazing baby grand." He stuffed his egg sandwich wrapper into its paper bag and looked at the door.

I knew the perfect place, an old-school piano dealer in midtown I'd recently wandered past on a pilgrimage to ogle Carnegie Hall. "I have seminar at two," I said.

He checked his watch. "Plenty of time."

I already knew I wouldn't be going to seminar. The night before was becoming a dream, one of those nightmares that make you feel energized afterward, fueled by the memory of terror along with blinding gratitude for real life. It was a high, so intense I could already sense the crash ahead, the storm on the wind of a sunny day. Or maybe I would never crash. Maybe this was the new me, invigorated to the edge of mania forever. I balled up my foil and followed him out the door into the bright white street.

As it turned out, an upscale piano showroom is actually not the best place to get free use of a piano. It's too quiet. Joe and I slid quietly onto an antique carved bench and he whispered, "How far away is Guitar Center?"

A salesman who looked like he had been there as long as the building sidled up. Joe explained he was a musician in town on tour.

The salesman nodded patiently. "Signed?"

"Yes." Joe looked at me, then back at the salesman, who seemed to be waiting for more. "It's an indie label. We were just hoping to try out your pianos."

"He wants to play me something," I said. "We can use your worst piano, it's fine, just tell us which one."

He nodded officiously, and led us to a shiny black upright in a back alcove where we had more privacy anyway. "Happy to help a young musician, provided you keep it both pleasant and brief," he said.

"Can I get some water?" Joe said. "Sir?" he added.

The salesman ignored him and sailed out of the alcove.

Joe and I shared a small laugh. "Okay," he said, and played a quick F scale, his long fingers rolling easily over the B-flat. "It's called 'Bay Window.'"

When he started playing I thought their worst piano had a wonderful sound actually, round and bright. Then he sang:

"From the woman I love's ba-a-a-ay window"—gorgeous melisma on "bay"—"I watch the world begin to end." He lifted his hands, not bringing them down until the next "bay," this time on a minor chord: "In the woman I love's ba-a-ay window . . . I see the good give up again." Major.

He looked up at me. "That's the chorus."

I had about ten thoughts at once, all of them racing in my mind, elbowing each other out for space. I focused on the least emotional one. "Is this about September eleventh?"

"Yeah. Is that lame?"

"No. I mean, I assume you won't be too on the nose about it."

"Right. And it doesn't necessarily *have* to be that day—it could be about the night Bush won, any of those cultural tragedies where you feel devastated, and disconnected, and a bit like, 'Am I allowed to be a person right now?'"

I nodded. "It's great. It's different for you, so plaintive and direct. It's that track five or eight that you skip for the first month because it's too grand and sad, and then later it becomes your favorite. Do you have verses?"

"One, but the lyrics need work." He turned back to the keys and sang slowly, with long, drawn-out syllables: "It's a movie, but it's happening . . . Eating black beans and avocado." He made a face at that line. "You said, 'I know that I want children . . . It makes me feel like a monster.'"

My breath caught. I looked down at my arm, where the hairs were raised. Joe followed my gaze and fought a smile. "What part?" he said.

I exhaled. "'It makes me feel like a monster.'"

"Lyric or melody?"

"Both. It really works, Joe."

He made a victory fist.

"Why does the girl get that line, though?" I said. "Why can't it be you who said that? We both talked about kids that day. You brought it up, actually."

He cocked his head, thinking.

"You just wrote it that way because you've absorbed giant piles of bullshit your whole life about—"

He held up his hand and sang it again: "I know that I want children. It makes me feel like a monster."

"Yes. Better."

"Okay. What else did we eat that day? I want to give that feeling of hunkering down."

"Chips, but what a terrible-sounding word."

"Eating black beans . . . And tortillas," he sang.

"Eating black beans . . . Margaritas," I tried. "Sounds like a party."

"Eating black beans . . . From the ca-a-an."

"Eating black beans . . . Hours passing," I sang. "That would sound good with 'but it's happening.'"

We settled on that. Then we wrote another line, and another. He had produced a small tape recorder and his notebook from his backpack. The whole time it felt like we were moments away from leaving or being kicked out; we never took off our winter coats, even as I felt sweat trickling down my ribs from my bra. "Real quick," we kept saying. "One more line, real quick."

When we had a full second verse, he said, "Let me just play the whole thing through." And he did, and it sounded great, it sounded real, I couldn't believe it. He looked triumphant. "Done!"

"What about the bridge?"

He sighed. "I'm thirsty."

"And I need to pee," I said. "But there's a larger issue here, which is you always want to skip the bridge."

"You and your bridges."

"They're important, Joe! They're the release. The emotional center. The climax."

He looked amused. "Which is it?"

"It doesn't matter! 'Creep' by Radiohead, that's release." I scooted my butt to the front edge of the piano bench, leaning over the keys like I was about to play something, which of course I did not know how to do, not without embarrassing myself. I wished so badly that I could break into a rendition of the "Creep" bridge. Instead, I kept talking. " 'Dock of the Bay': emotional center. 'Just My Imagination': that bridge is so devastating, it should've been a sign that Paul Williams was about to kill himself. It's *going for it*, Joe. Without a bridge, your song isn't up for its own challenge."

"What about the Magnetic Fields?" he asked. "Stephin Merritt's songs never have bridges."

"He's a genius at writing a half song. He's emotionally at arm's length, which is great, that's his deal and nobody does it like him— but that's not you. You're an emotional writer, you just lack guts."

He flinched so briefly I may have imagined it, then said, challengingly, "You think 'My Only Friend' is emotionally at arm's length?"

I paused. 'My Only Friend' was a heartbreaking Magnetic Fields song, an elegy for Billie Holiday that made me bawl the first time I heard it.

He let out a derisive laugh and shook his head. "Percy Marks realizes she might be wrong about something. Call the newspapers."

" 'My Only Friend' could be better if it had a bridge," I said weakly, but he was still performing that little jerky laugh. It made me want revenge, and with the nightmare fuel still burning in my veins, I knew exactly how to get it. I would write a damn bridge all by myself.

I looked at the piano. I knew we were in F. I spread my left hand over a D chord, then remembered how to make it a minor. The salesman entered our alcove and opened a metal file cabinet in the corner. With my right hand I began picking out a melody on the keys, correcting as I went, my fingers visibly trembling. Joe watched. The salesman left, lingering long enough in the door to make my hands freeze up. I started over when he was gone, whispering over the notes as I played them: "Zoe comes over in the afternoon."

Joe put his hand over mine and played it slightly differently, making the lowest note lower, much prettier.

I worked out a second line, over a G minor. Again he pulled the interval wider. Then I whisper-sang: "Zoe comes over in the afternoon . . . sucks the air right out of the room. She's planning protests with the bitter grin . . . of a pacifist who knows she won't win."

"Write it down," he said quickly, loudly.

He did more work on the chords as I scribbled in the notebook, then he played the whole song into the recorder.

At that point Joe began to look triumphant and it made me queasy. Was the song good? The bridge could work harder, I thought, especially given my earlier pontificating; I didn't love how it portrayed Zoe, and the last line was clunky. If Joe had written that bridge, I'd probably tell him it sucked. But my nightmare fuel was sputtering out, and the final chord of "NYC" was starting to buzz in my brain again.

I decided I needed beer. We left the showroom and walked until we found a bar with an old upright in the back, with chipped keys and a questionable middle C. The bar was nearly empty, just a couple construction workers at the counter, probably because the heater seemed to be struggling; even the bartender rubbed his hands together for warmth as he took our order. Joe brought his beer to the piano, and I sat down on a rickety, too-high barstool from which my feet were forced to dangle like a child's. The beer was bright and light and fulfilled its purpose brilliantly, bringing me back to this thrilling experience, the unfinished work of this song. On the back of two napkins, I wrote out the full lyric again. I felt a fleeting sense of being at home on this island, where it seemed I could find everything I needed—pianos, beer, a fresh blank page—for the mere cost of inserting myself into unwelcoming environments.

Halfway through my second pint I crossed out the bridge and wrote an entirely new one. It came to me quickly, before I began to feel self-aware (look at me writing lyrics on a napkin, do I think I'm Joni Mitchell, etc.). I thought maybe I could cross it out again and write a third version, something better and smarter than the second, but it sat there staring up at me from its napkin like a child refusing bedtime.

I brought it to Joe at the piano. "Instead of 'Zoe comes over in the afternoon.'"

"I liked 'Zoe comes over in the afternoon,' but okay," he said. He propped the napkin up on the piano's ledge and played the first chord of the bridge. "She tries to—" His voice dissolved into a grunt, and he shot me a stung look. "Guess we're not talking about Zoe anymore."

"Why bring a third character into it," I said. I moved behind him so he wouldn't have to see me while he sang.

He faced the napkin again and started over. "She tries to kiss me as the sun goes down—I only give her my cheek. I promise friendship and we face the screen again—what a day to be so weak."

He swallowed the "weak"; I barely heard it. His foot lay heavy on the sustain pedal. Finally he turned his head so I could see his profile. "I'd call that strength," he said over his shoulder. "Restraint."

"Use 'Zoe comes over in the afternoon,' then," I said. "It's your song."

I walked back to the barstool and started folding up the napkins. He had nailed the phrasing, fit in the extra syllables of the "again" exactly as I'd heard it in my head: muttering, defeated. Even the limp delivery of "weak" had worked. It was a beautiful bridge, and I was proud to have created it. But I was done.

He shuffled over to my barstool, empty pint in hand. He was watching me carefully, sideways. I thought he might be about to make a speech, but he just mumbled something about making it to Brooklyn in time for sound check.

I zipped up my black puffer coat. "When are you back in New York?"

"Two weeks. Boston, then a few stops in Vermont, then here again—just a warehouse party, but they're putting us up."

"Mind if I catch that one instead?" I said. "I need to rest, and my apartment and your show are at opposite ends of the city."

He nodded. He was still looking at me sideways, his body twisted in the direction of the piano.

"You guys must be getting good," I said.

"Yeah. Got a new drummer, a better one."

"Cool."

"How are things going for you, here, anyway?" he said. "Have I not asked that?"

I laughed politely. "I'm fine. Not really sure what I'm doing, as a writer—everyone else in the program is older and seems like they've already found their voice. But, you know. Figuring it out."

He scoffed. "If anyone on this planet knows their voice, it's you."

"No, I don't," I said. "It's tricky, what I'm writing—not quite music journalism, not quite personal essay. You don't understand."

"Ah," he said.

"That came out wrong."

"Come here."

He faced me fully and pulled me into a long, tight hug. I tried to relax my head against his chest, but I couldn't find my usual nook. And the longer he held me the more I felt myself stiffen. It was all the layers of clothing, I thought, muting the effect of the hug—these coats render everyone so sexless, just hordes of blackened marsh-mallows marching through the concrete jungle. But I knew it wasn't the coats. My body was petrified. It had made too many mistakes; it couldn't be trusted.

And then, out of nowhere, I laughed. It was suddenly too much: that he had named me as the woman he loves in a song, that I had helped him finish the song without ever mentioning this fact, that I had responded by calling him a coward for never consummating this love—and that after all this, we were standing in a bar, just hugging awkwardly and small-talking.

He pulled back and looked down at me. "Is something funny?"

"Funny strange, yeah," I said. "I mean, your chorus—that line—"

He spared me having to say it. "'The woman I love'?"

I nodded.

He shuffled his feet. "Yeah, hah." He looked right at me briefly, then away. "Sorry about that. It sounded good."

"Right," I said. A relief, really. It did sound good, just as "chips" and "margaritas" had sounded bad; you had to choose what worked for the song. I said goodbye and hauled my wooden limbs to a sub-way station.

A Case of You

Prepare to Bleed

I can't remember ever hearing the song "Chelsea Hotel #2" by Leonard Cohen without knowing it was about Janis Joplin. I wonder how I'd feel about it if I could, just once, remove that knowledge. Cohen expressed regret later—not about the song itself, but about the indiscretion of naming Janis as its inspiration. But I suspect it wouldn't matter who inspired it, Janis or just some unfamous gal: I would still despise this song.

I used to love it as much as everyone else. That painful blend of bravado and vulnerability that is always ascribed to Janis, brought to life in such vivid detail. I picture her adjusting her dress at the waist, for some reason, as Cohen observes her from his bed. Shaking her hair over her shoulder, maybe. Such life.

But on a recent listen, the last verse, in which Cohen dismisses Janis as one of countless fallen robins in his life, hit me like a gut punch. Seems a bit unnecessary, I thought. Even cruel. I reminded myself about dramatic irony, but I didn't believe it—he seemed to mean what he said. Then I skipped back to the beginning of the track and heard the whole thing anew. Oh my god, I thought. This is what men want. For a woman to give them head without caring that they're not handsome, that she's late for her own show, that they won't think of her often after this, even after her own spectacular death. "Chelsea Hotel #2" is what men want.

The only real compliment Cohen gives Janis in the song is that she doesn't bother him with emotionality. She doesn't whine about needing him, or not needing him, a presumably female tendency he refers to as "jivin' around." That this is about a once-in-a-generation genius who could sing two damn notes at the same time does make it sting a bit extra, but no woman deserves this as her biggest compliment. Because we've all done some "jivin' around": that endless game of trying to be heard without accidentally saying too much—of daring to express an emotion that might be subject to change, to a man who just wants you to service his parts.

The second verse makes me retch. He and his friends are spending their New York nights chasing money and flesh, a shuddery foreshadow of cokey '80s stockbroker energy. Then he shrugs it all off with a truly confounding line: "That was called love for the workers in song / Probably still is for those of them left." First there's the problem of a poet-musician labeling himself and his friends "workers" as their limousine drivers hold up traffic on 23rd Street, sweating through their polyester uniforms. And the phrase "for those of them left" is just bizarre given that this song was written in the '70s, a golden era for the industry of the singer-songwriter. Did Leonard Cohen anticipate our current age of nobody profiting from music but

Ticketmaster and T-shirt manufacturers? I doubt it. More likely he saw himself as a precious dying breed: the true artist always on the verge of extinction. Retch.

Janis did not write a song about Cohen, that we know of. But she did give this revealing and depressingly relatable confession, published much later in Richard Avedon and Doon Arbus's book, *The Sixties:* "Sometimes, you know, you're with someone and you're convinced that they have something to . . . to tell you. . . . So maybe nothing's happening, but you keep telling yourself something's happening. You know, innate communication. He's just not saying anything. He's moody or something. So you keep being there, pulling, giving, rapping, you know. And then, all of a sudden about four o'clock in the morning you realize that, flat ass, this motherfucker's just lying there. He's not balling me. I mean, that really happened to me. Really heavy, like slam-in-the-face it happened. Twice. Jim Morrison and Leonard Cohen."

So that's how Cohen's room at the Chelsea Hotel felt for Janis. She wasn't *saying* she needed him—maybe she didn't know how; maybe nobody had ever taught her the fine, exhausting art of jivin' around—but she did. She needed something from him, some kind of connection. And he was just lying there.

Janis may not have written about Cohen, but Joni did: in "A Case of You" she depicts him as a poison for which she has developed such tolerance that she can easily consume lethal amounts. Cohen's own mother warns Joni about him, in the final verse: "She said, 'Go to him, stay with him if you can / But be prepared to bleed.'" ("All the mothers warn me against their sons," Joni told her biographer.)

Decades later, in a magazine I bought from a garage sale as a teenager, Tori Amos said she would've given her arm to have written "A Case of You." I'm always struck by this notion. Any writer who's ever been warned off a man wishes they'd written "A Case of You." But what inspires this particular compliment, this feeling of not just loving a song, or any work of art, but longing to have created it yourself? It happens when you identify so intensely with the work it feels somehow wrong—sad, almost—that it didn't come from your own brain. Like if you had arrived at this expression yourself, you would have more effectively metastasized the emotions that made you love the song so much. Look what I turned that experience into, you could think, if you'd written "A Case of You." Your pain would have made the world more beautiful, would have made generations of women cry the most cleansing tears, the kind that open floodgates of endorphins when they're done. You would be forever connected to these women: your people. And your wound would be healed.

Of course, songs have been written about Joni too. The most famous is Graham Nash's "Our House," which illustrates that Cohen's "workers in song" were not all holed up in grimy hotel rooms; some of them were picking flowers and playing with cats. Joni stars as a radiant goddess of hearth and home, making everything seem easy. But even through Nash's rosy lens, I sense a wifely exhaustion in Joni—especially when he beckons her to sit with him, inviting her to rest for "just five minutes." Five minutes? She gets just five minutes?

Mere weeks after "Our House" was written, Joni

would turn down a marriage proposal from Nash, on the grounds that he just wanted her to "cook and clean for him." She would dump a bowl of cornflakes over his head in the midst of an argument. Nash's own description of one fight, and this is on the record: "Then I put Joni over my knee, and I spanked her. With all due respect, she took it very well."

"Our House" has remained frozen in the public imagination as an ode to domestic bliss. But the song's almost comic naïveté—the "very, very, very fine house," the bridge of la-la-las, the two jokey drum hits echoing the cats in the yard—whispers the truth in our ears: This is all a fairy tale. The song is a snapshot of one fleeting moment when a man's life was easy. We all get these moments, if we're lucky, and we stay with them if we can. But we must prepare to bleed.

It's like Nash knew when he wrote the song that his greatest fantasy had come to life and it was still just that: a fantasy. Worse, that it was more *his* fantasy than hers. Because "Our House" isn't about Joni Mitchell. And "A Case of You" isn't about Leonard Cohen, and "Chelsea Hotel #2" isn't really about Janis Joplin either. We are all just writing about ourselves.

"It's interesting," said one of the journalists, tapping her pencil eraser on my pages. "I'm never bored, per se, when I'm reading Percy's stuff. But as with her previous pieces, I find myself wondering what the point is. It feels a bit scattered. We don't even have the focus on one song this time."

"It was dark as hell was my impression." This from one of the younger girls, meaning my age, who was writing a memoir about her mom. "I don't know any of these songs, I'm not into old white-people music, but I did like the use of the three songs—like a literary triptych, or an after-the-fact love triangle."

The teacher, Tracy, nodded. She wrote long-form magazine articles and had published one epic narrative history of the Underground Railroad that had taken her twenty years to write and research. "I do know these songs, and I'm not sure I'll ever hear them the same way again," she said. "Which is definitely saying something."

Tracy had perfect gray face-framing locs that never moved. "Definitely saying something"—a deadweight compliment, almost backhand. It hung in the air.

"I agree with that sense of, like, what's the point?" the young girl continued. "What is she writing about, really? Is she writing about the music, or is she writing about herself? Because if she's writing about herself, we need more of her. And if she's writing about the music, we need less of her."

Heads began nodding around the table like dominoes, picking up speed. Only Raj, the food writer, stayed still.

Nomi was looking at me. "I would agree, generally," she said, and folded her long fingers thoughtfully over her chin. "But I would also acknowledge that maybe you're carving out some new territory here, and that's what's making us uncomfortable."

The nodding around the table stopped, replaced with the back-and-forth head tilting of fake consideration. Nomi was being a friend. I felt, as always when my stories were being workshopped, like my entire system had arrested—brain, organs, all the gears just paused mid-crank. I wrote everything down verbatim in my notebook, my wrist aching already. I would process it later.

"Raj?" said Tracy. "You look like you have a different perspective."

"Oh," he said, and leaned forward, clearing his throat. "Yeah. I guess so. I feel very clear on what she's writing about, actually, because she announces it in the last line: she's writing about herself. So I would vote for inserting more of herself, not less of herself.

She's writing about people, really, how people use music to get clarity on themselves. It's clear to me that Percy's subject is not music— music is just her channel to get at people. Channel's not the right word. Her medium. Not medium." He widened his eyes, annoyed at himself. "Anyway. I thought it was devastating."

"I'm buying your beer," I told Raj afterward at the Lion's Head. We were waiting to order at the bar. "Do you have your chili or whatever?"

He patted his pocket.

My gears had started turning again, creakily, eager for lubrication. We all sat at the big long table at the back. The Lion's Head had attempted holiday decorations, hanging real pine garland that was already brittle, dropping needles on our table. Half the class had come, but nobody mentioned my story; we talked about our plans for winter break. Most people were leaving. Even Nomi had sublet her apartment for a month and was going to stay with her mom in Philly. I couldn't afford a ticket home, having run out of my cost-of-living loan—a $5K check that came in September and January—so I'd gotten a job waitressing at a touristy restaurant near the Museum of Natural History.

I nodded along to the conversation and thought about Joe, who had called the night before to tell me he wasn't coming to Brooklyn after all. Some music blog in London had given the album a five-star review, which led to an invitation to open a UK tour. I was excited for him. Neither of us had ever been to Europe.

Raj gave me some dumb "penny for your thoughts" comment, so I told him about Joe. "Sort of my best friend," I said, in an attempt to avoid the same mistake of calling him my collaborator, though that was truer now, post–"Bay Window."

"And you were looking forward to seeing him?"

"Yeah. I mean, it's no big deal, he'll be back through New York. I'm just regretting not going to his show last week."

"I always find it curious when a man and a woman can be best friends. I was in that situation once, in college, and I was just desperately, pathetically in love with the girl."

"Oh, that's me," I said, laughing as if this was no big confession. "*Was* me, I should say. Finally coming out of it now."

He folded his arms. "If you don't mind me asking, did anything ever happen between you?"

"Nope," I said.

"Nothing?"

"We talked about it. Held hands, spooned. But no, nothing happened." I felt my cheeks warming, catching up to the conversation.

He gave a definitive nod. "Good. You're fine then."

"Oh yeah? Why?"

"Because you don't know what he tastes like. When there's nothing concrete to miss, that makes it easier to get over, in my experience."

This had a nice ring to it—the ring of a truism if not quite the truth. I smiled. "What he tastes like. You're such a foodie."

He shuddered.

"Sorry," I said. The term had only recently gained popularity; it was my first time using it. "It does reek of class, doesn't it?"

"Indeed. And of restaurant-as-sport. Of appropriating food as a hobby when you have found, in your thirties, that you have none."

I laughed. "Is that so bad?"

"No. It's just not me." He tipped his beer can back as far as it could go, even after it became clear it was empty.

I was out of things to say. I turned back toward the other students.

"I'm enjoying the Neko Case CD," Raj said, and that's when I knew: he had actually gone out and bought the Neko Case. As soon as I had the thought, I papered over it in my mind. I would deal with it later, along with my workshop feedback. "I feel I should give you a food recommendation in return," he was saying.

"Sure," I said. "Hey, what's up with those Indian restaurants in the East Village that have all the chili pepper lights? Are those good? Because they look fun, in a lame way."

He grimaced. "It hurts me to hear you say this," he said. "What time is it? Are you hungry?"

I said I was, and then he was pushing back his chair and leading me up Amsterdam Avenue and down to a subway platform. He had to consult the map; we were going to Queens.

The train was loud and crowded. I watched Raj clutching the subway strap, eyes darting around, as new to the city as I was, and had an impulse to hug him. Instead I said, over the rush-hour din, "Thanks again for today."

He shrugged. "It was honest feedback."

I'm not sure why I believed him, given my new suspicion that he was into me. But I did. He seemed oddly incapable of lying.

"The idea of inserting more of myself into my writing does not appeal to me, though," I said. "Unfortunately."

"Just throw in a little bit. A line here, a line there. Readers don't need much."

"I don't think I can do a little. I tried to write autobiographically once and it was mortifying, how personal I got." I winced at the memory of the pieces I'd never submitted to *Ring Finger*. "I'd end up telling a whole big story."

Someone with a boom box arrived in our train car. "What?"

"I'd say too much," I said loudly, into his ear. "It would be a whole book."

"So write a whole book," he shouted.

The train lurched. I looked down at my feet, my black boots on the speckled gray floor, trying to restabilize myself. Lines from my buried Archives folder—"'Communist Daughter,' second verse, searing pain"; "Her butt was in the air, her hands in a gopher hole"— appeared in my mind, jackknifing each other. No way, I thought. I would never write that book.

We arrived in Queens at a large, nondescript Pakistani restaurant next to a closed sari shop. The food was good, but curry is always good. He explained in detail what made the naan so chewy as I fought a profound lack of interest. I asked where he was from and he said Los Angeles, which I found surprising.

"Why is everyone so shocked by this?" he said. "Should I be offended? Do I not seem like I could come from a place with celebrities, is that it?" He held up a knife and looked at his reflection. "I have a good face. I have analyzed my face and I'm pretty sure it's inoffensive, at worst. Is it because I'm not very tall? What about Tom Cruise?"

I laughed. It was true: he did have a good face.

"I'm serious!" he said. "I'm sorry, if you were the first person in New York to *gasp* upon hearing where I'm from, it would not be an issue. But you are not. You are the third."

"New Yorkers hate LA," I said. "Take it as a compliment."

"Yeah, but I'm not hanging out with real New Yorkers, am I? I'm not hanging out with rappers defending their coast. Half our class is from somewhere in California, including you."

"I'm from Indiana."

"Well that's just random. And don't change the subject."

I thought for a minute while he trained that expectant face on me. I knew my answer, I just had to figure out how to say it. He was still holding his knife up like a conductor freezing the music. "Your vibe is not superficial," I finally said. "Like, at all. I think that's why."

He seemed to like this explanation enough to resume using his knife for eating. He chewed for a minute and then he said, "I live in the realm of the senses."

What an odd thing to say. Later that night, home in bed, I considered what he'd meant. The senses are pure experience, I decided; there is no sense for how things *seem,* which is what matters to the superficial.

I rolled onto my back and tried to tune in to my senses. The faint circular pressure of a bedspring against my shoulder blade. The smell of prewar plaster and dust, notes of unwashed laundry. The sight of four empty walls leaning toward a ceiling, the clang of an ancient heater, Colgate mingling with the sour remnants of beer and cumin. And then I thought about how my life *seemed* in that moment—a young writer in her spartan New York phase, studying where Allen Ginsberg had studied—and I felt much better actually. Raj and I were probably not a good match.

Bring It on Home to Me

We were together by Christmas. I would've been embarrassed by the swiftness of it if anyone had been around. Upper Manhattan was like our own private snow globe.

Raj lived in a university-owned building too, just a few blocks from mine, but he and his roommate had bought rugs and a rice cooker and multiple lamps with dimmer attachments. I was constantly marveling at the lighting. The first night I slept over, he put up tea lights along a crown molding ledge near the ceiling—one tiny flame every foot or two, down the hallway, around the living room and his bedroom, even in the bathroom. It tinged everything with hushed, flickering sepia.

I had packed a toothbrush that night. I felt very aware of my toothbrush in the backpack as we ate the dinner he'd cooked, a whole roasted chicken with lemons and rosemary. Otherwise I had taken no special measures for the evening. I was wearing the plain black T-shirt and skinny jeans that I had started wearing every day and would wear some version of for the next several years, having decided that my bangs could do the heavy lifting in signifying the existence of a personality.

We kissed in the sepia that night for a long time, standing on our knees in the center of his bed. I liked how he kissed me. Sweet, short kisses on the lips, threaded together by compliments and self-effacing jokes. He had a George Harrison smile, toothy and bashful, lopsided. Several times he kissed me through the smile.

"I keep picturing you putting up these lights," I teased, between kisses. "Did you use a ladder?"

He looked down, hiding the smile. His nose brushed against my lips. "Stepladder," he whispered.

"Mmm. So grown-up."

"Mmm."

A playlist traveled from a laptop through real wired speakers installed above his bed, lots of Cat Stevens and Carly Simon, like a classic rock radio station's chill-out hour. I didn't mind it. It was impossible to mind anything in that lighting. Then Sam Cooke came on, "Bring It on Home to Me," the exact song you want to hear while kneeling on a soft surface with a man in a candle-rimmed room.

I collapsed onto him, hoping he understood not to say a word until the song was over. He held me quietly through the first call-and-response with Lou Rawls. I felt his chest draw in, about to speak, but I shushed him in time. People think of Sam Cooke as a voice more than a songwriter, but he wrote this shit. Sam Cooke was a miracle.

We started to sway in the second and third verses, as the strings got louder, building with the gospel longing in his voice. The increasingly soulful swing of the drums. I noted the absence of a bridge, but this was soul; it didn't need one. For a song about brutal rejection and heartbreak, it's strange that it makes me feel so heart-swellingly happy, always, just drowning in joy to be alive on this earth.

By the time it ended I had decided I never wanted to leave this apartment. At least not until spring. In spring we could wander out to Central Park.

We didn't talk about the song. I was sort of relieved not to have to hear myself go on and on about it. We resumed our kisses, which grew longer.

"What do you want to do?" he said eventually. "I mean, I'm happy to spend the whole night kissing, but."

"Right," I said. I'd overindulged his generosity.

"Just checking in."

I sat down on my heels. "Sorry," I said.

"Don't be sorry."

"I didn't mean sorry," I said. "I just—I'm not super, you know, experienced."

"Okay. Well, you're young."

"Am I? I feel too old to have had sex only one and a half times."

He sat down against his pillows.

"Thanks for telling me that," he said. "I'm more experienced, but I'm twenty-nine. At your age I had only slept with one person, I think. Anyway, I figured there was something, based on your last submission for workshop—I figured something had happened to you."

"Oh god." I saw the piece again in a terrible, embarrassing light. "Did I come across as completely damaged?"

He tried to look kind. "It was quite a bit of vitriol for Leonard Cohen."

I groaned. "Honestly, nothing has happened to me. That's the problem with my life, more than anything, probably: nothing has fucking happened. I don't deserve to write a piece like that. I didn't have some terrible boyfriend or father or something, if that's what you're thinking. My dad wouldn't even hug me once I grew breasts." This wasn't a thought I'd had before, at least not so clearly. But I realized it was true. A memory arrived, fresh from the deepest well of my mind, of my dad hugging me while walking home from kindergarten. I had tripped on nothing and scraped my knee. Dad's chest was warm and so broad I could barely get my arms around it.

Raj was waiting patiently. "Of course, something has happened to everyone," he said.

"I mean, sure. There has been some unpleasantness at the hands of men."

He didn't say anything.

"And the one and a half times I did have sex were terrible, absolutely terrible. But mostly it's just been Joe, or the fantasy of Joe, and that's lasted for so long that I'm worried it's gotten to a point where Joe has become . . ." I couldn't say the rest out loud. It was too predictable.

Raj pulled a pillow over his lap and retrieved his glasses from the nightstand. "So, okay, let's attack this. First, there's this Joe loser, touring Europe with his band—ugh, sounds like a real waste of space. You'll forget him soon."

I smiled.

"Then there's the terrible sex. Can I ask what part of it was terrible?"

"All of it."

"Specifically, I assume, the intercourse?" He wrinkled his nose. "Sorry for that word."

I nodded. "Yeah. That."

"Okay. We won't do that."

And we didn't. I stayed until summer.

Hey Ya!

The summer of 2003 in New York was dripping-wet hot, I guess like always, though I swear people said it was especially bad that year. I was waitressing and trying to write, when I wasn't camping out for Shakespeare in the Park tickets or sitting at outdoor tables of restaurants drinking well margaritas with Raj. He had a job key-wording *New Yorker* cartoons for a searchable database. I don't think either of us got any real writing done all summer.

I remember it as the first great summer of my life, like an urban version of a Beach Boys song, although I recently found a journal we'd kept together that evidenced a more realistic story. I'd forgotten the thing until I saw its worn red cover: we'd started it as a jokey little diary of what we seemed to know would be a summer worth remembering, but it quickly became an all-purpose notebook, filled with phone numbers, doodles, inside jokes, and notes left for each other that we would not tear out but just leave sitting there in the book, splayed open.

> *June 19: Today we went to 125th for a street fair but it was already over, so Raj got a shirt at Old Navy. I said, "Should this lame day go in the journal?" Raj said we do not keep things from the journal.*

1. Cancel NY Times *subscription*
2. Get a job

Things Percy thinks I'm bad at: wearing shorts, cooking without making a mess, covering my toes in public, talking about music, owning my word choices, eating for satiety, communicating plans with sufficient advance notice, reading subway maps, telephone etiquette. Things Percy thinks I'm good at: lighting.

My job search has ended in success; for more details see "Heaven Knows I'm Miserable Now" by the Smiths.

July 16 or 17 or 18: Today was like every day in that we worked our respective jobs but then Percy had the idea to take the subway down to Chumley's for a nightcap, around the corner from which we heard a man on drums "makin' omelets," as he called it, and singing "Who'll Stop the Rain." He had perfect posture and a rear-to-front comb-over.

Rajie! I know I said I'd stay home and write but my talents appear to have waned. I went for a walk or something. Meet at Nacho Mama's at 6:00?

July 17: Despite now having a job, I woke up this morning feeling terrified of money and I couldn't shake the feeling. All day I spent like this, terrorized by the money I'm borrowing from my future to attend this ridiculous writing program. But then on my way home from work, on the bus, I met a woman who had just had a brain tumor removed. They tipped her head on its side and drained all the fluid out, so her brain fell smack against the side of her cranium, then they filled it back up again. Only half of her face could tell me this. The other half was just a stone-cold badass staring at me.

Presently Percy is reading Didion in bed with her shirt off (hot). While I am looking forward to my roommate returning so he can contribute to the rent, the ramifications in the area of shirtlessness concern me.

I like Raj's face the way I like the feel of his barely capable AC blowing on my sweaty skin: elementally.

Percy! Gone campus-ward (hot in here). Call my cell if you want to have coffee or a drink or just company. Sorry I called you dramatic. You are, but so is life.

August 10: Today we talked about how we have no friends here this summer except each other and what that means for each of us. I had good friends in LA and I miss them, I miss them desperately, and I miss my family, whereas Percy does not miss anyone except Joe who is a loser so whatever. But then we got some food from the grocery store and I cooked it up and we ate in bed whilst reading. Then we drank a very dry rosé and assembled a playlist of summery songs. We have a very pleasant time together, that's the thing about this.

He made me feel so good. He went down on me after dinner as a matter of routine. One time he got under the kitchen table, crawling up between my legs while I finished my glass of wine. I learned what he liked too, and did my best. Occasionally he asked if I wanted him inside me, and I always told the truth: I did not. I wore a backpack of guilt about this, but he never said anything. We gave each other a lot of space, emotionally.

The blackout in August is absent from our notebook, but a highlight in my memory. I had just gotten back to Raj's apartment after working a lunch shift and was sitting in front of the AC window unit, drying my sweat, when the unit stopped working. Slowly I realized everything had stopped working. People were spilling out into the street. Ten minutes later, the landline rang: Raj would make his way uptown from his key-wording job and we would meet on Broadway and 113th. I waited there for hours, just talking to strangers, watching the spectacle, eating a pint of ice cream that had been thrust into my hand by a bodega worker along with a plastic spoon. An older man I recognized from campus, maybe a professor, was directing traffic in the middle of the intersection, laughing at himself. People were standing on the backs of delivery trucks, hitching rides like garbagemen. Raj finally arrived and we embraced ecstatically. At a small grocery on Broadway, we were allowed to take anything frozen, along with sweating bottles of cold water. We loaded up and walked back to campus, where we sat on the steps of Low Library in the pitch-dark eating melting Choco Tacos and deli meats. I heard a woman say to a friend, passing by on College Walk, "It's like September eleventh but fun," which seemed like something that would never, ever be said again. It made me want to write a song, an inverse of "Bay Window," about the specific camaraderie of New Yorkers in moments of anarchy.

Cell towers became functional again as we sat on campus, and our parents called with all the stories they'd seen on the national news: commuters trapped in the subway, overheating grandmas from here to Pittsburgh. There had been no way for us to get that information at the time. I felt retroactively scared. "It was caused by drooping foliage," my dad reported through the phone. "They think," my mom added, on the extension. "Also maybe a bug in the alarm system."

I looked at Raj, my eyes wide. I didn't have speakerphone on, but it was clear Raj could hear my parents; everything sounded louder in the complete darkness. "There but for the grace of drooping foliage and a buggy alarm system," Raj whispered. My mom said who was that, and I said nobody.

I liked a lot of popular R&B that summer, a fact that seemed geographically ordained. Beyoncé's "Crazy in Love" played seemingly from the lampposts a few blocks away, where the bright line around Columbia gave way to Harlem, and I never tired of it. I had the original N.E.R.D. album on rotation for weeks, burned for me by Nomi—the bootleg version with samples and programming instead of the rap-metal instrumentation on the studio version (tragically this treasure would disappear within a year or two, into whatever black hole claimed the bulk of my CD collection).

And then, mere days after the blackout, OutKast dropped two singles simultaneously: "Hey Ya!" and "The Way You Move." Instantly they became the songs of the summer, so much so that I associate them with memories as far back as June even though I know that can't be possible. I told Raj we should have a party; I wanted an excuse to dance to "Hey Ya!" on a loop. He agreed, because summer was ending and people were coming back into town, and he wanted to make appetizers.

The morning of the party I got my first-ever text from Joe: some hipsters in bklyn r paying us 5k to play their wedding!! labor day wknd- be my date? I miss u.

I hadn't spoken to him since he'd left for Europe. I was copied on his mass email updates, according to which he was both physically and mentally exhausted but having fun, meeting people, grateful for the opportunity, blah blah. In every email he seemed to be restraining himself from whining about why Caroline's popularity overseas wasn't translating back home. There were fewer photos and travel narratives than his domestic tour.

He'd been on my mind lately, in the context of the collaboration between the two members of OutKast on the new album *Speakerboxxx/The Love Below,* which fascinated me to the point that I read every magazine that featured them—often standing in the subway station newsstand, missing my train so I could get to the end. Best friends and partners since middle school, André 3000 and Big Boi were growing apart musically, and this latest release was the most striking illustration of the rift: a double album that was basically two solo albums, each with its own title and lead single. André and Big Boi weren't in the studio at the same time; they didn't even sing on each other's tracks. But the label insisted both albums be credited to OutKast. And in interviews, no matter how much they griped about each other, it was clear they still saw themselves as a team. A maddening, dialectical union. They needed each other, if only as listeners to their own solo work—that crucial first ear.

I loved this idea. I'd been blabbing about it to poor Raj for days. How many more Beatles albums could we have gotten if they'd taken this approach—if they'd set each other free but kept lending their ears? John would've forced Paul to step up his game on his first solo album; Paul would've tempered John's self-seriousness in the mid-'70s. *Speakerboxxx/The Love Below* seemed quietly revolutionary to me, in this way, a new solution to the age-old problem of the ego in artistic collaboration.

I'd been thinking of Joe in this context only abstractly, the way I always thought about him when I thought about songwriting. But when that text came in, the connection sharpened instantly in my mind: I had never responded to the CD of fragments Joe had left me. I'd listened once, and had plenty to say about it, but then I'd met Raj and shoved the CD into a low drawer. I had refused to give Joe my ear.

I decided to deal with the text and this revelation later. I was busy buying booze and putting toothpicks into tiny stacks of food.

We invited only nonfiction writers and a few poets to the party. This was not just an effort to exclude Harrison, whom Raj hated even without knowing our history, but a genuine desire to pack the place with our nonfiction family. I'd developed more of a liking for them as I'd realized that nonfiction was for people who felt about something, anything, the way I felt about music. But the fiction writers came anyway, waiting until the party was in full swing and then trickling in two by two, Harrison among the last of them. By then he was easy to avoid, a dance I'd perfected by this point, even though he always pretended—or believed—that nothing even slightly inappropriate had happened between us.

"Hey Ya!" was requested anew with each arrival, so we must've played it a dozen times. What a jam that was. Within weeks it would be so overplayed it would sound like nothing, but that summer, whenever it started I felt like someone had tapped my spine with a hammer and activated an entirely new sensory system in my body. I loved how it started at ten out of ten, no time to waste. I loved that the lyrics, for those who listened, were about the impossibility of love, the inevitability of heartbreak—but just fucking dancing in the face of it. I loved the extra 2/4 measure that kept you on your toes. "Hey Ya!" was the first time I learned that I liked to dance; I wasn't sure if I was any good, but I liked how it felt. Raj's one move was a glorified walk, small steps taken on the beat, hands raised to fighting position. I found it indescribably cute that night. He weaved between the sweaty bodies of our classmates, filling drinks, sharing bites.

People were starting to leave when Joe called my cell phone, which I'd put in my jeans pocket in case anyone had trouble with our building's buzzer system. I went into the bathroom and answered on what must've been the last ring.

"Joe! Hi! I'm hosting a party!" I saw myself in the mirror, flush with flavored vodka and OutKast.

"Oh, sorry," he said. The connection was bad. "Is that why you didn't respond to my text?"

"What?"

"I texted you."

"Right, sorry, I meant to respond. I hate texting!"

"I can't believe it's been so long that—entirely new method of communication."

"Hah, right."

"—in a week."

"Sorry? You're going to be here in a week?"

"Yeah—come?"

"Yes, I can come to the wedding."

"—you?"

"I can't really hear you."

"Can I stay with you?"

I watched my mouth open and close in the bathroom mirror. "The Way You Move" was starting outside the door. The connection cleared up.

"Percy?"

There he was. Now he sounded almost too close. "I have to tell you something," I said. I thought of how a woman would phrase it in a movie, a real woman with a career and high heels. "I'm seeing someone."

"Oh," he said. Long pause. "I wondered, when you didn't text back. Is it serious?"

"No," I said. I glared at myself in the mirror. "Maybe."

"So you'll come to the wedding but I shouldn't stay with you, is that what you're saying?"

"Yeah," I said. "I guess that's what I'm saying."

"Okay," he said. "The wedding is at a hotel, and they're comping our rooms, so I can just stay there for the first night anyway. Not sure how long I'll stick around in New York, but I can figure something out."

"Okay," I said.

"Percy, I miss you," he said, suddenly sounding intense. "I'll see you in a week, okay?"

I went back out to the living room and sat next to Nomi on the couch. Raj was in the kitchen with the fiction writers, including Harrison. I told her about the phone call.

"Ooh, city wedding!" she said. "Do you have anything to wear?"

"No," I said. "I gave my dresses to Goodwill. But I'm just the plus-one of the wedding singer, does it really matter what I wear?"

"Yes it matters what you wear," she said, offended. "Dressing for weddings is one of the great joys of life. Lucky for you, my apartment is basically a giant closet with a bed in the middle. Stand up?"

I stood.

She put a hand on my hip, lightly turned me. "I have just the thing. Black Prada, too short for me."

"Can I wear a bra with it?"

"Yes, actually."

"I don't know what Prada means, other than fancy. What if I spill on it?"

"I don't care if you throw it in the East River. It's a gift that doesn't fit."

I sat back down and got comfy on the couch. I miss you, he had said. Twice. "Raj will be weird about me going."

"I mean, don't throw it in the East River," she amended. "It's Prada."

"He won't make a big deal about it, but he'll be subtly weird."

She sighed. "You couples are so boring. You were supposed to be my single friend—remember Erykah Badu?"

"Yeah, sorry about that," I said.

She looked over at Raj, who had emerged from the kitchen and was handing out cans of sparkling water. "It's like people who dress for comfort," she said. "I don't understand it, but I can respect it."

"You're too beautiful to understand," I said. Raj proffered water to a drunk poet, then threw his head back with laughter when it was rejected. "Us mortals, we need someone else around to verify our existence. Make us feel worthy of being here."

Nomi slouched down into the couch so the back of her head was next to mine. "One could argue models feel this even more, having been validated only for our appearance our entire lives."

"Bullshit," I said, and she laughed.

I took her hand. Instantly I was unsure about it—Zoe and I used to hold hands like this all the time, especially in these late-party moments, but maybe that wasn't normal.

Nomi looked at our hands, let them sit there together a minute, and then she slipped hers out and folded it between her legs. I felt a small wave of embarrassment.

"Prada means intellectual," Nomi said, and the wave washed away. "Clean, intellectual simplicity. It makes you feel feminine and powerful at once—a perfect fit with your bangs. I would advise a bold lipstick."

"I'll need to borrow that too."

You Said Something

Labor Day weekend I returned to my apartment for the first time in weeks. Raj had decided to visit a friend in Boston for the long weekend, and his roommate was back: summer was officially over. As predicted, Raj made an awkward show of being unbothered by my attending the wedding, and I avoided mentioning the borrowed dress and lipstick.

Sunday I took two subways to a hotel on the edge of Brooklyn. The lobby had tufted couches and lots of those lightbulbs with the filaments showing. Nobody stopped me, so I rode the elevator up to Joe's room, 601. I felt like someone was going to accuse me of wearing a stolen dress. I could count the number of times I'd been in a hotel on one hand, and they had all been Holiday Inns or Best Westerns.

When he opened the door in his wedding best I couldn't hide my shock at how good he looked. I coughed. Had it been that long? Was he always this tall? Had I ever seen him in a suit?

"Perce," he said, and rested his head against the doorframe. There was some product in his hair making his curls pile higher. The eyebrows at attention, two black rainbows.

"Hi."

"You look so good," he said, his breath catching on the last word.

"It's called Prada," I said, holding out the fabric of the skirt so he could see its rich texture. "It makes you feel feminine and power-ful, according to the girl I borrowed it from. Fashion is her music."

He lifted the tip of his slim black tie. "H&M."

I smiled. He put his hand on my shoulder in what I thought was the initiation of a hug, but no hug followed. I was still standing in the hallway. The wedding was starting in minutes, on the roof of the hotel; he had been clear, in a logistical email he'd sent the day before, that we were to attend the whole thing.

"Should we go?"

He nodded. But his hand moved from my shoulder to the back of my neck, under my hair. Now the eyebrows were angling toward each other in a way I didn't remember ever having seen before. He pulled me into the room and the door closed behind us.

"I'm ready," he said.

I felt disoriented to the point of dizziness. He bent down until our faces were touching, his nose lying alongside mine. He smelled like shaving cream and toothpaste. "I have a boyfriend," I said.

"Fuck him," he said. "I'm your boyfriend."

I tipped my mouth into the kiss. I couldn't stop myself, I was entirely flooded. The kissing was so good as to be instantly unsat-isfying, a ladder up to a whole new level of longing. I pulled off his tie, then his shirt. He unzipped my dress so it pooled at my feet and he almost made me come right there, with his finger, though it was mostly the sight of his dipping shoulder as he worked—the stretching tendons in his neck, a small mole on the knobby end of his collarbone, this totally new view of his body—that turned me on so fast. All I wanted was more, everything, and maybe that's how I became a person who has an affair in a hotel room—maybe it was the sheer relief of the fact that I wanted it.

We fell on a wide, square bed, sending a chocolate mint sailing off a pillow. He said he loved me, which did not come as a surprise; of course Joe loved me, of course I loved him. But hearing him say it as he sank inside me made me hysterically happy.

Then it was happening. For the first few seconds he stayed very still. The pain I remembered was mostly but not entirely absent.

"This good?" he asked softly. His eyes were so close they nearly filled my field of vision. One of his curls came loose, a shellacked brush on my forehead.

"It's you," I said. It was all I could think: This was Joe, this was real. He lifted his head and I saw a small smile. And then the pain disappeared, bowled over by a pleasure that felt like nothing less than the secret of the whole insane universe.

Afterward we lay on the bed on our backs, laughing a little, looking back and forth from the ceiling to each other. I felt blown out now, blown up, like I might see bits of my brain splattered on the walls.

He pulled himself up to look at the digital clock on the nightstand—I watched his abs working, small folds of skin over muscles, surprisingly tanned—then fell back down. "We missed the ceremony and half the cocktail hour," he said. "Do you want to come with me now? Or join me later for dinner?"

I panicked at the idea of being alone with my thoughts, which I knew would turn to Raj. Legs wobbling, I stood up and put the dress back on, reapplied Nomi's lipstick. The room, I noticed now, was cold and modern, all right angles and gunmetal gray. Once his suit was back on, he pulled a CD from the pocket and handed it to me.

"The last one I burned you is out of date," he said.

I winced. "Sorry," I said, with a look of what I hoped was genuine apology. The CD wouldn't fit in Nomi's tiny purse so I left it on the desk.

We made it to the roof in time for cocktails. The humid air and hanging lights reset my mood, like falling back into a good dream after briefly waking. I mingled surprisingly easily both with and without Joe. It helped that I didn't know anyone; I was just the wedding singer's date in a killer dress, anonymous and intriguing. A quality sound system played a loud, excellent playlist, 90 percent contemporary indie and 10 percent "You Can Call Me Al." I learned that the bride and groom were New Yorkers who loved music festivals and had tech jobs that allowed them to work from anywhere. They'd spent the summer floating around Europe and were "obsessed" with Caroline. I hated them on principle, but happily partook of their open bar.

After a while I peeled off to stand at the railing, watching dusk settle over Brooklyn, smiling behind my bushy mint garnish. I remember deciding I would be happy to stand here all night, I would be happy to stand here forever, on the roof of room 601. I kept thinking of how different the same act could feel, depending on the whims of desire: a revelation that felt obvious, embarrassing to admit at my age. But nobody had ever told me this. Nobody had even implied it to me. When sex had been presented positively, it was always a rational decision—"you'll know when you're ready," "wait for the third date, fourth is too late"—all those TV scenes of leg shaving and exfoliating. There was nothing rational about it. Not if you wanted it to feel good.

Joe came up behind me and kissed my neck. I angled it to improve his access, a thrill shooting down my spine. The new Spoon single bounced over the chatter and laughter. Across the roof, amid a group of people gathered around the black-tableclothed bar, I noticed a blond girl in a fedora watching us. She said something to another girl, who turned and looked at us, then said something back to the girl in the fedora.

"Joe," I said.

"Yep, stopping." He stood next to me at the railing and we turned our backs to the party. The sun had set, just a dense stripe of orange behind the low skyline.

"Congratulations on all this," I said, gesturing over my shoulder.

"Thanks." He smiled. "But mostly we're still sweating it out in the medium-terrible time slots. Luckily we're done with Europe—looping back through the States this fall now that we have a bit more of an audience, and then we'll take a break to make the second album. I think we're going to find apartments here. The guys want to be a New York band."

I nodded casually, as if this weren't huge. The news was snowballing.

"Of course, I need to *write* the album before we can record the album."

This was a reference, I knew, to the disc downstairs. "I'll get you my thoughts soon," I said. "Promise."

"Thanks," he said. "Luke's writing now too, and the longer I take, the more he seems to come up with."

"Whoa." Luke Skinner had greeted me earlier with a gregarious back slap. I looked over my shoulder and saw him standing with the rest of the band, his once long hair trimmed to a dark mullet, pretty-boy features arranged in a slight pout. "Is he wearing eyeliner?"

"He wants us all to wear eyeliner," Joe said. "It's a real big issue for him that I won't wear eyeliner."

"Are his songs bad?"

"So bad," he said, and I believed it; even from across the rooftop, with his dramatic gesticulations and self-conscious hair flips, Luke Skinner radiated style over substance. "I'd be willing to help him get better, if he weren't such an asshole about it," Joe added.

I decided to change the subject. "So what's your set list tonight?"

He touched some whiskey off his upper lip with his cocktail napkin. "We learned a couple of classic wedding songs, you know, earning our five grand. Otherwise it's all originals. Oh, and for the first dance they asked for 'You Said Something' by PJ Harvey."

"No way! I love that song!"

He sent a rueful smile out to the horizon. "I know."

The song, I remembered, was set on a Brooklyn rooftop. "I don't even mind how obvious it is."

"I wondered if you would."

"Always loved that line about the smells of our homelands."

"Me too," he said. He slung his arm around my shoulders, relaxing again. "What are the smells of Indiana?"

I leaned into him and thought. "Freshly mowed grass, wet in spring. Soil from my mom's garden. My brother's football gear in the back of the van." Nostalgia stirred in me, raising its head from a long hibernation. I wondered what it would be like to bring Joe home. "What about you?"

After a minute he said, "Freshly poured asphalt, baking in the heat."

I saw him sitting on a curb in brilliant summer, his sensitive eyes squinting in the brightness, waiting for his mom to get better.

A waiter came by with a tray full of squat glasses. "Johnnie Walker Black?"

I took one automatically, because it was free; Joe shook his head. I was about to make fun of myself for holding two drinks when Joe said, a little anxiously, "PJ Harvey is actually really tough to cover."

"It's just a wedding!" I set one of my drinks down on a nearby table and put my hand on his chest, feeling for his heartbeat. "Are you nervous?" My fingers slid between the buttons of his white shirt.

"Only because you're here."

"Don't do that," I said. "You're going to kill it."

He leaned down until our faces were touching and said quietly, into my ear, "Did I kill it downstairs?"

The question embarrassed me, but I murmured assent. I tasted the light sweat on his freshly shaven cheekbone.

They called us to dinner. Seated at our table were Luke and the other Caroline guys, none of whom had been granted a plus-one, and a pair of wedding photographers who wolfed down their meals and disappeared. I had known the bandmates only slightly in Berkeley, and one of them was new, a replacement for the original drummer, who had started smoking heroin on the road. But they knew a lot about me. I fell comfortably into the role they wanted me to play, arguing about music and probing for stories from the road. They were easy to talk to, though there was a taut line of tension between Joe and Luke, like a rubber band the guys had all learned to avoid. I accidentally tripped it a few times, once when I inquired about the next album—"We're struggling with finding our *sound*," Luke said, and Joe rolled his eyes—and once when Luke invited me to come see him DJ at Don Hill's, and Joe looked like he might murder me if I said yes. It was a bit of a relief when all four of them left to set up their gear downstairs, in the hotel's top-floor restaurant, where the cake cutting and dancing would be happening next.

It was dark by this point but still warm. I sat alone at the table and stared at my hands, whose stubby fingers and bitten-down nails looked ridiculous against the rich fabric of my dress. I was grateful for the quiet; Joe's snowball was careening around my head, waking up all sorts of feelings, one by one. I was about to go to the bathroom when the girl in the fedora appeared, her shoulders squeezed up around her ears in what appeared to be an expression of her enthusiasm to see me.

"Hi!" she said. "I'm Raina! I met Joe at ATP!"

ATP, I had learned earlier, was All Tomorrow's Parties, an indie rock festival in England. These people had their own language.

"My best friend and I went together. Rebecca? We met Leanne and Greg at Primavera."

"Cool."

She paused. "Anyway, just wanted to introduce myself. We think Joe is a genius." She looked over her shoulder quickly, as if about to say something controversial. "I mean, obviously they're a band, but it's pretty much a one-man show, right? Those *songs*!"

She leaned so close I could see the uneven shape of her lipliner, a crust of foundation in the outer ridge of her nostril. The only conversation I wanted to have with this person was an extremely immature one in which I quizzed her on Caroline—What was her favorite lyric? Had she ever noticed the way the drum pattern changes in the third verse of "Somebody Said"?—just to watch her fail.

"I have to pee," I said, and left. I blamed this behavior on the Prada. A person could do whatever she wanted in a dress like that.

The indoors portion of the wedding was a different vibe, dark and air-conditioned, background jazz. The band stood on a small black stage during the cake cutting, pretending to be invisible because everyone should be looking at the bride and groom, which I guess everyone was. Then Joe began strumming his electric as the happy couple walked to a dance floor signified by parquet tiles and a spotlight. I recognized these rituals from movies, of course, but here in real life they seemed plainly absurd. The little toy figures on the cake! The white dress! Were we not all adults here?

"On a rooftop in Brooklyn," Joe sang, and a few of the guests whooped. My breath caught at the sound of his singing voice, which was dramatically improved, more controlled and expressive.

But he was right: it was tough to cover. It occurred to me for the first time that "You Said Something" is a perfect track more than a perfect song. There's not a lot to it, musically; the magic is all in PJ's delivery, the wisdom and emotion dripping from her voice. Joe's solution was to mimic her phrasing verbatim, which just made me miss the real Polly Jean. And the new drummer held a generic rock beat through the post-verse refrain that was all kinds of wrong. I was a bit embarrassed for Joe. Did he feel whorey up there, playing requests for cash, butchering this classic for a bunch of hipsters and their uncles? On the final repeated string of "you said something"s, which he delivered with decreasing intensity, I felt a strange flare of anger. Leave PJ alone, I thought irrationally, as if each phrase was an insult hurled at her face.

I could feel his relief when he reached the end. Everyone clapped, and Joe said, "Congratulations, Leanne and Greg!" with the manufactured charm of a game-show host. Then the band ripped into "Funny Strange," and Leanne and Greg and their friends went nuts.

Briefly I enjoyed myself again. I had helped bring this song into the world, and now I was in a room full of rich people acting like it was "Hey Ya!" I would've joined them if it weren't for the attitude I'd just given the fedora girl, who was holding court in the center of the dance floor.

Watching Joe perform was like observing an animal of a different species. How could someone I knew so well, someone who had just been inside my body, be so comfortable up there? So natural with his instrument, with his voice, with all his limbs? He owned the mic from every angle, laughed at himself, jerked his shoulders emphatically before standing totally motionless to deliver a line. I wouldn't even be able to speak into that microphone, even in the Prada; my voice would crack and dissolve on a single hello. I wondered if seeing him live would ever stop making me feel inferior, if I would ever be able to just enjoy his talent, or if that required a strength of character I lacked.

By the bridge, the song was dredging up its usual memories: the cold night air on that creaking Berkeley porch, the pissy way he picked his guitar; the hardness in his eyes when he said, "What do *you* do, when you write a great hook?" Strange how recent it felt, how brightly it still stung. What would this song be if I hadn't forced him to rewrite it, almost from scratch? What good is a great hook if it rests atop a steaming pile of Billy Joel's garbage? "Those *songs!*" the fedora girl had squawked. Her little pet genius. She probably thought "Funny Strange" had sprung straight from his heart, perfectly formed, like a tulip from soil.

I sat down at a table with two grandmas and a niece making origami out of napkins. Raj would like this table, I thought. He would help with the origami. He would rescue all the mint garnishes that had been cast onto the table, squeeze the oils onto my wrist, put a sprig in his lapel.

Joe didn't play "Bay Window," probably because its subject matter would've been wildly inappropriate for a wedding, but I was disappointed anyway. He covered "The Book of Love" by the Magnetic Fields solo on the guitar and then, as a closer, I couldn't believe it:

Graham Nash's "Our House." The band gave it an almost new wave treatment, and Joe sounded great, amped up the sweetness with more passion. But something soured on my tongue as he sang those lyrics I'd just analyzed so intensely. I couldn't stop it from happening. His romantic performance seemed to swallow my own interpretation of the song. Meanwhile, the fedora girl and her friend stood at the edge of the dance floor, swaying in unison, staring up at him. His limbs became even looser in their gaze; he hung the mic by its cord a couple times, swung it, winked. I hated how objectively desirable he had become—his off-center attractiveness now rewritten as plain fact, no longer my little secret—but of course that's the old line about why guys learn to play guitar, isn't it: get your chicks for free.

I waited for him on the roof. Downstairs the bride was DJing from an iPod to a handful of diehards while Joe packed up.

Finally he appeared in the white light of the stairwell door with a slumped posture. "Jet lag kicked in around 'You Said Something,'" he said. He dragged a chair to where I was leaning on the railing and fell into it.

"You were great."

He pulled me onto his lap. "My favorite thing about right now is that our bedroom is in this building."

"Can I ask you something?" I turned to face him, but we were too close, so I stood up. "Why now? You said you're ready, but what did you mean by that? Ready how?"

He sighed and rubbed his eyes with his palms. "I don't know. More confident now, I guess. I've always been so scared I'd mess it up with you."

I looked out at Brooklyn again. More confident how? I remembered him asking if he'd "killed it downstairs." I turned back around. "Joe, who are Raina and Rebecca?"

His gaze was steady through its tiredness. "Let's remember you have a boyfriend."

"Yeah, but I was up front about that."

"I have to be up front about the fact that I've slept with other people in the past year? Fine. Raina is Rebecca's friend, and Rebecca is nobody. She and I hooked up a few times in England."

"She's not nobody. She's a person. Is Rebecca the one with the fedora?"

"Is a fedora a hat?"

"Yes."

"No. That's Raina."

"Raina was annoying."

"She was acting weird tonight. Offended on her friend's behalf, or whatever. Becca seemed fine." He yawned.

"Raina probably likes you too. Probably likes you more, I'd bet."

He made a face at this like it was insane. "Nothing ever happened with Raina." Then he waved his hands in the air, erasing the whole subject. "I'm sorry I didn't warn you."

"I want to ask you something that might seem like none of my business."

"Fine."

"How many Rebeccas have there been?"

He sighed again, heavier this time. He stood up from the chair and leaned on the railing.

"Fewer than ten? More than ten? More than a hundred?"

He bent his head far over the railing and let out a frustrated growl. Then he straightened and said, "More than ten."

I calculated this to mean roughly ninety-nine. A cramping void opened in my gut. "Is this what you were thinking that night in my hallway, after your first show? 'I'm hot shit now, I'll get back to you after I go bang a bunch of groupies real quick?' It was, wasn't it?"

"I was twenty-one, and I'd only ever slept with a lesbian who hated my body!" He said it fast and loud, defensively.

"I didn't know anything about sex either! We should've been figuring it out together all this time!"

He rubbed his forehead. "I wasn't ready."

"Stop saying that." I picked up Nomi's stupid purse. "It makes me sick to think about, Joe. Using other women for practice."

His face darkened. "I didn't say it was practice. Don't flatter yourself."

"Wow. You really are just a dude, aren't you? Following your dick around like a blind man's walking stick. If you put that thing anywhere near me again, I will *throw up* on it."

I was about to storm off, but the look on his face stopped me— pure, acute shock—and then he started laughing. Softly at first, then harder. My mouth twitched against my will. I collapsed onto the chair he'd pulled up.

"Put that one on *The Greatest Hits of Percy Marks*," he said, as his laughter faded to a smile.

After a moment the smile faded too. He slid down against the railing wall and sat on the ground facing my chair, his elbows on his knees.

"I know I waited too long," he said. "I've been in such a panic since you told me you were seeing someone. I did try, on my last visit—but you were in a weird mood that night, and then we got caught up in writing 'Bay Window,' and I wasn't going to mess with that. Next time, I figured. I didn't know I was about to be shipped off the continent."

Our snowy day in Manhattan played briefly in my head like a home movie in which you are unrecognizable to yourself, shot from another angle. But it was already too late by then. I'd already puked on a frat lawn listening to Radiohead; I'd already leaned my shoulder into Harrison's. Who would I be now if I'd been with Joe all that time? I looked at his sad, exhausted face and tried to muster forgiveness. When it didn't come, I tried to find the excitement I'd felt earlier that day, but the memory just gave me a shameful stab of desire for Raj.

He must've seen it on my face. "Is this about that guy?"

I looked away.

"If you're feeling guilty, I have to say, I don't think it should count as infidelity when it's with the person you were always meant to be with."

This annoyed me—the idea that Joe and I were each other's answers, no matter how we arrived; that he got to travel the world, playing music and gorging himself at a groupie buffet, while I waited patiently at our inevitable destination. What had I gotten to do? I had been a blow-up doll for a fiction writer at a show. I had dragged words around a screen in a claustrophobic bedroom. I had spent a summer with Raj.

Tears stormed my eyes. I had found happiness that summer. It wasn't as exciting as Joe's adventures, but at least it was mine.

"I want to go home," I said, my voice sliding up an octave. "I want to go home to Raj."

For a second he looked confused. "What? Who?"

I hadn't planned to say the words. But there they were, hanging in the air: game changed. I wiped my eyes before tears spilled. "That's his name."

Now his mouth and eyes were hanging open, his whole face slack. "You said it wasn't serious."

"I said I didn't know." I caught another spill of tears just in time. "We've been together since Christmas."

His skin turned white. "What?"

"I was ready to leave him," I said, my face hot with shame. "That was my plan, all night. But—" I didn't finish. A noisy mess of hooks clashed in my head: turn on the bright lights and bring it on home to me and our house, with two cats in the yard.

"Jesus," he said quietly. "I will never be good enough for you, will I."

I shook my head—that wasn't right, that shouldn't be his takeaway—but I was really crying now, struggling to get a full breath. "He makes me feel good," I managed. "You make me feel small, and bitter."

His face was still hangdog, unresponsive. Finally, slowly, he put a hand down and pushed himself up. His long body unfolded to a standing position. He picked up an abandoned glass of scotch from a table and tossed it down his throat, then found another and did the same, then walked across the roof to the stairwell. His steps echoed into a fade-out.

I sat in that chair a long time. A waiter cleared the glasses into a black plastic bin. I did want to go home to Raj—to one of his scratch-made meals and our red notebook, to the warm, enveloping light of his apartment. But of course I couldn't. He wasn't there. And I had just wrecked our home.

I was shuffling through the hotel lobby, shoes dangling from my hand, when I remembered the burned CD and froze. My bare toes curled on the lacquered hardwood floor. Quiet jazz fell from the ceiling like snow.

I couldn't abandon those songs again. Better to go back, to say something lovely and sad in his doorway and slink away with at least that one single thread of our bond—the music—intact. I slipped on my shoes, cleaned myself up in the lobby bathroom, and took the elevator to the cherrywood door of room 601.

No answer, but I heard movement in the room. I knocked again.

"Yeah?" came Joe's voice.

"Just wanted to grab that CD," I said. "Sorry if I'm waking you."

A girl's giggle cut off abruptly.

Blood rushed to my head. The heel of my palm pounded on the door, drilling a bright pain down my forearm. The fedora girl—no, the other one. "I hope you washed me off first," I shouted.

Footsteps inside. The CD shot out from under the door into the hallway.

"Guess she makes me *feel good,*" he said through the door, pitching his voice high, mocking me.

"Play her the original demo of 'Funny Strange,'" I said. "See how good she makes you feel then." I snapped the CD in half and shoved the two shards back under the door.

The Heart of the Matter

Once the idea arrived I followed it dumbly, taking the subway straight from Brooklyn to Port Authority and boarding a 1:30 a.m. Greyhound heading west. I rubbed my arms for warmth the whole night, staring out the smeared window. A bruise ripened slowly on the heel of my right hand. When the sky lightened over Ohio I called my parents, who agreed to pick me up in Indianapolis once they recovered from their surprise. "This is so unlike you," my mom repeated the whole drive from the bus station.

"It's really helpful how you keep pointing that out, Mom," I said.

My bedroom had become the treadmill room. This was new: on my last visit the walls had still been lined with my music posters, most of them from record sleeves and CD cases, their fold lines still visible. I didn't ask where they'd gone. My brother's room had been left untouched, right down to the life-sized Michael Jordan poster and assorted winner medals hanging from the curtain rod, clanging lightly in a breeze through the open window. If they'd known I was coming, Dad kept saying.

"This is fine," I said. I entered his room and closed the door on my parents' strange faces. I scanned the shelves of team photos—those other families he kept, his easier siblings—then sat on the bed and opened the nightstand drawer, where I found a framed glamour shot of his high school girlfriend resting in a cloud of gum wrappers. I wasn't sure what I was looking for. Maybe some clue to the stability my brother had always embodied—the self-belief that seemed to ballast him against emotional highs and lows—as if he'd won it in a deal with the devil. But his room was the room of a good person.

Mom knocked on the door with the only two pieces of my high school clothing she'd saved, a sundress made by my aunt and a pair of Christmas pajamas from a matching family set. I put on the pajamas and instantly fell into a sleep so deep it took me minutes to remember where I was when I finally woke.

Dinner was vegetables from the garden and a bland chicken breast. There was talk about salt, cholesterol; I told them I was glad they were thinking about these things. Dad tried to veer into politics a few times and Mom changed the subject. We called my brother, who still lived in his college town, had some assistant coach job that seemed anticlimactic only to me; after hearing about my surprise morning arrival, he whooped so loudly I took him off speaker.

"Sorry," he said. "I just think of you as my nerdy little sis, and this—is this an epic walk of shame?"

"You know I don't do things halfway," I said. "Which, by the way, is basically what it is to be a nerd."

He laughed and asked me to put Dad on; the two of them had money on the game that night.

After dinner, Mom and I did the dishes while Dad watched what turned out to be college football, hanging on every toss and fumble of a bunch of teenage boys. I gave Mom the rough outline of the wedding, though I left out the part about the girl's giggle in Joe's hotel room—I told her the bruise was from falling down the stairs at Port Authority.

"So you're torn between two men," she said flatly as she dried a ceramic platter. "Less dramatic than I was expecting."

"I'm not torn," I said. "I decided."

"Did you? Sounds to me like you just picked the impossible option. The option you ruined. Which means you decided on neither." Her mouth set into a grim smile I'd seen more times than I could count. When emojis became a thing, years later, the one with the straight line for a mouth always reminded me of Mom. "Doesn't mean it was the wrong decision. Maybe it was a great decision. There's still soap on this."

I rinsed the platter again, leaning my elbows on the edge of the sink. I felt, as I had all day, like I couldn't find my sea legs. "Can't a person make a mistake?"

She clucked her tongue. It rang an unpleasantly familiar bell, like when she'd discover I'd cleaned my room by shoving everything under the bed.

"I'll finish later," I said, and walked outside to the front porch, drying my hands on my pajama bottoms. The old porch swing was still hanging on; I sank into it, enjoying its creaking music. Otherwise it was unbearably quiet outside. The houses in our neighborhood were all set back far from the road, a stretch of lawn around each standard-issue rancher, but I didn't remember this level of stillness. Where were all the kids? Had we not been replaced? There was a chill, fall arriving, streetlights on already.

Mom came out and sat in her favorite chair with the worn cushion. "How's the writing program?"

"Fine. I feel a bit out of place there, but I guess I do everywhere." I pushed my toes against the deck, activating the swing. "Actually I hate it."

"Really? I love the idea of you as a music critic."

"Music writer." I tried not to be too annoyed, since I'd never worked too hard to disabuse her of the idea that I was trying to become a music critic. I lacked the patience, or the clarity of mind, to explain to her that writing and music could be combined to create something other than criticism. Maybe I wasn't sure that they could.

"You know criticism is its own form of art," she said.

"Why do people always say that?" I snapped. "Have you ever heard anyone say, 'That Robert Christgau takedown of the Eagles really changed my life'?"

Mom adopted her bewildered "how did this child come from me?" face.

I decided to change the subject. "Where did you live, when you lived in New York?"

"Different places. Hell's Kitchen for the longest stretch."

"Uptown, ever?"

"No. Lately after dinner I've been enjoying a nice Perrier in a wineglass with a lime wedge—would you like one?"

The is how it was to talk to Mom: like one of those old-fashioned dances where your partner steps back whenever you step forward, choreographed to maintain distance. "Sure."

She stood up from the deep chair and I noticed she straightened her legs a bit slowly. How awful, to get old. As if it wasn't bad enough being young. At least our knees responded to our commands.

The Perrier was, indeed, nice. We sipped in silence awhile. The insanity of my visit seemed to demand a Big Conversation—she was clearly waiting for it—so I asked, "Do you ever regret making the safe choice?"

"What makes you think that's what I did?"

"It seems obvious. You were in New York. I'm sure you had some excitement there, hot flings and career prospects, and then you came . . . here." I gestured to the empty tree-lined street. "To him." I jerked my thumb at the living room window, lit by the green glow of an on-screen football field.

"If by 'hot flings' you mean conductors putting their hands down my shirt while they adjusted my bow positioning," she said. She snorted. "As if my bow wasn't always perfectly positioned."

I winced with sympathy.

"Of course I wonder about the road not taken, honey. That's part of life. But I don't regret it nearly as much as you think I do."

"How do you know what I think?"

"Your disdain for my life choices has been palpable to me since you hit puberty."

I twisted the swing so I could see her better: she was squinting out at the street like there was sun in her eyes, but the sun had set.

"I'm sorry," I said. I hadn't known how obvious it was. "I guess I just wanted more. Maybe that was silly."

She met my gaze finally. "Depends what you mean by more." And when I didn't immediately answer—I meant more, *more!*—she stood up and ambled inside.

I sat at the computer table in the corner of the living room, rolled out the keyboard tray, and signed in to my email. Raj was trying not to worry.

> *Hi, I'm back. Boston bros weekend was fun. Got home last night and something felt off, I guess because you left no message or note (where's the red notebook?). I hope you had a good time with Joe at the wedding or whatever it was. I know he's important to you. Just let me know if you want to connect, otherwise I'll see you in seminar on Wednesday. Can't believe the summer's over. It was lovely, spending it with you.*

I didn't labor over my response; I felt like I owed him the courtesy of speed, at this point. I read it over once and pressed send:

> *Raj,*
> *Your off feeling is right, because I did things I regret at the wedding and I've been paralyzed ever since. I don't know how much to tell you because I'm scared you'll hate me forever. Yes, Joe is important to me, foundationally important, and I suppose that's my excuse for making this mistake. But by the end of the night I chose you. If you'll have me.*
> *I love you,*
> *Percy*

We'd never said the L-word before, and it had a whiff of too-late desperation about it, but I had to try. Was it true? I was pretty sure it was true, even though what I felt for him was so different from what I felt for Joe, it seemed like it should get a different name. What did this say about our culture, that we had invented only one word for all these feelings? If we truly valued it we would label it more precisely, like Eskimos and snow.

I busied myself in town the next day, running errands for my mom, buying some clothes at the Salvation Army—a shirt that said INDIANA SCIENCE OLYMPIAD 1982, gray Dickies, and flip-flops. I hung Nomi's dress carefully in a garment bag. I felt stunned, numb, like a pause button had been pressed down in my brain and would not pop up until Raj's response. My next login yielded an email, but it was from Joe.

> *did you see the review?? you know i don't get hippie about this stuff but it did kinda feel like the universe doing me a solid when i needed it most. look i'm not going to apologize for the other night, i was sad and she was there and she has a way of seeing the best in me- you wouldn't understand. anyway it didn't work because i'm still sad, and pissed, you probably are too. here's an FTP where you can download all the mp3's from that cd you broke. i have to know, are you still on my team with this second album, as a friend, a partner? this is big- i need you.*

It had just posted that morning, not a full review, but a paragraph-long mention on a massively consumed blog.

Real-Deal Alert: Caroline, *Funny Strange*
7.5/10

This impressive debut out of the Bay Area is a year old, but hasn't gotten the attention it deserves in the US despite fitting snugly into the new '60s-tinged indie sound (though the title track owes more to '70s rock; the influences are broad enough to surprise). Luckily they fared better in the UK and spent the summer on the European festival circuit. On the album's twelve tracks, a tragically lo-fi production tries but fails to obscure the considerable pop sensibilities of lead vocalist and songwriter Joe Morrow; live, his potential shines even brighter. No word yet on a follow-up album, but we'll be tracking it closely.

I smiled for a good ten minutes after reading it, but then the memory of the girl's cut-off giggle returned. I didn't reply.

Raj's email came the next day. As soon as I saw his name, I knew it was going to be awful. My mom was right: I had chosen neither. I took a long, steadying breath before I opened it, but still, I was not ready.

Percy,

The idea of you choosing me is frankly hilarious. Why, because you like my air-conditioning? If my "one who got away" (you never ask about her, but she still exists) suddenly wanted to try again, I would not choose you. Why? Well, it's not me, Percy, it's you. (Cruel, but too good to delete.) You don't love me. You don't even love yourself. You're too busy editing to write; no wonder you didn't finish a single page all summer. You're obsessive about inconsequential things, like song lyrics, and dismissive of things that matter, like food and sleep and other people's feelings. Who can live like that? And now this. Your refusal to give any specifics of what happened with Joe leads me to presume the worst-case scenario, and this scenario makes me so angry that I am legitimately considering buying some

*sort of voodoo doll of you and stabbing it repeatedly.
I don't know what your problem is—girls have always
found me sexy, all-the-way sexy, until you. But I am
still a self-respecting South Asian man who grew up in
America, and your twisting this particular knife isn't
something I expect I'll ever get over. Fuck off. I wish
you well.*

    Raj

I bolted out of the house, trying to outrun a horrible heat inside
me. It was late afternoon and gray clouds were gathering, shutting
down the sun. I saw Mom in her garden and ran across the lawn
toward her.

"What happened?" she asked as I approached.

"Raj dumped me."

"Ah."

I glared at her, pacing the edge of her garden.

"What? You're mad at me because I predicted that?"

"What the hell, Mom!"

"I know it's hard, honey," she said. "It's hard to lose someone, no
matter the reason. And you're losing two people at once. I am sorry
this is happening. I just want you to see that you chose it, because I
think that might mitigate the pain."

I whirled to face her. "Remember our piano lessons?"

She flapped away a bee. "Sure. You weren't very interested."

"Bullshit."

We looked at each other a long moment, and then she resumed
her hoeing, half-heartedly. "I didn't have the impression that you
had any great innate musical talent, if that's what you're implying."

"When did you know? When did you make this decision, on my
behalf, that I would be useless at the thing I loved most? That the
best I could be was just a barren appreciator of music?"

She abandoned the hoe again and looked at me like I was a child.
"Barren?"

"Yeah. I'm going to stick with 'barren.' It's like the power of giving life, to be a songwriter."

"You know you also have the *actual* power of giving life, don't you?"

"Mom, gross. I'm twenty-three." I sat on a decorative stone stool in the mint bush.

"I'm sorry you didn't get the music genes, honey," she said. "But that was a relief to me. When music is your profession, everything becomes outer directed. It's all about pleasing people—men, mostly. I wanted you to be inner directed. To know your own opinions."

"My opinions have brought me nothing but problems!" I said it so loudly, my voice propelled me to a standing position.

She shielded her eyes to look at me; the sun had poked through the darkening clouds. "You're so *smart*!" she said accusingly. "I never understood it! Why would someone so smart be so fixated on pop music?"

"I don't know! We don't get to choose what we love, any more than we can choose our talents. Don't you get that?"

She looked down at her weeding.

I sat back down on the stool and yanked off a sprig of mint to chew on, the roughness of the gesture sending pain oscillating through my bruised hand. "I co-wrote a song with Joe, actually. It's going to be on his next album, which is already getting buzz."

"That's wonderful," she said. "And you have other talents too."

"Joe doesn't talk about talent, you know," I said. "It's like the idea never occurred to him. He trained himself to sing in tune." This last part was not true—Joe had come out of the womb singing in tune, I was pretty sure—but I had read it once about Sufjan Stevens, and it always fascinated me.

"Good for him," she said, still concentrating on the dirt. "I do think these things are easier for men."

I stared at the back of her head. She was right, of course. "Boys are less afraid of being wrong," I said. It was a line from *My So-Called Life*—she wouldn't remember, though we'd watched that episode together in high school: the sensitive redhead observing the boys in her classroom as they shouted dumb guesses at the teacher. This was why men got to run the world, even as it became slowly obvious they were terrible at it. But who was molding all these chickenshit daughters?

Mom said something about rain coming and pushed herself up to stand. But she didn't walk away. She stood looking at me, holding her hoe in one hand and a bouquet of uprooted weeds in another.

"What?" I said.

"Oh, it's just," she said. "It's the players. My friends. That's what I gave up when I chose this life. My best friend, we lived together— her name was Jennifer, before everyone was named Jennifer. I think she still plays in the city. Miss her sometimes, that's all. Nobody understands you like a violinist, what it's like living up on that high wire. Odd ducks like me, all of them. But, honey," she said, with a significant look, "that is not something you get from a man."

My impulse was to scoff. Not men like Dad, I wanted to say— there were better men out there, interesting musical men who could talk forever. But the past twenty-four hours were making me second-guess my impulses. Maybe she was right—maybe even the most interesting men would always be too distracted, too fixated on the whole thorny realm of sex. So I met her eye, nodded. She responded with a hug, which I accepted. The hug felt good. I supposed, as I held her tighter, it was what I had come for.

Inside, I watched her cook dinner. I should help, I thought. Instead I wandered into the living room and gazed absently at its familiar brown furniture, my face on the wall alongside my brother's in a series of school pictures—mine following a progression of "say cheese" smiles to more natural attempts to not smiling at all. A sadness took root in my bones, deep in the marrow. New York yawned like an abscess at the edge of my mind.

Some inner compass pointed me to the old CD rack, where I scanned the plastic columns for something nonclassical—*Blue,* or *Kind of Blue,* at least. I should've bought music at the Goodwill; I needed it more than I needed clothes. Finally I found a block of Dad jams and selected a Don Henley solo album, then poured myself a finger of scotch and sank into the recliner with the lyrics booklet.

On the cover Henley had long hair, lines in the face, a cigarette. The first track was grating, lots of that classic boomer hand-wringing for the world they were hell-bent on destroying. But the studio polish and his strained, weary voice felt just right. Finally I found the one I wanted, "The Heart of the Matter," which I remembered vaguely as a good song, though I was not nearly prepared for *how* good. I couldn't have understood it the last time I heard it. It was a grown-up breakup song with a central question ripped straight from my weekend: Why do we listen to those voices, calling from just outside our door, that tell us to reject contentment in search of something more?

My mom thought she had the answer; she thought the voices were simply to be ignored. Close the door, was Mom's advice.

But old Don doesn't know. He just throws the question on the table and lets it sits there, satisfied to have asked it so beautifully. He's tired. He's not sure he knows the heart of the matter, though he knows what it's not: It's not pride, or competition, or work. It's something to do with forgiveness.

Rain was slapping the windows now. The smell of sautéing onions came from the kitchen. "Forgiveness, forgiveness," called the background singers from a fading outro.

I refilled my scotch glass and sat back down at the computer table, opened Internet Explorer. I hit reply on the Raj email, but I couldn't focus on the blank space where I was supposed to write; my eyes kept sliding down to what he'd written, and it made me feel so horrible I could barely breathe. So I opened up the Joe email and found it made me feel horrible too. I deleted both emails and logged off. I couldn't imagine eating. I couldn't even finish my scotch. I stepped slowly up the stairs and crawled into bed in my brother's trophy room.

Running Up That Hill

I stayed in Indiana through the first week of fall semester. My boss at the restaurant in New York fired me in a voicemail. When Nomi called, I picked up and told her the whole story, which she absorbed with kind yet baffled patience. I considered dropping out of the writing program—staying put, paying off my debts, finding some stern midwestern therapist to fix my brain. In the end, it was the sunk-cost fallacy that got me on the bus back to Manhattan. I was in thirty grand deep at Columbia; the least I could get for it was a degree.

My old room was brutally depressing. It had always been depressing, but after a summer at Raj's and a week in a real house with a yard, it felt roughly like a prison cell. The door to my room had been left closed so the air was warm and stale, even though it was late at night when I arrived, and the jeans I'd changed out of the morning of the wedding were still crumpled on the floor. I hung up the Prada dress and then I couldn't make it across the room to the bed. I just sat down on the floor next to my dirty jeans. I tried to cry but the misery had become too flat inside me, too normal. Finally I pulled myself up into the chair by my desk, where my laptop was open, screensaver undulating.

I addressed an email to Zoe Gutierrez and started writing. At first I didn't think I would send it; I just needed a project. I told her everything, beginning with an apology for what I'd said to her at Cafe Milano and going all the way up to Interpol and the Brooklyn hotel. I begged her not to yell at me for not reporting Harrison, the shame of which was already unbearable. I told her I could see what she must've seen that day in the café, and what Raj saw now: that I was, on some level, a terrible person. I asked her to tell me what to do—with my life, with my hands when I walked, with my face when I saw Raj in class. I worked on it all weekend, deleting and revising, and then, because my project needed a conclusion, I sent it.

She wrote back the next day.

Oh babe. I wish I could hug you, roll around a nice California park with you. Remember when you let me feel you up? That was so sweet of you.

Your apology about Milano is accepted. You can let it go.

I'm okay. Uganda is weird as hell, not the country itself which I love, but my job and the expat scene here. Everyone does too much coke and nobody's gay—it is actually illegal to be gay—and the nonprofit is doing the kind of work that may not actually be helpful in the long term (I won't go into the details, which I am positive will not interest you, but suffice to say the experience has been questionably fulfilling). No, I don't have a girlfriend, but I did before I left. She lived in San Francisco and worked at a coffee shop. We broke up for no good reason other than my move. I've already decided I'm moving to San Francisco next, once I've put in enough time here, having determined it is the only place where I can be surrounded by lesbians while also being a short drive to my dad's cooking.

Honey it's your own damn decision whether you tell people about being dry-humped at Interpol, I won't yell at you about that, but I would scream this straight into your face if I were there: SHAME ON HIM, NOT YOU. Don't you dare feel shame about any part of this horrible thing he did to you, including your own stupid shame. Ugh. Hugs.

You want me to tell you what to do? Sure. How fun.

With your life: fight back. No, fight forward. Forget him: fight forward. With your hands: put them in your pockets. Don't wear clothes without pockets. When you see your ex, give him a smile but don't speak, even if he does, just keep walking once you administer that smile. On the weekend, do whatever needs to be done for school and then rent a bunch of mindless DVDs and get some Chubby Hubby. If the store doesn't have Chubby Hubby, walk to another store (the salty sweet is key, and the walk will do you good anyway).

I expect a report back that you have successfully done these things. You've always been a bossy bitch, it's fun to role reverse. BTW being a bossy bitch is not the same thing as being a terrible person, nor is infidelity. Being a bossy bitch is how women learn to be heard in this world, duhhh. Infidelity is, in this case, probably, your body telling you something you needed to hear. Just forgive yourself, it's too exhausting not to.

I love how authoritative I sound right now. Should I become a therapist?

Forgiveness, forgiveness: I hadn't thought of it for myself. The idea seemed so insane I almost laughed. Forgive my*self*? *That* crazy bitch?

I must've read Zoe's email fifty times that day. By night my sadness seemed to be morphing into a more manageable shape, something I could fit into a livable existence. As long as I could get emails like this, I thought, I would be okay.

In my reply, I asked her what to do about a gathering that a professor was hosting the following night, which both Raj and Harrison were certain to attend. Zoe instructed me to show up late with unwashed hair, drink exactly two glasses of red wine, and talk only to women. I did as I was told. Nomi asked if I needed to borrow shampoo, but the embarrassment was not mine, entirely; I was just following orders. When Raj and I encountered each other in the bathroom line, he gave me a long look that began as cool, then turned slightly tender, then flashed with confusion when I forced a smile and walked away. I left the party, as instructed, at 11:00.

The next night I asked her what to think about before falling asleep, which was the only time I ever missed Raj. Most of the time, if something reminded me of him, his words would quickly follow—*Fuck off. I wish you well.*—and then the feeling of missing him would self-destruct before it had fully formed, swallowed up in a blaze of horror. But at night in my small bed, his absence seemed to pool around me, outside of thought or reason.

Zoe's reply: *Think about the saddest thing you remember from childhood.* And the following night: *The first time you got turned on.* I enjoyed having an assignment and I tried, but I could never remember the things she wanted me to remember. My own past was indecipherable to me, like some invisible forearm had smeared the ink before it finished drying. All I could locate were random scenes adjacent to each ask: watching my mom beam with pride at my brother's first big game and hating him with an intensity that scared me, or the time some high school boys had rated me "gross hot" in a survey. Typical stuff. I had been lucky, I would end up thinking, though inevitably I fell asleep crying. (Zoe, of course, had very clear memories of these milestones—that's why she assigned them. The first time she felt turned on was watching Peg Bundy shimmy across the screen on *Married . . . with Children,* which made me laugh so hard I forgot to be depressed for nearly a day.)

She seemed to have lightened up since coming out, traded in the chip on her shoulder for a wary enthusiasm for life. One day a couple weeks after I'd returned to New York, I emailed her with the subject line "Running Up That Hill."

> Do you know this Kate Bush song? It's about wanting to swap places with someone, temporarily, so you can understand each other's experience. The *experience*—that's the key, that's what you can't get through conversation or talking about your feelings, you can share the facts but you can never really get across the full weight of how it felt to be you in that moment. And it's the experience that matters, not the facts. It's the experience that drives the stupid things we say in relationships, all the nitpicky fights and the weird decisions and those moments when lust takes over.
>
> I know it's well-trodden in any number of *Freaky Friday* rehashes, but this is why music is so much better than books and movies, because you've got Kate Bush's art-rock singing and intense production making it feel all raw and fresh, and because there's no need to resort to dumb magic tricks to tell the story—you can make a whole masterpiece just out of a wish.
>
> I've been thinking lately that if I could make a deal with God and swap places with Raj, he'd forgive me, fully and completely. And if I could swap places with Joe, I'd forgive him. Maybe.

Her reply came in minutes:

> See I don't relate to this song because I have so little need to understand men anymore. Women don't need a deal with God. You and I have already been doing this in our emails, from our lonely perches in our re-

spective exiles—we've been exchanging our experiences, and I don't feel confused by yours at all. Like for example it makes complete sense to me why you didn't tell that creepy fiction writer to stop. I can hear the droney music pounding in my ears, I can feel the terror, the shock of it, like those first seconds of an earthquake when you just sit there thinking, "Is this really happening?" and then it ends and you realize you didn't do all the things you'd planned to do in the event of an earthquake. I understand why after such an event, Joe's sluttiness on the road bothered you so much. I understand why you're writing me every night instead of writing stories for your expensive MFA program. Kate Bush must be straight is what I'm saying. If I could trade places with you I'd just play with my boobs all day.

ileanpercy: should we IM?

ringfingrr: YES!!

ringfingrr: whoa sorry that was overly exuberant

ringfingrr: i had too much coffee this morning

ileanpercy: remember when joe drank so much red bull he thought he needed to go to the hospital

ringfingrr: hahahahaha i still can't believe you had sex with that nerd, and that it was good

ileanpercy: ugh it was so good

ringfingrr: i can't handle this new sentimental you

ileanpercy: it's not sentimental because it's irrelevant!

ileanpercy: imagine you had the best burger you've ever had, but later you found out it was made of cockroaches— would you be sentimental about that burger?

ringfingrr: insects are high in protein and commonly consumed in many countries

ringfingrr: and what's this about burgers anyway, aren't you a vegetarian

ileanpercy: i've been making exceptions

ringfingrr: gross dude. i'd rather eat cockroaches than the flesh off the neck of a cow bred for slaughter using precious resources, but anyway

ringfingrr: here's a theory:

ringfingrr: maybe joe did learn something from all those groupies

ringfingrr: maybe that's how he got so good

ileanpercy: ew

ringfingrr: i'm telling you he was not good two years ago

ileanpercy: you were gay!

ringfingrr: okay, yes, i was gay

ringfingrr: i just don't think it's the worst thing in the world that he wanted some experience, you know?

ringfingrr: before he stepped up to the plate with you

ileanpercy: and AFTER, let's not forget

ileanpercy: THE SAME NIGHT

ileanpercy: i was but a mere interruption in a steady stream of groupies

ringfingrr: you know the word groupies is misogynistic right?

ileanpercy: why are you defending him?

ringfingrr: i don't know

ringfingrr: because maybe i'm the one who messed him up?

ileanpercy: ooooh he's making you blame yourself! like a republican! right?

ringfingrr: omg do you ever forget anything

ileanpercy: but it's not just the groupies, zo

ileanpercy: it's this feeling i've always had

ileanpercy: this feeling of wanting to BE him

ringfingrr: oof

ileanpercy: right? who can live like that?

ringfingrr: yeah that's gross

ringfingrr: okay here's my question:

ringfingrr: can you get off to it?

ringfingrr: to the memory of your cockroach burger sex?

ileanpercy: haha

ringfingrr: i'm serious

ileanpercy: that's private!

ringfingrr: whaaa

ringfingrr: are you seriously so repressed you can't talk about masturbation

ringfingrr: guess you didn't have the most sex-positive upbringing out there in indiana

ileanpercy: i mean it wasn't sex-negative

ileanpercy: i had tori amos

ringfingrr: thank god

ringfingrr: well what i'm saying is if the memory of the sex can get you off, then it has served a positive purpose

ringfingrr: and maybe that's all you needed from him

ringfingrr: maybe this is the legacy of joey morrow

ileanpercy: the memory can get me off

Almost daily, since I'd returned to New York. Standing in the shower, cooking eggs, writing at my laptop. His hand would appear on my shoulder, rest there a minute—the memory arriving like a PA announcement: Put down your pencils, folks—then slide, slowly, up to my neck. I'd become instantly wet. Then I'd let the whole hotel scene unfurl, with occasional fictional flourishes, as I finished: my first successful jerk-offs, if you must know. That much of what I did to myself had been learned from Raj was something I tried not to think about. Afterward I felt a dark mix of shame and anger, though this exchange with Zoe had the effect of dampening that feeling somewhat, like a hand in the bell of a French horn.

Joe,

The review is so exciting. Impressive debut! Considerable pop sensibilities!

But my answer is no. I hereby terminate my position as your muse/collaborator/whatever I am. It's not good for me, this job.

Anyway, I've been wondering lately what you might produce without my influence. Didn't you get tired of my shit, when you were writing *Funny Strange*? You were always either not trying hard enough for me or trying too hard. Hah! If there was any truth to either of those complaints, it's because the standards I held you to were ludicrously high. I mean, do you lack discipline as a writer? Compared to Cole Porter, sure, you're a lazy piece of shit. Do you sometimes overwork things at the cost of naturalness? It's like I expect you to be Robert Johnson, possessed by the spirit of some otherworldly talent-demon. God, I'm the worst.

You're all you need, Joe. I'm all I need. This is America, land of the individual. Lay off the women and get it done.

I can't wait to hear the new album for the first time, like the fan I am.

Eileen Percy Marks

SF/NYC/LA/MIA

This Side of the Blue

Zoe was obsessed with Joanna Newsom. So was I, so was everyone in San Francisco in 2005, but Zoe brought a real gay energy to the whole thing.

"You can't post pictures of this," she warned when I snapped a photo of Joanna's harp, gorgeously lit on an otherwise empty stage.

"What? Why not?"

She shot me a preemptive look and ran a hand over her new buzz cut. "Because I didn't tell Melissa I was coming."

I gave her the response she had expected, which was ridicule. "You know Joanna Newsom is straight, right?"

"I don't believe it," she said. "She plays a *harp*."

We'd been sharing a carpeted two-bedroom in the Haight-Ashbury district of San Francisco for the past year. Zoe had reentered her first relationship when we'd arrived, but it ended soon after; for weeks I'd held her sobbing head on my shoulder. Then one night I dragged her out to a lesbian bar in the Mission and watched her acquire a new girlfriend with the ease of ordering a drink. I'd been dismissive of the new girl, Melissa, until I realized how much I liked her; she was perfect for Zoe, a community organizer with a Dolores Huerta tattoo and an ability to recognize a good thing when she found it. These were the kinds of charming problems they had as a couple: Zoe not inviting Melissa to a show in order to drool freely over a categorically unattainable woman.

The venue was too humble, a music hall above a club, booked before Newsom's recent shoot to stardom. A few rows of chairs had been set up near the front, all of them claimed by people who seemed to actually know Newsom: friends, family, former teachers visiting from her Northern California hometown to witness the return of their prodigal daughter. Zoe started chatting them up like she had a shot in hell at the after-party.

I waited at the bar for a drink, mulling the angle I might take on the show on my blog, *Walgreens Songs,* where my twelve to fourteen readers would be eager for a report. The press was calling her music "freak folk," so I could use that as a starting point, how inadequately it captured what Newsom was doing—how the ren-faire affectations and squawking voice were actually the *least* interesting part of her music.

I appreciated this about my blog, how it gave my thoughts about music another destination beyond live conversation. The initial concept was to write about the uncool music my generation ignored, the songs you never think about until you find yourself in a Walgreens aisle fighting tears—but when that became limiting, I relegated "Walgreens Songs" to a tag, an occasional category of post. I kept the title because it provided a hook: I would be the proud dork of the music blogosphere, if anyone ever noticed me.

The girl ahead of me in line was wearing vintage Levi's and an eye-catching crushed velvet blazer. She was drinking a Hamm's, which was the new PBR, and tossed her wavy hair with an ease that made me want to buy her shampoo. I wasn't supposed to be working tonight, but I got out of line and found Zoe. "Do you have a pen and paper?"

"Did you score one of your undercover agents for capitalism?" Zoe fished through her tote bag and produced a small notebook and a pen. "Show me." I pointed to the blazer girl. Zoe nodded begrudging approval. "See if she knows Joanna."

When I got to San Francisco I'd worked as a waitress and then, as the six-month grace period on my student loans gave way to desperation, landed a temporary job as a writer at a trend agency that specialized in providing "intelligence" for brands (mostly alcohol, some clothing). They loved me at the agency. "You're so much more than a writer," they said. They gave me a raise and a new role: intelligence specialist. My job was to recruit "trendsetters" in four coastal cities—SF, LA, New York, and Miami—which I did through a combination of Myspace stalking and approaching people in bars and clubs. Once I'd collected their contact information and loaded them into our database, I sent them monthly online surveys mining their "intelligence" ("intelligence" basically meaning what song should play in a vodka commercial; I could never say it without air quotes). With this well of knowledge I would then write articles for our clients, real meaty pieces with titles like "The Next Old-Man Drink" or "Nu-Rave Is Dead, Long Live Nu-Rave."

I can't lie: it was fun. Zoe disapproved, but she didn't understand the bleakness of the post-MFA job hunt. Nomi was logging long hours at *Nylon* magazine for a salary that worked out to well under minimum wage; others were teaching ESL part-time, still eating oatmeal for dinner. And I rationalized that my job challenged me— I had to learn to be a slightly different person, to split myself into two Percies and be able to jump into the new one at a moment's notice, the more brazen one with the capacity to approach strangers in bars. It helped to remember that I would be, almost always, the highlight of their night. That flash in their eyes: Finally, I've been discovered!

Clutching Zoe's pen, I took a deep breath and repeated my mantra in my head: People love this shit. People love this shit. Then I tapped the blazer girl on her shoulder and gave my standard speech—"couldn't help noticing your style," "fifty dollars per survey," "are you between the ages of twenty-one and twenty-nine?" I got the eye-flash right away. Very interested. Maybe too interested. Easy tiger. I asked her about music, where she shopped, trends she'd noticed in drinks and clothes: B-minus answers across the board. I skipped the contact page, just wrote down her Myspace so I could check out her network.

"Meh," I told Zoe, slipping the notepad back into her tote. "Weirdly obsessed with the Strokes."

"What's wrong with the Strokes? The Strokes are generation-defining!"

"The Strokes are 2002-defining. I said, 'Anything else?' and she said, 'Any bands that sound like the Strokes,' and I said, 'So, like, the entire British Invasion?' She didn't get it. She's only here on a date."

Zoe looked at me with awe, shaking her head. "You found a way to judge people for a living. It's amazing, really."

"I know."

"What a terrible use of your God-given talent for being a total asshole."

"I know. I'll quit soon."

"Promise?"

I shrugged. "We can't all be social workers for at-risk youth."

"You could totally be a social worker!" she said, and, when I looked at her incredulously, laughed. "Okay maybe not."

The crowd grew noisy; Joanna had arrived.

We stood with our mouths ajar for the next hour, too ensorcelled to speak. She kept a full band in that harp, plucking syncopated beats and lead-guitar melodies while simultaneously strumming rhythm chords. And the *songs*. This was before she got weirder, when she was still molding her radically unique sound into perfect pop structures. The lyrics, sharp and literary and existential, fit their melodies like hands in gloves.

The friends-and-family rows were beaming up at her; Joanna occasionally reciprocated with a knowing smile aimed down at them.

Oh hello, jealousy. I'm trying to enjoy this show; could you leave? No? Well then. Please try to stay quiet. (A lesson from some mindfulness podcast I had overheard from Zoe's bedroom: "Label your thoughts, talk to them." If nothing else, it brought me mild amusement.) Yes, Joanna probably did have an encouraging, supportive mother. Yes, her waist is Barbie-degree tiny—Christ, what does that have to do with anything? We're standing here witnessing actual genius, and I'm supposed to focus on the cinch of her belt?

During a relatively up-tempo song, I heard a hoarse whisper: "Zoe Gutierrez! Holy shit!"

Carlos, apparently. Eyes bugged and mouth gaping, hand crushing a plastic Crystal Geyser bottle. Zoe hugged him and then explained to me that we'd known him at Berkeley, where he'd lived with Caroline's bassist. I made a show of remembering him even though I didn't. Zoe was always running into acquaintances like this, the special club of the Bay Area born.

Joanna was having an issue with her strings onstage, so Carlos got chatty with us. "Literally every hipster in the city is here," he said, eyes darting around. I realized dimly I did recognize him—not from college, but from the bars where I recruited: one of those people who never stayed home. "Hey," he said. "You guys have any updates on the album?"

"What album?" Zoe said.

He staggered backward in mock shock. "Dude! Caroline's! Does this mean you aren't tight with Joey anymore?"

Zoe said some stuff—email sometimes, you know how it is.

"Why?" I asked him. "What have you heard? Is it finished?"

"It *was*," he said, taking a swig of water and then wiping his brow. "But they decided it needed a single, you know, a big single. The suits weren't satisfied, or whatever. So now they're taking some time, trying to come up with one more song. The album is called— ugh, I forget—Jeremy told me . . ."

I took a step forward.

Carlos squinted. "Something and something, I think?"

"Something and Something?" I said, aghast.

Carlos laughed. "No, no, like—" He started laughing again, could barely talk through the laughter. "Like, two words I can't remember, with an 'and' in the middle."

"Oh."

"Your face," he said, wiping his eyes. "Hey, you guys want some coke?"

"That's *Joanna Newsom* up there," Zoe hissed. "Show some respect."

I faced the stage again, where Newsom was resuming her plucking, but had a hard time paying attention. "Something and Something" was a tantalizing puzzle that made me think mostly of lofty abstractions: *Love and Mercy,* "Ebony and Ivory." That wasn't Joe. Maybe it was two proper nouns, like Belle and Sebastian or *Teaser and the Firecat.* I felt another stab of jealousy, this one sharper than the ache I'd felt for Newsom. How fun it would be to name an album.

When I was late to applaud at the end of a song, Zoe elbowed me. "Stop thinking about Joey," she whispered.

I did, but only because Newsom began strumming my favorite of hers, "This Side of the Blue." It was a series of scenes about people just doing their best over here on this side of . . . the San Francisco Bay? The Pacific Ocean? The sky? The bottomless pit of misfortune hovering just one wrong step away from all of us? It's a miracle just to be here, the song seemed to say, on this side of the blue. Don't torture yourself trying to understand why. Know what you know. Do what you have to do.

That's what Joe is doing, I told my jealousy, as the lights dimmed and the last chord gave way to applause. He's struggling to nail his single, doing his best on this side of the blue. It's what my mom is doing. It's what I'm doing too, with my evil job and my useless degrees.

My jealousy did not, at least this time, argue back. Instead it propelled me to walk straight home after the show, over to Haight Street and up its hill—alone, as usual; Zoe had admitted after-party defeat and walked south to Melissa's—composing in my head an ode to "This Side of the Blue" and then unloading it onto my keyboard once I got home.

I had put some effort into my room this time: installed a Raj-inspired dimmer attachment on a floor lamp, inserted a desk with a green banker's lamp into the squared-off window. I liked looking out at the street as I wrote, at our neighborhood mix of tourists and panhandlers and vintage clothing enthusiasts, or, on a Friday night like this, swarms of buzzed twentysomethings hunting down cheap drinks.

I structured my "This Side of the Blue" post as a thank-you to Newsom. I wrote about how its existentialism made me feel liberated from my expectations, my stupid hunger to be capable of a greatness like hers. I couldn't quite squash that ambition, I wrote, but maybe there was a way to braid it with self-acceptance, with peace.

When I pressed publish and reread the post, I felt, as always, a light dissatisfaction. Just black marks on a screen, floating in an unwelcoming void. I kept waiting for my words to land somewhere real, to mean something more.

Mis-Shapes

Later that year I wheeled my suitcase through a door held open by a valet and entered a sunlit art deco lobby, feeling a rush of stupid, obvious happiness. Garish mistletoe everywhere. Donald Fagen's "Walk Between Raindrops" began playing in my head, always cued up for Miami: a classic Walgreens Song I'd written about on my last visit. I checked in and began my cherished work-trip routine.

First there was a deep breath in the hotel room, an assessment of the vibes and the cleaning products: lovely here, fresh, not lemon scented. Then I ate an eight-dollar piece of candy from the minibar (Good and Plenty) while standing at the window (courtyard view, a pool, pink-and-white-striped umbrella tops). Instead of working in the room, which I had learned could invite a creeping loneliness, I took my laptop down to the restaurant.

It was early so I spent a couple hours down there at a poolside table. Got a big fancy salad and dug deep on Miami's Myspace: Who seemed intriguing, who had that whiff of a wannabe? Whose captions were the most witty, informed, hip to the shifting tides of 2005? Who appeared most often in top 8s? I made a list of names, tried to memorize their profile pictures, and looked up the bars and parties I'd seen mentioned, sketching out a route. Then I went back upstairs to shower, smudged on some eyeliner, grabbed my backpack of supplies—screening questionnaires, a Polaroid, hand sanitizer—and hailed a cab.

I had a problem in Miami. After the mojito explosion, our alcohol clients had demanded we add the city to our roster, but the trendsetter density turned out to be painfully low. The cool people all knew each other, and worse, they were starting to know me. Half of them were on the panel already, which meant they saw my name in their inbox once a month when I sent them surveys, called me at the office when their check didn't arrive in two seconds. Sure enough, I'd barely arrived at my first destination when I felt an arm around my shoulders.

"Hey mami!" Jesse Jams, he called himself. A DJ, eternally clad in a suit with pants as skinny as his tie, one of the first trendsetters I'd recruited in Miami.

"Hey," I said, suppressing my irritation. I was supposed to fade into the scenery like a wildlife photographer. I turned my back to him and surveyed the place: mostly generic, only cool tonight because of the DJ, who looked like the female version of Jesse. I spotted two others in the crowd currently on the panel.

"It's early," Jesse reassured me. "I have someone I want you to meet later, total trendsetter. You're going to Poplife later, right?"

Poplife was more of the same, hipsters dancing to Britpop and electroclash. I decided to come clean with him. "Can I buy you a drink, Jesse Jams?"

"Girl," he said. "You know I'm Jack and Coke."

I brought him to a quiet corner table near the back, the kind of spot where people would be making out in a few hours, and gave him a leveling look. "How many people will you know at Poplife?"

He seemed to think it was a trick question. "Everyone?"

"You see how that's a problem for me, right? I need to diversify."

"Uh, good luck with that. Don't trendsetters tend to know each other?"

"Not necessarily. Say the Miami panel all becomes ironically obsessed with Michael Bolton, or whatever—I might report this to my clients like it's an actual trend, and suddenly they're paying Michael Bolton to shill rum when all that happened is you and your friends got high one night watching VH1 Classic, you know?"

He laughed gleefully. "Not rum though. Michael Bolton should sell champagne, like a champagne that's cheap, but like pretending to be fancy, you know? 'How am I supposed to live without this smooth mouthfeel.' Write this down, girl!"

I smiled patiently. He was coked up already.

"Okay," he said, focusing his eyes on his drink. "I know you already have the soul and hip-hop crowd. So like—maybe the industrial goths? There's a warehouse party downtown tonight."

"Those people don't buy anything. Love them, but they've been wearing the same clothes for ten years."

"True."

"I shouldn't be telling you this."

"Right?! You're all, like, bringing me behind the curtain!"

"You're welcome."

Eventually I pried a couple good ideas out of him: edgy lesbians and techno ravers. But the lesbian bar he suggested was filled with thirtysomethings, none of whom had the slightest interest in becoming a trendsetter. At the rave, I acquired a headache and two decent panelists whose circles seemed unlikely to intersect with Jesse Jams's. Enough to call it a night, but I cabbed over to Poplife anyway.

It was past midnight by now. "Laid" by James was playing, everyone pogoing during the chorus, their greasy mullets splaying in the spotlights like pineapple tops. I bought myself a real drink, then found Jesse Jams and made him point out everyone he didn't know. This tactic yielded my favorite score of the night, a film student named Hannah who was making a documentary about Miami artists and was only here for the music.

"I hate scenesters," she told me loudly over the noise, eyeing the crowd. "But I love dancing to Britpop, so." She shrugged and sipped the drink I'd bought her. She was wearing a sack dress and a pair of

Amy Winehouse–worthy dirty flats. "I come alone so I don't have to talk to anyone."

I scribbled this in her screener. The seats were all taken so I was writing against the wall. "And why do you love dancing to Britpop?" This was off script.

"What?"

I leaned toward her ear: "Why Britpop?"

"Well, it's basically dance music, but it's *songs,* you know? *Great* songs. With melodies and words and images that mean something. Why anyone would want to dance to *oonce-oonce nnta-nnta* is mystifying to me, but that's what's dominated clubs—that's what it's *meant* to go out dancing—for as long as I've known." She gestured at the dance floor. "Until these assholes came along."

"And why do you think they're assholes?"

She sighed and leaned against the wall. "Oh, fuck me for saying that. They're not. Just a bunch of nerds who've finally found their place. Let's be honest, I'm one of them."

I put my screener down and watched them with her. She'd made quick work of two fundamental truths about hipsters: that they had all been miserable kids, the boys too sensitive and the girls too willful for the social systems of the late twentieth century; and that nobody wanted to admit they were one of them.

"I think what bothers me," Hannah said, "is that we found our place, and then we immediately went and turned that place into basically another version of high school. Only we get to be the kings this time. Like, it's a little . . . embarrassing?"

I had her fill out the contact information page. These answers would raise my boss's eyebrows, but was a little self-awareness too much to ask for in a trendsetter?

As I packed up my screeners, the DJ started playing Pulp's "Mis-Shapes," and I felt Hannah's hand on my wrist. Her eyes were wide, entreating. I nodded to show that I understood: the song was about the outcasts she'd just described. But she didn't let go. She was jerking her head to the dance floor.

I would've refused if she hadn't been so damn cool in her interview. Hastily I stowed my backpack under a bench and followed her out into the throng of bodies.

Hannah committed hard right away, striking poses, commanding space; I did my best, but the first verse is mid-tempo, tricky. Then the pre-chorus arrived like a trampoline, sending us all bouncing in unison. Some girl grabbed me by both shoulders, shook me once, and sang loudly in my face about sweet revenge. I sang it back at her; we were intimates, co-conspirators. She slipped by me and I never saw her again. Next I felt Jesse Jams hug me from behind, and he folded me into a circle of people with their arms around each other. I pulled Hannah in too. It was deliriously fun, everyone scream-singing the lyrics, releasing buckets of pent-up angst into the sweaty air. A boy in a black mesh T-shirt locked eyes with me from across the circle, then walked over to me and rested an arm on my shoulder, caressed my cheek with his hand. "You're gorgeous," he shouted into my ear, then snapped his head around like a ballerina and marched back to his place in the circle.

Hannah was wrong, I decided, as I shouted along to the final chorus: I loved these people. I loved this city, its weirdos finally beating out its bimbos. I was glad they'd put themselves on top of their new world order.

In the cab ride back to my hotel I felt the song still pulsing inside me. I knew it was the first track on *Different Class,* Pulp's '90s masterpiece, and I knew it had inspired the name of a DJ team and club night in New York, but I hadn't listened to it in years. There was an element of physical discomfort in how badly I wanted to hear it again as I rode the elevator up to my room. I dropped my backpack on the floor and found the song on YouTube and then played it three times in a row, dancing in front of the blackened window, not caring about my silhouette on display for all of Miami Beach. Then I let the album play and sat down to write.

Years later, the scene I had inhabited that night, and so many of my nights on the job, was christened "indie sleaze" by the internet. Entire Instagram accounts were devoted to remembering the era; I showed up in the flash-heavy photos occasionally, usually in the background with my giant backpack. Indie sleaze is remembered as an attitude—a fuck-it-all embrace of grimy fun—as well as a musical moment defined by the party-friendly indie acts of the aughts: Yeah Yeah Yeahs, M.I.A., CSS. This is accurate but incomplete, omitting the massive amounts of '80s and '90s Britpop those kids consumed every night like so many cans of caffeinated malt liquor. History always forgets that it doesn't exist in a vacuum. New Order was everywhere; "Age of Consent" seemed to play automatically upon entering a bar, and the *Unknown Pleasures* T-shirt was ubiquitous. There was Erasure on sunnier days. Orange Juice and Echobelly for the more informed. And above all, if you ask me, there was Pulp. "Common People" was the ultimate closer, a song so great it couldn't be followed; "Mis-Shapes" and "Babies" were mid-set go-tos. It seems clear to me now that Jarvis Cocker, Pulp's front man, created indie sleaze when we were all still teenagers—he came up with the whole damn thing, the attitude and the aesthetic and at least part of the sound, and then my generation acted like we invented it ten years later.

I didn't write about indie sleaze that night in the Miami hotel room because it didn't exist yet, at least not by that name. But I wrote about how Britpop was everything that year. I wrote that only the English could capture the ironic humor, style, and detachment necessary for a young person to survive the aughts in America. I described how it felt to be on a packed dance floor screaming along to "Mis-Shapes"—wailing, I said, like a lost animal who'd found its family—while realizing the loneliness that has characterized your life so far may in fact be optional. I went into the whole album, calling it the hipster manifesto of our time, *On the Road* for a generation who didn't want to end up living in their parents' basement like Kerouac. I wrote that it had taken a decade-old record to help us figure out what we wanted, and what we wanted was fun—*real* fun, which requires freedom, and belonging, and affordable housing, and peace from wartime. The Bush years were ending, I wrote; you could feel it on the dance floor.

It was a little much. But at four a.m., after two Heinekens from the hotel room minifridge, I did something Zoe had been telling me to do for months, something I swore I'd never do, mostly because the idea embarrassed me: I emailed a link to the post to Jesse Jams. By morning, he'd reposted it on a Myspace bulletin and on a dozen individual walls. By the next night, when I returned home to SF, Zoe greeted me with the announcement that she had seen it reposted on multiple bulletins, and underneath the original post were 468 comments.

I sat at my desk reading comments all night, giggling at my reflection in the window. A few of the comments showed actual insight. Some were from people who'd been at Poplife that night. Some took issue with something I'd said; others took issue with those who had taken issue. I loved them all. My audience!

The next day I got a few emails from people who'd seen the post: Nomi, with predictions that my blog could land me a book deal; my brother's girlfriend in Indiana, whose hipster cousin had mass-emailed the link to her entire family; and, late in the day, Luke Skinner, with the subject line "Question." It took a second for my brain to attach his name to a face, first the long-haired suburban kid playing "Here Comes Your Man" in Zoe's garage, then a pair of kohl-rimmed eyes shooting daggers at Joe on the Brooklyn rooftop.

> percy marks! saw your pulp piece, been wondering what you were up to, love it! hey so not sure if you've heard but i quit caroline. got my own band now. would you be willing to listen to a few of my songs, see if you have any thoughts? not sure if you know this but i heard some of joe's original demos way back when, i know your feedback can really help.

I laughed out loud. Hey not sure if you've heard but I have a life, I wanted to write. Not sure if you know this but servicing the songs of Caroline and all its spin-off comma-splicers is not actually my reason for being on this earth! Not sure if you know this but Joe's original demos were the work of a true raw talent whereas you are a pompous wannabe! God it felt good to ignore this email, to be so bolstered by success that I could laugh off a musician and really mean it.

Everybody Needs Somebody to Love

We were listening to *The Best of Wilson Pickett* on the kitchen iPod dock. It was 2006 now, late spring. Melissa was out of town so I had Zoe to myself on a Saturday night, an event so rare I had over-planned for it, ordering her favorite deep-dish and buying the ingredients to approximate a complicated martini I'd had once at a hotel bar. I'd even gotten the proper glasses, though they looked out of place in our kitchen, whose bizarre lack of cabinets had prompted us to buy a metal shelving unit that encroached on the floor space and attracted objects from all over the apartment: paperbacks leaning against stacks of mismatched plates, airplane-issued headphones slung around a mug. We were nearing the end of the album and our second round when I casually mentioned Soul Night.

"It's every first Saturday, so it's tonight," I said. "At the Elbo Room?"

"Soul Night," Zoe snickered. "You can dance to Black music, kids, but just for tonight."

"Come on," I said. "I've only been there when I'm working, and it looks so fun."

"But we're having fun here!" She gestured to our milky drinks.

I confessed: I needed blog fodder. It had been months since my breakthrough "Mis-Shapes" post and my readership, which had grown steadily for a while, was stagnating. I'd tried leaning further into my job, got a backstage pass through a client connection—but

I was just your basic music journalist back there, and too nervous to be a good one. It wasn't my beat anyway; the space I'd carved out, among all the *Pitchfork* wannabes, was as a personal music blogger. I used the music to write about real life, pulling from a half century of songs instead of fawning over every latest indie breakout.

The problem was, I told Zoe, the personal part was hard to maintain. My audience wanted stories from the dance floor, not my introspective musings on lyrics. They didn't know I was just a mole in their scene. I needed to get out there, for real.

"Fine," Zoe said, downing the last of her martini. "But I'm not dressing up."

I was. I knew what the girls wore at Soul Night: vintage dresses, toe-cleavage flats, lipstick, and messy hair. I wanted to be one of them, for once. I quickly changed into a spring-green polyester number I'd picked up earlier that week on Haight Street.

Zoe maintained an air of doing me a favor throughout the cab ride, the line to get into Elbo Room, and the slow ascent up the creaking wooden staircase behind the bar to the guy collecting our ten-dollar covers. But when we emerged into the party, she smiled.

"Told you," I said.

It was just another upstairs venue space, but there was something magical about that room on Soul Night—like an old secret dance hall, long and flat and so teeming with noisy bodies it seemed illegal.

Zoe laid her palm on the red wall. "The bass is tangible," she said.

I pulled her through the crowd to the bar in the corner of the dance floor. It was hard to know where the dancing ended and the waiting for a drink began; some people appeared to be doing both. We positioned ourselves near the back of the mass and leaned in.

"Frank Wilson!" I shouted at her, as a new song began. "In the UK they used to do these crazy athletic dances to—"

"I don't need every song live-blogged, thanks!" she called back.

The crowd around the bar was even louder than the music.

There was a couple in front of us engaging in high-intensity flirting, screaming things like "I *knew* you would love that song!" and then stomping their heels on the floor, their hands flattened against each other's like drunken mimes. Behind us were two dudes, clearly a wingman arrangement, who were inching closer to us as though they could move the line forward through force. One of their chins kept knocking the top of my head.

"Zo?" I pressed my hand to my chest to tamp down a swelling panic.

She looked at my face, then at the guys behind us. "Back the fuck up," she shouted at them, and her buzz cut probably went a long way toward the fact that they obeyed.

"Zoe!" Her friend Carlos was on the dance floor, waving and hollering. "And what's-your-face! Over here!"

I nodded at Zoe—I needed to get out of the horde more than I needed a drink.

He introduced us to his date, who pulled us both into a weirdly long three-way hug. I tolerated it only out of a bold hope that she, or Carlos, might lead me into blog-worthy territory.

"She's huggy tonight," Carlos said, chuckling. He hadn't stopped dancing.

I extricated myself from the hug. "Hey Carlos, have you heard anything new about Caroline?" It had been over a year since Carlos had told me, at Joanna Newsom, the album was nearly finished.

He looked confused. "Who?"

"Caroline!"

"Caroline Harmon? She's in jail, dude!"

Zoe gasped, and then they were shouting at each other about some cheerleader from their high school whose life had taken a dramatic turn. Carlos's girlfriend and I were left to dance together, except I wasn't really dancing, I was sort of just bobbing my upper half and thinking about the music, some obscure track that sounded like it had been recorded through sweat-drenched microphones. The girl was grooving hard and grinning at me like we'd just had sex.

"Are you on something?" I finally asked.

"E!" she shouted through her grin. "Twenty a pop if you want some!"

Instinctively I shook my head. Then I looked at Zoe, who had clearly overheard.

"Sidebar!" Zoe announced, holding up her finger like a director pausing a scene. We stood cheek to cheek, speaking directly into each other's ears.

"I've never done it," I said.

"It's fun," she said, her breath hot in my ear. "We wouldn't have to wait for drinks. You feel terrible afterward, though."

"I heard it wrecks your immune system."

"It does. I can't believe you're considering it. Is it because you're looking for something to write about?"

"Yes. I can't believe you're considering it either. Is it because you're trying to support my writing so I'll quit my job?"

"Yes."

We pulled back, smiling.

The girl gave us two small pills and a half-empty bottle of water, and we handed her two twenties. I swallowed mine quickly before I had time to think.

"Dude!" Carlos bolted out of a dance move and grabbed my arm. "You meant Caroline the band! Sorry! All I know is it's coming out very soon—and that they booked a freakin' late-night talk show!"

"Oh my god." A vision of Joe on a slick navy stage dropped into my brain like a premonition: skinny tie, professionally tousled curls, a sexy half smile as he opened his mouth to the microphone. "Which show?"

He didn't answer. The DJ had dropped the original "Tainted Love," and Carlos and the girl had levitated to a higher plane of consciousness.

I turned to Zoe, feeling uncertain about the drugs in my body. "Is Joe going to be famous?"

She shrugged in an earnest, hopeful way, excited for her old friend, and led me deeper into the dance floor, where the music was clear and loud and incredibly physical. Movement was the point: the swing of the drums and the messy hand claps and the smooth horn shots and what they all did to the body. After a few songs my body began shedding the baggage of my mind, becoming only the physical manifestation of happiness: warm and loose and shot through with perfect energy. Zoe's enormous smile bobbed in front of me, such a pleasing sight.

"I love your face," I shouted, hugging her.

"I love your body," she shouted into my hair.

"I was just thinking how I love my body!"

She laughed. "That's high-person talk."

"Definitely," I said: my mind was clear. "But make me remember this later, okay? Because my body is amazing. It's healthy and it understands music and I'm lucky to be inside of it."

"I promise!"

They played Pickett's cover of Solomon Burke's "Everybody Needs Somebody to Love," which we'd heard earlier in our kitchen, and we danced so hard to it, so closely, that a bead of sweat flew off her nose and into my mouth. They played "Ain't No Mountain High Enough" and the crowd thickened instantly, impossibly, but the mood was so joyful I didn't mind, and anyway I had Zoe. Carlos appeared at some point with the kindest two bottles of water I'd ever seen, and then we needed to pee.

In the bathroom line we stood face-to-face, petting each other's forearms. "Even a twelve-thirty talk show would be a big deal," I said to her.

She gave me a look. "You haven't mentioned him lately," she said. "I've been wondering if maybe you're, you know, over it."

I considered this. "I do go days without thinking of him now. Or *a* day, anyway."

"I hate to say this, Percy, like I *really* hate to say this," she said. "But you may need a boyfriend."

I grimaced. "The fervor with which I'm expected to pursue this boyfriend goal is so alien to me. Sure, it'd be nice to have what you have with Melissa, but I'd be totally okay if it doesn't happen. Is there some gene I'm missing?"

"No," she said, but her tone was unconvincing. "Whatever happened with that client guy?"

I sighed and leaned against the wall. I'd slept with three men since my night with Joe: a trendsetter from our panel, an activist friend of Zoe's, and a brand manager for one of our clients. The trendsetter had lost interest in me halfway through our third date, abruptly and observably, when he realized I would not be a boon to any of his fledgling creative careers. The activist had hung around a bit longer, but was insanely busy with his job as a political staffer—he was my first encounter with a smartphone, with dinner-date pings and emails whooshing from bed—and liked prog rock to a degree that slowly revealed itself to be a deal-breaker for me. The client had been the most recent, handsome and insecure, and I wasn't sure what had happened.

"I think I hurt his feelings," I said. My last communication from him had been an emailed link to some expensive jacket he was thinking of buying online, with the message *time sensitive q: cool hipster or burningman fixie?* I had not responded. "My job does make dating weird."

"Quit!" She said it like it had just occurred to her, like she hadn't said it a hundred times. "You're a music writer, not a—whatever you are!"

"Trendsetter intelligence specialist. A job I quite like. And freelance writers work long hours for peanuts, Zo—I have seventy thousand dollars in student loans." I started shivering. I felt suddenly stiff and lifeless, as if the drug's curtain had been pulled back. My jaw ached.

Zoe pulled me closer, rubbing my back for warmth. "I just want the world for you."

I nodded against her neck. "I'm fine," I whispered.

"Do you still—?" She pulled back to face me and wiggled her eyebrows. "With Joey?"

Joe's hand materialized on my shoulder. "Sometimes."

"Really?" She wrinkled her nose. "When you're solo, or when you're actually doing it?"

I ran my finger down the length of her nose, ironing out the wrinkles, admiring her face. Her new look was so spare: no hair, no makeup, just her long thin nose and straight dark eyebrows and skin so clean you could eat off it. "Both," I admitted. "Is that terrible? But I make the fantasy very abstract. It still works if I chop Joe's head off his body."

She laughed and hugged me again. "We all have our tricks."

It was our turn for the bathroom, and we spun our way in, still hugging, laughing. The curtain was dropping back down; my muscles were relaxing again to that perfect warmth. We enjoyed our hard-won allotment of time, chatting and checking ourselves out in a grease-streaked mirror.

Later, as we filed downstairs to enter the fierce competition of hailing a cab, I felt a rush of love for Zoe so strong it almost knocked me down the steps. Her fuzzy scalp bobbed just below me. What would I do without her? Was it okay to love someone this much who was not actually your partner? Was this why she wanted a boyfriend for me, because she couldn't bear the burden alone?

The chill returned, but I willed it away. I felt a strange ability to control my thoughts, to push them around the room of my brain like furniture. I was grateful for Zoe: that was the feeling to focus on. No: I was grateful for the love I felt for Zoe.

At home Zoe went to bed and I dove straight for my laptop. I could feel the chill nearing again and I wanted my post to be infused with the ecstasy, not the comedown, and definitely not the day after. Zoe was picking up Melissa at the airport first thing in the morning.

But then I wasted the next fifteen minutes of my dwindling high googling "Caroline band" and "Caroline band new album" and "Joe Morrow new album." No reviews or release date, but Myspace was teasing a drop in summer. There were professional photos of the band I'd never seen, staged and airbrushed, a new guy in Luke Skinner's place. Joe with his fists balled in his jeans pockets, leaning against an industrial building.

When I finally started writing I managed just two paragraphs before the chill took over. I blamed this on Joe, haunting me from across the country. I posted it with the MP3 and fell into a hard, headachy sleep.

Everybody Needs Somebody to Love

Everybody needs somebody to take dancing. Everybody needs somebody to hail a cab to Soul Night on a first Saturday in San Francisco. Everybody needs somebody to feel the bass in the walls with their palm, to let it shimmy through their limbs and into yours. Everybody needs somebody to tell a creeping bro to back off when you need some space, when music threatens to wield its power over our bodies too recklessly—to help you feel the beauty of what music can do, while protecting you from its danger.

Everybody needs somebody to take ecstasy with you, then allow you to pet their beautiful face in line for the bathroom while Wilson Pickett wails the simplest, truest truth: "everybody needs somebody to love." Queen said it too: "find me somebody to love." Who else? More have whined about *being* loved, but these dudes understood it's the giving—the love you make—that matters more. Because where do you put the love you make, if you're all alone? You don't give it to yourself, in my experience. You take it out with the trash every day until it slowly stops regenerating inside you, and friends, let me tell you, that is no damn way to live.

The next day I woke with the sensation that all the moisture in my body had been vacuumed out, leaving my organs pressing up against each other, my skin shrink-wrapped on my bones, my brain crumpled into a dried-up ball, begging for serotonin. When I saw myself in the mirror looking relatively normal, it shocked me. I wasted the whole day in bed, chugging water, reading books and the internet on an alternating basis.

In the evening I got an interesting comment on my post from someone named Alma, in Germany: *I like how this blog is about the way music inhabits and shapes every part of the life, not just emotional but physical too. This is not something that happens with other art forms, no? One does not typically read books or observe an abstract canvas while dancing or having sex—we can only think about them while doing these things, which is not the same because the art is not as present. You're right it is a power both beautiful and scary but mostly beautiful.*

I like you, Alma, I replied under her comment. I couldn't find any more information about her, but I decided that from now on, I would think about Alma, not the scenesters, when I wrote.

Britpop Night

July 1, 2006
Caroline, *Strong & Wrong: 6.9*

That the belated sophomore effort by Caroline is plainly inferior to their debut, 2002's *Funny Strange,* may hardly be remembered in the long run. Because to paraphrase Petty, the A&R man hears a single. "Britpop Night," the album's opener, is a rollicking anthem for today's whiskey-swilling hipsters, bright and sincere and deceptively complex while also being just *fun,* so damn fun it made this author practically fume ("What's wrong with music being *fun?*" I demanded of everyone in earshot through a giant, uncontrollable smile). It's quite a feat this song is pulling off: retro-themed, yet arrestingly au courant; six minutes long, and still it zips by; packed with candy-floss hooks, but emotionally resonant at its core. "New Order on the rocks, two shots of Siouxsie / And I am an animal who's found his family," goes the chorus: a sweet expression of belonging, fueled, in the grand human tradition, by the seamless fusion of music and booze. Never have we needed this more. You heard it here first, nerds: "Britpop Night" will be indie's song of the summer.

The rest of the album fails to reach the heights of its opener, though it's not without some nice moments. "The Pond" is a long-distance love letter in which the ocean represents emotional distance: familiar but well executed, with an easygoing melody sailing over a sea of jangle-pop guitar. And "Bay Window," a piano ballad about one man's intensely personal experience of an event much bigger than him (9/11, presumably, but not too obnoxiously), hit me right in the gut.

A more polished production brings Joe Morrow's elastic vocals forward in the mix, unlike the first album, which smothered them in reverb—a welcome change, but one that puts more burden on his lyrics, which are spottier this time around. "Soap Scum" appears to be a song about how nobody cleaned his house for a year in high school, with metal guitars attempting to fill the holes created by broad metaphors and vague storytelling. And the second-to-last track, a power-pop ditty called "You You You," features a lyric so terrible as to be subtractive from the album as a whole: "I love you you you / I sure do / More and more and more / For and for and for / Ever"? It's hard to imagine this coming out of the mouth of the man who made *Funny Strange*.

Morrow has my forgiveness for these missteps, though. Because with "Britpop Night," he gave us the instant classic we deserve this year. Excuse me while I go back to my uncontrollable smile.

"No," I said, my body rising from my chair.

"No to what?" said the designer who sat across from me.

I stared at her face without processing what I was seeing. I'd forgotten I was at the office. Finally I shook my head and walked to the office bathroom, where I locked the door and sat on the toilet.

"I am an animal who's found his family" was from my "Mis-Shapes" post. "Bay Window" wasn't one man's experience; it was our experience. "You You You" didn't seem like it came from the mouth of the man who made *Funny Strange* because *Funny Strange* had been my mouth too. None of it, suddenly, seemed okay. At the same time, I felt drunk with exhilaration.

I put my head in my hands, forced myself to untangle my thoughts. First: "I am an animal who's found his family." He was clearly reading my blog, which was thrilling at first, but the more I thought about my line in his song—my *published* line—the more confused I felt. Was this Joe's way of reaching out, trying to tell me something? Or was my blog just a convenient resource for him, a public-access portal into the brain he sometimes borrowed?

And "You You You": over my dead body would that monstrosity have made the album if I'd been involved. "For and for and for / Ever"?! I could hear the quarter-note melody with some stupid music-theory change thrown in somewhere: one of those songs he would dash out in five minutes back in Berkeley and decide was genius, until the next day when I would shit all over it, and nobody would ever know it existed. He really does need me, I thought meanly.

Then came a rush of pure, heart-stopping excitement for Joe. Oh, Joe. I lifted my head from my hands, a smile cracking open my face. This was a gushing rave, if not for the album then for its single, which I knew enough to know was huge. This would change everything. I saw him as that little boy waiting on the suburban curb and felt like I might choke on my joy.

I went back to my desk and began googling fiercely, breathlessly. Press was already trickling in even though the single wasn't out yet, and the album release date was still two months away. There was even a feature article in a Bay Area lifestyle magazine—"East Bay Boy Eyes Indie Fame"—that read like a *Rolling Stone* cover story, with descriptions of how he held his fork ("lightly, like he might be asked to leave the restaurant at any minute") and this revealing bit:

"I went through a period of writer's block," Morrow says by way of explanation for the four-year gap between albums. Pressed to identify the source of the blockage, he hesitates and says, "There was a girl," before laughing at himself. "It's not quite how it sounds, but let's just leave it at 'there was a girl.' I don't mind being a cliché."

As pressure mounted from the label and his bandmates, Morrow found the best way out of his block was to "flip the fuck-it switch." "We started giving ourselves more permission to mess up," he says. "Me in particular. 'Britpop Night' is basically a pastiche of hooks. A Frankenstein's monster, which never works, but this time it did. That's why we called the album *Strong & Wrong,* which is something that musicians say when a player comes in real loud with the wrong notes—not a good thing at all, it's sort of the ultimate embarrassment, actually. But we wanted to own that, because some of the best stuff on this album came from fuckups." He laughs and rolls his eyes again, a dryness creeping into his voice. "It's my fuckup album."

And then, at three p.m. that day, the single dropped. There was a typo in the post—clearly the release was someone's hasty decision, an attempt to ride the buzz from the review. Who was in charge of these things now? Did Joe himself push the button, or one of the suits Carlos had mentioned? I knew little about how the business worked; he was on another level now. I jammed my headphones into the laptop port.

"You okay?"

My boss was standing at my desk, her bob still swinging from a brisk stride.

I lifted out an earbud. "Hi! Need something?"

"Oui. The final for the Miami deep dive."

"First thing tomorrow," I said. "Sorry."

She called me a millennial and clipped off.

The song was pure and brilliant and totally new for Joe. Updated synthpop with a snaking bass line that made me wiggle in my desk chair, my hips even more excited than my brain. The vocal line was so melodic I could hardly identify the main hook: Was it the McCartneyesque verse, the jarringly different pre-chorus, or the rousing chorus, where my "animal who's found his family" line scaled an octave and a half before landing on a pillowy resolving chord? The full lyric contained no other direct lifts from my "Mis-Shapes" post but was thematically almost identical, the same sense of awaking from loneliness on a dance floor, the same winking generational call to action.

There was a video too, blessedly low budget: vintage Madchester-style club footage interspersed with the band performing on a black box stage. If it had been some shiny MTV cheese I might've passed out at my desk. Joe's showmanship came through, though, his swagger behind the mic exaggerated for the camera.

I yanked out my earbuds and put my head back in my hands. I would've killed "You You You," that was for sure. But would I have killed "Britpop Night" too, inadvertently? The way that pre-chorus sounded like it was spliced in from another song—I would've fought him on that, and I would have been wrong. Had I been keeping him in some sort of middle lane, avoiding catastrophes but falling short of his full potential?

I sent an apologetic email to my boss and then I unloaded to Zoe over IM. She convinced me not to confront him yet, to wait until the album came out. A single on the internet was devoid of context, she said, which I decided was fair. Maybe he'd credited my line in the booklet; maybe he'd mentioned my blog. And there was still "Bay Window"—which bridge had he chosen? How many copies of the CD should I buy? At least three, I decided—one for listening, one for posterity, one to FedEx overnight to my mom.

The days before the album's release dragged. I kept busier than usual, meeting up with co-workers for happy hours, filling weekends with museums and shows. It would've been a great time for a business trip, but I was in the "analysis" portion of my work cycle, writing reports and PowerPoints, packaging up all that trendsetter intelligence. I permitted myself only a handful of "Britpop Night" plays a day, in an attempt to keep my head above a tide of emotion that rose higher inside me with every listen. The precise nature of the emotion was always shifting, moving from rage to embarrassment to magnanimity, but always building in intensity. The rage would simmer at low heat until the embarrassment arrived: Who was I to get so puffed up? I wasn't Dylan; I wasn't Shakespeare. "Like a lost animal who'd found its family," I had typed into my work-issued laptop at three a.m. in a Miami hotel. An average line, at best. But of course, it wasn't average in the song, with that melody and his warm voice and all the lush instrumentation sprouting up around it like wildflowers, a whole ecosystem of beauty. Then came the magnanimity: How lucky I was to be part of it! To have had any hand at all in this masterpiece! To hear my average words transformed into such magic! And that is when the rage would return.

On the album release day I left work at lunch and bussed to the San Francisco location of Amoeba. I found the CD right away on the NEW RELEASES rack, a black-and-neon graphic cover with two stickers: "NEW" and "Featuring the single BRITPOP NIGHT." I bought four copies and tore off the cellophane as soon as I got outside.

Just the lyrics, the studio credits; no extras.

"All songs written by Joe Morrow, with special thanks to Percy Marks."

My hands shook. A loitering punk asked me if I was okay. I started walking, first toward home, then veering off Haight toward the Panhandle. I was still holding the jewel case open in one hand; with the other, I found his name in my phone.

He picked up after one ring. "Percy!"

"Hi."

"How are you?"

"A little pissed?"

He swore lightly under his breath. "We were up against the wall to deliver a single, and the whole lyric just came out of me after I read your Pulp post. Didn't realize I'd bitten a line until we'd laid down the track, and by then it was like, well, that's our hook. The band all decided you'd understand. We're loving your blog, by the way."

"Clearly," I said. "First question. Why no heads-up? 'FYI, old pal, you're about to be plagiarized'?"

He paused for a second, and when he spoke it was heated. "I don't know, Percy, same reason I haven't called you five hundred times over the past three years? Because you told me to leave you alone!"

"Did I?" I said. "I believe I said I wanted to stop helping you with your music, a request you somehow found a way to violate entirely on your own. Well done."

He was quiet, and I felt a moment of triumph at having articulated the betrayal so perfectly. I jaywalked across a busy one-way street, beating a rush of oncoming cars, and entered the park.

"Anyway, it's, what," he said tiredly, "eight words?"

"Fine," I said. "Forget 'Britpop Night.' What about 'Bay Window'?"

He sighed. "What about it?"

"I co-wrote that song and you know it! I wrote the bridge entirely myself!"

"Well, the bridge melody was mine—"

"No, it wasn't."

"I made it good."

"Classy. And totally beside the point. Even if I'd just written the lyrics, that's a co-write."

"For normal people, yes, it's a co-write!" His speech was finally quickening to meet the pace of mine. "But that's not our arrangement!"

"Our arrangement?"

"Yes! We talked about it back at school—you said you didn't want credit, that the songs were mine, you weren't a songwriter. 'I just like helping,' you said."

"Did I! Sounds like something a twenty-one-year-old would say to her crush." I glared at a man who crossed my path in pursuit of a basketball. "And of course you never questioned it, because girls have been doing your homework for you your whole life."

He exhaled noisily, a wounded scoff. "You don't know half of what I know about self-reliance, Percy."

He knew how to get me. I yanked off my cardigan—I had worked up a sticky, cold sweat. "'Bay Window' was different," I said.

I heard some shuffling, a relocation, and he sighed again. "It was a little different," he admitted.

"Why not credit me, then? Was it just too awful, the thought of not seeing 'All songs written by Joe Morrow' in your liner notes?"

"Percy."

"Were you worried people would think you're not really writing your own songs, because you have a co-writer? Don't you know that only happens to singer-songwriters who are women?"

"Percy. I really thought you wanted nothing to do with me. I actually wondered if you'd be annoyed that I even gave you the special thanks. I mean, honestly—it's been *three years*."

The way he said it sapped the energy from my stride. The catch in his voice was so familiar. I sat down on an iron bench.

"I do love how 'Bay Window' turned out," he said, when I didn't say anything. "A bit out of place on the album, but oh well."

"It was always out of place in your oeuvre."

"I guess. What do you think of it?"

"I haven't heard it yet. I just walked out of Amoeba."

He started laughing. "How do you know I even used your parts?"

"I just know," I said, but I bit my lip. Why did I call so quickly? I didn't even remember making the decision to dial. I looked down at the four identical jewel cases in my hand. "Did you?"

"Don't worry, you were right. It's the same bridge."

"Which one? 'Zoe comes over in the afternoon'?"

"No. 'What a day to be so weak.'"

I smiled slightly, against my will. He was filing the edges off my anger, but the bulk of it still loomed inside me like a tumor, hard and immovable. He wasn't copping to it, but he'd wanted "All songs written by Joe Morrow." Of course he had. Just like he wanted the girls. He wanted it all. I put my sweater back on and started walking again, looping back around toward Haight. A mom jogged by with a crying baby in a stroller.

"Where are you?"

"Panhandle."

"Mmm. Foggy?"

"Like a graveyard scene in a horror movie."

"New York is roasting. I'm living in Greenpoint now—"

"That's nice."

He sighed. "Did you at least hear the single?"

"Yeah," I said. "It's brilliant, but you don't need me to tell you that."

"Yeah?" he said, waiting for it.

"Okay fine. I can't get over how different each piece of the song is, and yet they all work together. I don't even understand how this song is possible. I've listened to it probably a hundred times and I'm still not sick of it."

I could feel him glowing through the phone.

"The title is dorky, though," I said. "I would've gone with 'Animal' or 'Animals.' But nobody else is mentioning it, so whatever."

He cleared his throat. "Since when do you care about dorkiness? You blogged about 'Just the Way You Are' last week."

"You asked for my opinion," I glowered.

He sighed. "Fine. What can I do? 'Bay Window' isn't a single—we might only get one single. It won't earn much in the way of royalties."

"It's not about royalties," I said. I was back on Haight now, walking into a tide of tourists. "It's about how it feels to be used."

"Oh, come on. Used?"

"Is that so crazy? I had my hands deep in those early songs, very deep. And who gets all the glory?"

"I do," he said forcefully. I winced; it was the wrong word, "glory." "Because I did all the work, Percy. I was up until four a.m. every night making *Funny Strange*. I played every part. Then I had to teach three randoms how to play those parts, how to show up to rehearsal on time, how to not become drug addicts on the road. I lived in a van with them for a year of my life, for God's sake."

I turned onto a side street and sat on the bottom stair of a Victorian stoop. I wanted to say that I wasn't asking to be credited for playing the parts or being his road manager; I was asking to be credited for writing. But I was scared of what other petty accusations might be waiting in my mouth. Who cared about glory? I wanted the pride.

"I know you deserve the glory, Joe," I said finally, quietly.

"But it still makes you mad."

"It does," I admitted. "And jealous. I can't help that. The jealousy was what tipped me over the edge that night at the wedding. It was always there. I will always be jealous of you."

"Fine. I will always be inspired by you, even when you tell me not to be," he said.

"And I will always be critical of you too. I can't stand it when you don't live up to your talent."

"And I will always be destroyed by your criticism."

I pulled the hot phone from my ear, fighting an impulse to throw it into the street. What more could be said? When I told Zoe later, she said it sounded like we had exchanged a perverse version of vows. I can't remember exactly how the conversation ended, who hurled the first goodbye; it was just extremely, obviously over.

The Weakness in Me

The *Strong & Wrong* tour was scheduled to come through SF late that summer. Zoe and Melissa had tickets; even Zoe's parents had tickets. I didn't want to go, and I didn't want to explain why not, so I decided to be out of town. It was time for my recruiting tour anyway—"tour" being my boss's word, not mine, I swear, for my semiannual trendsetter scavenger hunt around the country—though I did bump it up a week. I made LA my first stop, booking a four-day stay at the Mondrian on Sunset starting the night of Joe's show.

It seemed like a clever plan until Zoe pointed out, quite brightly, that I could still see Caroline—they were going to LA immediately after SF! They'd be playing two nights at the Troubadour while I was there! Joe Morrow was entirely inescapable! I kept my face neutral when she delivered the news, though of course she knew exactly what she was doing.

She called me the morning after the SF show. I was driving around Hollywood in my rental car, drinking spa water from the hotel lobby out of a thermos and shuffling LA music (Laurel Canyon, Rilo Kiley). My only experience driving as an adult had been in LA, and it always made me feel a mellow sort of alienation, almost pleasant.

"That was insane," Zoe said, instead of hello.

I pinched the phone between my ear and shoulder and turned down the stereo.

"People were flipping out. I kept wanting to say chill out, you guys, it's just Joey! But it wasn't just Joey. He's on another level now."

Yet another level, I thought. "Who came?"

"My entire high school, for starters—some of them had pictures of their babies, so that was weird. Joey's dad lurked in the back for a bit."

"Really? Is he . . ."

"What, in AA?" She snorted. "He had a good year or so a while back, apparently, but no—I talked to him for five minutes and almost got drunk off the smell of him. Still, he was very proud, which was sweet."

The idea that his dad showing up drunk for only a portion of Joe's big show could be considered "sweet" was unbearably depressing to me—and "proud," really? Did he get to be proud? But Zoe had moved on.

"Lots of Berkeley people, of course. Some of them said to say hi. Your old roommate was there!"

"What? Megan?"

"Yeah! I told her what you've been up to. She didn't even know about your blog."

This made me feel guilty, though I couldn't say for sure that I was to blame for losing touch with her. She had disappeared without protest.

"I saw Joey before the show too," she said, a bit cautiously. "He came out to my parents' house for lunch. Melissa too. It was really—man, it was really special. My dad was so stoked to make Joey his tamales. My mom had two mimosas and got all tipsy. I wish you could've been there."

I turned onto Santa Monica Boulevard, one of those blocks you see in movies, lined with towering palms. Mr. Gutierrez had cooked for the three of us once or twice, back in the fall of '00. Melissa had probably sat in my chair, the one that was the cat's favorite, warm and covered in tiny hairs.

"Are you still there?"

"Sorry. I'm driving." I cleared my throat. "Did you go backstage after the show?"

"Yeah, but that was hella chaotic because he let in all our friends. It'll be more chill tonight."

I didn't say anything.

"Percy," she warned. "He knows you're there."

"Oh, does he? Thanks, Zoe." I passed the Troubadour, rubber-necking as long as I could at the CAROLINE in black block letters on the marquee. "It's sold out anyway."

"Send him a text," she said. "Seriously. I don't care if you go backstage, but go to the show. I don't know why you would deprive yourself of this."

"Deprive myself! Hilarious!"

" 'Bay Window' was the highlight of the night. Everyone agreed. Just him and the piano, near the end of the set."

I put on my turn signal so I could circle back again. "Fine."

I waited until I was back at the hotel, comfortable on the massive bed. Zoe said you might have a ticket for me tonight in LA?

His response was instant: Great! Just give your name at the door, I'll put you on the list for All Access.

K, I wrote back. Probably won't stick around tho—I'm here on a work trip.

Noooo at least come back for a hug, came the reply.

This felt oddly friendly given our last conversation. Maybe I should go backstage, I thought. It did sound exciting. And then he wrote: My girlfriend will be there, if that's what you're worried about.

I dropped the phone into the bright white bedsheets. A minute later it lit up again: Her band is our opener.

And again: Just sayin there's no danger of us accidentally sleeping together like the last time we saw each other hah.

My gut spun with nausea. I googled the opener—the Trouba-dour marquee had said THE CURLERS—and knew right away it was the bass player. I'd seen her in a photo with Joe a few months back on Last Night's Party, while scouring the party blogs for pictures I could use in my trend report. They were just standing next to each other at a warehouse party, not touching, so I hadn't thought much of it. But now here was her face again on the cover of the Curlers' self-titled debut, pale flawless complexion in the camera's flash, hair a fiery shag. I found the warehouse photo again, and this time I could see it: the intimate lean in their shoulders, which were almost the same height, and a matching sheen of sweat, like they'd just been dancing, or performing.

Joe was still texting. Bay Window is bringing the house down- have you seen the updates online? Lawyers made it happen fast, they're sending you papers.

I pulled up the iTunes Store and there it was: "Bay Window (J. Morrow/P. Marks)."

Morrow/Marks!

Now I was smiling broadly and also still nauseated. God, it looked glorious. I took a screenshot on iTunes, and then Wikipedia, and everywhere else I could find it online. On the band's Myspace wall, a recent post:

> Due to a rather extreme example of human error, the song "Bay Window" was improperly credited on the first CD printing as being written by Joe Morrow. "Bay Window" was actually co-written by Joe Morrow and Percy Marks. Check out her blog *Walgreens Songs*. Thank you, Percy.

I picked my phone back up: Special your welcomes, Joe.

I sent the screenshot to my mom, ordered a plate of room service pasta, then sat at the desk and looked at myself in the round brass-rimmed mirror for the entire time it took the pasta to arrive, watching the emotions cross my features, then vanish the moment they were spotted. My face was beginning to change a bit in the latter half of my twenties: leaner, not so round. I didn't mind it; my full cheeks had always been slightly embarrassing to me. In all the promotional photos I'd seen of Joe, and in the one with the redhead, he had looked the same. But Joe had never really looked young.

The pasta was tepid and chewy, and I couldn't get much down. Briefly I tumbled into an internet hole about the bass player—Brooklyn born, then painted abstract canvases at Central Saint Martin's; shared equal co-writing credit with the other Curlers on their songs, which were mostly unremarkable but featured tight, melodic bass work—before deciding I wanted no more information about this woman, ever, and jammed the back button on my browser repeatedly as if it would erase the pages from my memory.

Next I looked up Raj on Facebook. It occurred to me he may have moved back to his home city, that he might be all alone in some little bungalow not far from me, stirring a pot of sauce on a stove. I was right: he had moved back. And he was married.

Married! His bride was beautiful, in a strapless white gown on a boring-ass beach. *I'd say it felt like a dream but I've never had a dream this good,* Raj had captioned.

I slammed the laptop shut. "Who gets married?" I growled into the mirror. I was suddenly so sick of these rooms. I swore I'd seen this mirror in a hundred different hotels.

At nine-thirty I drove east to some terrible event DJed by Steve Aoki, recruited a single subpar trendsetter, and then, when the Caroline set was certain to be well under way, came back across town to the Troubadour. Parallel parked my rental car on the side of a hill after only twelve attempts. The doorman found my name on a list and handed me an all-access badge on a lanyard.

"I won't need that," I said. "I'm just here for one song. Have they done 'Bay Window' yet?"

He stamped my hand wordlessly.

I entered to "Funny Strange" sounding better than I'd ever heard it, Joe's guitar line neither buried, as it was on the album, nor distractingly up front, as it usually was live. I couldn't see him, just heads of the crowd silhouetted against a rainbow of stage lights, but his voice did what it always did to me. I ordered a shot of tequila and a dark beer from the bar and began working my way through the audience.

The band ripped into the next song, one of the power-pop yawns from the new album, just as I emerged into a clearing. He was scruffy, his curls too long to achieve their usual height, a half inch of beard growth softening the angles of his face. He stepped up to the mic and sang the opening line while chugging his electric: "I'm only a humannn . . ."

I was startled to hear a girl behind me singing along loudly. I turned to look: college age, at most, with the starry eyes of a su-perfan.

"Not even one of the good ones," sang Joe and the girl in unison. She was really belting it, a direct line to my ear.

"Isn't this song awesome?" she shouted to her friend during an instrumental break.

"I don't know," came the friend's voice, dubious. "They shouldn't have done 'Britpop Night' so early. It sets a high bar."

I thought her friend was probably right, but I was relieved to hear I'd missed "Britpop Night." I ordered a double vodka tonic from a miserable cocktail waitress prying her way through the crowd and checked out the ceilings of the place, the bar behind us, the ram-shackle balcony. When I looked at Joe singing, I felt overwhelmed and tormented—the image of the last time I'd seen him, silhouetted in the fluorescent light of the rooftop stairwell, kept superimposing itself over the scene onstage—but when I looked away, I could feel a certain amount of peace about everything. I could be happy for him. He had done his best to right his wrongs against me. And he had moved on.

Raj had moved on, too.

The more I drank, the more I expected to be approached. Surely some guy would try; I wouldn't have been choosy. But nobody so much as nodded at me—a woman alone at a show! All those nights in stealth mode at clubs seemed to have given me an invisibility superpower.

The waitress appeared with my vodka just as the stage darkened and the band walked off. A moment later, twin spotlights lit up on Joe at an electric Wurlitzer. I shoved a twenty at the waitress and waved her off. Joe was squinting out at the crowd, a hand shading his eyes. A tattoo on his inner forearm, or maybe it was his set list in Sharpie.

"Is Percy here?" he said.

I heard myself laugh with shock. People started looking around at each other, but nobody looked at me.

"I wrote this song for her, and also with her, which is exactly as complicated as it sounds," he said, to some laughter. "Perce? Holler if you're here."

"I'm here." I thought I'd shouted, but my voice came out sounding downright elderly. "Here!" I tried again, with a limp wave.

The superfan behind me and her friend started hopping up and down and bellowing, "She's right here, Joe! Joe! Over here!"

Joe nodded in our direction, pleased, though I could tell he couldn't see me in the glare of lights. Then he looked down at the keys and started to play. "It's a movie," he sang, which got a surprisingly loud round of recognition applause, even some whooping. He stayed focused, sang the next line right over them: "But it's happening." The girl behind me was quiet now; I could feel her keen awareness of my presence. "Eating black beans. Hours passing."

I remembered feeling dissatisfied with that line when we wrote it, and now who cared? People were entranced. Was it not actually that hard to write a song?

"I said I know"—he winced on the high note—"that I want children. It makes me feel like a monster."

A girl standing to my left brought her hand to her collarbone, overcome.

"From the woman I love's ba-a-ay window . . ." He moved the

melisma through his whole body. "I watch the world begin to end." The place was pin-drop quiet now. "In the woman I love's ba-a-ay window, I see the good give up again."

He lingered there, his body slightly slumped, before straightening and returning to the chords of the verses. The girl in front of me still had her hand on her chest. Her boyfriend put his arm around her.

"The anchor's stumbling. He thinks he's dreaming." Those were my lines. Joe's eyes were closed, his forehead creased, shining. "The music doesn't come. So I start cleaning." Then the melodic shift: "The phone rings, but it's always for her. Everything I do is for her."

At least three women in my vicinity turned to look at me, quickly, snapping their heads back into place. I felt a warmth traveling up from my fingertips. When he'd sung that phrase at the piano store, it had just felt right—a nice repetition of the previous line while also being enough of a non sequitur to be interesting. The idea that it held any real truth had not occurred to me, not really, until that moment. But of course, somewhere backstage—maybe watching from the wings, out of my sight—was a bass-playing girlfriend who knew the truth: this was all ancient history; "the woman I love" just sounded good; Joe was hers.

He sang the chorus again, bigger and more building, then he pounded on the bridge chords. "She tries to kiss me as the sun goes down—I only give her my cheek." His voice was bruised and bold, wailing, majestic. "I promise friendship and we face the screen again. What a day to be so weak." He savored the last word, his voice dripping with despair. He hung his head for a beat of silence before singing the chorus again, quieter this time, and then he leaned back and lifted his hands.

The audience exploded into applause. "Thanks, guys," Joe said humbly, shaking hair off his forehead, and the bandmates returned from the wings. "Can we do one more?"

I turned on my heel and pushed through the crowd for the door, desperate for air. It was warm outside for the hour and the sidewalk was bustling with men in tank tops. I walked fast without really knowing where I was or where I'd parked, though I seemed to be in no shape to drive anyway. I felt like I'd done two fat lines of coke. My cheeks hurt from what I realized was a massive, deranged smile; I massaged my cheeks as I walked, trying to calm them down, but they kept springing back up.

That audience had loved our song. Loved it. My bridge had been perfect. My bridge! Was it possible it could be a second single?

I turned toward Sunset, abandoning my car, scampering up the long hilly blocks in time with my racing heart. I was trying to walk to my hotel, but when the shops and clubs became dark mansion driveways I realized I'd turned west instead of east on Sunset and had to double back. As I passed through West Hollywood again, a voice called out to me from a side street.

"You're the girl in the bridge!"

It was the superfan. She was about to get into a parked car with her friend, who was opening the driver's-side door.

"I *wrote* the bridge," I said.

She shook her head, a look of awe on her face. "Damn. 'Bay Window' is basically my favorite song ever. Did all that really happen?"

I nodded. "Down to the black beans."

"Amazing. That is the best 'fuck you' in the history of 'fuck yous.' Like, okay, you don't want to kiss me? I'm gonna make you sing about this mistake for the rest of your life, dude. You're going to be singing about this at the fucking Troubadour in a fucking decade, dude."

I laughed. "Well, September eleventh was, what, five years ago?"

"He'll still be singing about it in five years. He'll be singing about it when he's forty." She shook her head again. "Anyways. Honor to meet you."

"You too," I said lamely, and resumed my march down Sunset.

The interaction inflamed my adrenaline even further. At a

fluorescent-lit shop called Pink Dot, which appeared to be Sunset Boulevard's version of a bodega, I bought a tall bottle of water with electrolytes. My calves were tight and sore. I sat down on the curb in the store's small parking lot and held the cool bottle to my throbbing hot face, but sitting seemed to be making my heart pound even harder. I got up and kept walking, faster now, trying to outrun the beating against my ribs. The famous Sunset billboards towered above me, bizarrely bright and awkwardly angled, not designed for pedestrian viewing.

In my hotel room the loneliness seemed to be there already, waiting for my arrival. I indulged an overwhelming desire to scratch my scalp and the skin of my arms, pacing the limited walkable area, semicircling the foot of the bed. When blood began to pool under my fingernails I grabbed my phone. I knew Zoe would be asleep at Melissa's, so I called the Indiana house.

My mom answered groggily. "Are you okay? What's wrong?"

"Sorry. I thought maybe you'd be up in the garden already."

"What's wrong?"

"I don't know. I think I might be having a panic attack or something."

I was still pacing. I heard her say something to my dad, switch on a light.

"I saw Joe perform the song we wrote and people *loved* it, like they lost their actual *minds,* and it made me so happy, Mom, I—is it possible to be too happy? I feel like I'm malfunctioning from happiness. My heart is beating so fast it's kind of scaring me."

"That doesn't sound like happiness."

"Thrilled, maybe? It was so incredibly thrilling."

"Drink some water."

"I tried. My throat is, like, sealed."

"Where are you?"

"My hotel room, on Sunset Boulevard."

She made a chuckling noise that meant my life was so glamorous, that I was taking it all for granted. "Honey," she said. "You're fine. Take a deep breath. Exhale longer than you inhale."

I leaned my forehead against the thick glass of the full-wall window. LA was such an uninteresting city at night, the palm trees lost in the darkness, the boulevards reduced to spotty lines of light. I wondered where Caroline and the Curlers were staying. I forced a deep breath into my lungs, and the air seemed to bring with it a clear, piercing pain, like a long needle inserted into my core. On the exhale, I felt my shoulders relax.

Those intricate bass lines. The tall, lean body of a woman who could handle her instrument.

"I'm okay," I said into the phone. "You can go back to bed."

"Are you sure?"

"Yeah. It helped to hear your voice."

"It's just a boy," she said tenderly. "It's just a pop song. Now get some rest."

An actual musician. They probably wrote songs together all the time, their guitars in bed with them like pets, harmonizing. And I had given up my chance to ever write with him again. I had handed it to that girl on a gleaming silver platter.

I pushed myself off the window and found my iPod. A pop song: that would help. I tugged off my jeans and slid my exhausted legs between the sheets, spinning through my music library. I needed serious medicine, that stuff they administer to stop an overdose. Then I saw it: Joan Armatrading, "The Weakness in Me."

Her voice was like a rich, warm oil massaged into my muscles. Journalists always called it "throaty," or "mannish," or "guttural"— words that all struck me as horribly incorrect and probably homophobic. To me her voice was just right, completely pure, and that made it impossible to describe; words would always go too far in one direction or another.

And what she was saying, with that voice. What she was asking. Is this hold you have on me, Joan asked her lover, because of you—because of your power, your magnetism, the force of you? Or is it because of my own weakness?

We fell asleep together, me and Joan, curled up with our arms around a long pillow, and just before I drifted off, I had an idea.

Dawn woke me just an hour or two later. I hadn't shut the curtains, and a bright slice of orange light had fallen directly on my bed. Then I remembered. I went to the desk, opened my laptop—Raj's wedding picture had to be closed in a hurry—and searched my email inbox for Luke Skinner.

There were two emails from him, both unanswered: his initial request for feedback, almost a year old now, and another, more recent email. This one included a link to his mostly finished album on a password-protected FTP site. The tracks were unmixed, he warned in his email, and the last two might be dropped. The project was called Skinner—but it was a band, like Van Halen or Bon Jovi, he explained, as if either of these references was remotely culturally relevant. He was still on Caroline's label, but had a different producer and was going for a darker, cooler sound. No presh, but it occurred to him maybe his first email went to spam.

I entered the password on the FTP, pressed play, and ordered room service.

He described it as post-punk, but I would've said dance rock because of all the staccato synth lines screaming over the guitar and bass, and because post-punk gave the entire project too much musical credit. His singing was monotonous through most of the verses, then he'd attempt some kind of melody in the chorus. The lyrics were barely intelligible, goth-lite, a few outer space/alien metaphors. All the songs had long, pretentious titles. The third track was obviously the single, with more polish on the vocals and a reasonably catchy synth riff.

On Myspace the band was heavily made up, sporting jet-black mullets and matching military jackets. I could just imagine the A&R

man pitching it to the label: this would be so easy to market. Joy Division through the grinder of *American Idol*. Bowie without the inconvenience of art.

I listened to all thirteen tracks while wolfing down a stack of pancakes, then listened again. In the shower later that morning, only one of the songs was stuck in my head. It wasn't the single; it was one of the two on the chopping block. Its title, "Least Worst Night of the Century So Far," at least had some charm. And the chorus contained a real hook, though it was buried in a squashed production.

I called the number in Luke Skinner's email signature and left a voicemail. He called back a minute later.

"Am I too late to help with your album?" I asked.

"We're mixing, so probably," he said. "Why?" He sounded sharper than I'd expected, older; he was taking this seriously.

"I like 'Least Worst Night of the Century So Far.'"

"We cut that one."

"That's a mistake. It's the best song on the album."

He was quiet for a minute, then said, "We only have eleven tracks."

I crossed the room to the window. LA was a pastel layer cake now, topped with a thick shmear of smog under pale blue sky. "Give me a crack at it. If it's good, you've got your twelfth track."

"I don't want people to think we just eked this album out. *Strong & Wrong* had fourteen."

"Well," I said. "Half of them sucked."

His grin was audible. "Okay," he said. "Send me your ideas."

In the city below, I spotted the angled line of Santa Monica Boulevard, followed it down toward the Troubadour. "I don't send ideas without a contract," I said. "Fifty percent of the writing credit. And I want to produce it."

Least Worst Night of the Century So Far

The studio was in Brooklyn, an old building near the water. Before entering I tossed my half-full Dunkin' Donuts coffee in a garbage can on the corner. The caffeine hadn't been doing my anxiety any favors.

Luke Skinner was funding the day himself, which meant we were at a slightly cheaper studio in the same building as the one where the band had recorded their tracks weeks earlier, on the label's dime. I'd paid my own plane fare, spent the night on Nomi's couch, and had a red-eye out that night. My boss thought I was going to a wedding.

At the end of a long concrete hall, I found a smaller, more cluttered version of the studios I'd seen in music documentaries. Black cords hung in long loops from scattered keyboards. Luke was seated next to a guy I recognized from the internet to be Dennis, the studio's co-owner and engineer, both of them facing a large console and a computer screen. A half inch of brown showed at the roots of Luke's black hair. Dennis had a nose full of broken capillaries and was halfway through a cigarette that made the scene feel jarringly anachronistic, like entering a casino. There were no windows in the room. I stood with my roller suitcase until they noticed me.

"Here she is," said Luke, and gave me a quick hug. The engineer moved the cigarette to his mouth to shake my hand, rising only halfway from his chair.

I sat on a hard couch behind them as they ran through the logistical agenda for the day. I nodded along, always a half beat behind, struggling to decipher the industry lingo. Dennis said the day would be spent entirely on Pro Tools since the tracks were all recorded.

"Except vocals," I said.

Luke looked nervous. "That's right. We do have new lyrics."

Dennis leaned back in his chair, rocked it. "Iso booth makes this a longer and therefore more expensive day."

Then came a strained exchange I didn't fully understand, though I guessed that Luke was being dicked around. In the end we were allowed to record new vocals in the isolation booth, but we had to nail them in an hour, and would have to do so through a heightened tension that seemed to be coming not just from the ticking clock, but from Dennis's rapidly deteriorating opinion of both me and Luke.

Luke entered the soundproofed booth on the other side of a glass partition, and I sat in his vacated chair. Dennis showed me how to use the talk-back button to communicate with Luke. On a dark screen, the tracks of the song ran in horizontal stripes. A corkboard on the wall inches from my head was filled with handwritten notes, promotional buttons, and candid photographs of people hanging out at the studio that stung my eyes one by one: Karen O!—TV on the Radio!—was that *Bowie*?

I grabbed my phone. "Where's the bathroom?"

"Now?" he said, but jerked his head toward the hall.

The bathroom was empty and weirdly warm. I went into a stall and called Zoe.

"Hi babe."

"My pits are dripping," I said. "This is my shot, and I'm already blowing it."

"Really, though?"

"I'm stumbling around like a new kid at school, wasting time. The engineer hates me, and he knows everybody, he'll talk, I can tell. What am I doing here, Zoe? What did I think, I could just click my heels and make myself into George Martin?"

"Hang on," Zoe said, and I heard some rapid typing. "No, you're not a George Martin. George Martin was a classically trained symphonic arranger which informed his production style greatly. You're a Rick Rubin."

"I can't believe you know who Rick Rubin is."

"In anticipation of this call, I did some research."

I understood her point: Rubin was famous for getting out of the artist's way, most recently with a series of absolute legends. "I'm not exactly dealing with Johnny Cash here," I said.

"Rick Rubin also produced Limp Bizkit."

I laughed and left the stall, washed my hands at the sink. Through a grated window in the ceiling came a welcome gust of air, a crisp early-fall breeze off the water.

Zoe was reading aloud now: " 'Rubin has little in the way of musical or technological ability. His talent—and it is immense—is his taste.' "

I looked at myself in the mirror. Nomi had loaned me a brown-red all-business lipstick that morning. I wiped it off on the back of my hand.

"Did you hear me?" Zoe said. "Are your pits drying?"

"Yeah," I said. "Thanks, Zo."

I walked quickly back to the studio, where the engineer was typing on a BlackBerry with one hand and lighting a fresh cigarette with the other. "Hope you enjoyed your thirty-five-dollar pee," came Luke Skinner's voice over the talk-back speaker.

He sang the song from top to bottom in his affected growl, holding a printout of my emailed lyrics. I had replaced all the abstractions and spaceship metaphors in the verses with concrete details clarifying the song's central story, which was, like much of the album, about striking out alone after years of feeling suffocated. I calibrated my edits so that it could read as a romantic breakup song even though the breakup in question was clearly with Caroline. Luke had surprised me by agreeing to the changes in an all-caps response: *HELL YAH*. He'd also liked my slightly tweaked melody— I'd sent him an audio file of myself whisper-singing it, pulling the notes apart like Joe had done on my "Bay Window" bridge—though Luke was muddying it up again now, in the vocal booth.

When he finished, the engineer looked at me with his eyebrows raised. I pushed the talk-back button and cleared my throat. "Can you do it again, but this time just, like, *sing* it?"

Luke stared at me through the iso booth's window. I heard the engineer laugh slightly, cruelly, though I wasn't sure if it was at me or Luke.

I stood and made my way to the booth so we could talk privately. Luke waited for me with arms folded, one eye on the clock that hung in the center of the main room.

"Listen," I said. "It's okay that you can't sing."

He scoffed. I was standing in the open doorway of the booth, propping it open with my hip, but we were still uncomfortably close.

"No, really, it's okay. Think about Dylan, Cave, Mangum—you don't need me to tell you this. The difference is, those guys didn't care. You need to start caring less, right now. Don't dumb the melody down to meet your range. Aim for the notes I sent you. We'll fix it later." I wasn't actually sure how we were going to fix it later, but I had trust in Pro Tools.

Luke looked up at the clock again, then back at me, holding my gaze a long second. "He's going to be so pissed," he said, and pursed his lips as if savoring something delicious. Then he pulled his headphones on and faced the mic.

I walked back to the control room feeling slightly sick. It's not that it hadn't occurred to me, that I had been a revenge hire, at least partly. It was the kind of dark and unprovable thought that reared up occasionally at night, that I had learned to cram back down in the cracks of my brain before it mutated into self-destruction. But it was true this time. It was as true as Luke's prediction: Joe was going to be so, so pissed.

As I sat back down behind the console I felt a blaze of hatred for them both. Let him be pissed. Let Luke be smug. I was producing a song.

"Are we good?" Dennis asked.

I shook my head, loosened my shoulders. "Yeah," I said. "Sorry."

"He's a hack," he said.

But Luke's next take was better. Even though his voice faltered at the edges of the melody it sounded okay, it sounded emotional. The third and fourth and fifth takes were even better, and then, just as our returns began to diminish, the hour was up.

Luke went out to get us all food while Dennis and I sat down at the screen.

"I want more *space*," I told him. "More room for each instrument to breathe, especially around the hook."

I explained my reasoning—it's a song about loneliness and freedom, it shouldn't feel so crowded—but he was already nodding, dragging chunks of music around the screen. Each playback sounded better. Luke came back with food and two friends, and then proceeded to entertain them in the main room. This seemed insane after all his ticking-clock histrionics, but there really wasn't much for him to do. On our side of the glass, we were focused and efficient. When I told Dennis to chop off the back half of a synth riff that went on too long, leaving only the melodic refrain, his energy shifted visibly. He was leaning in now, responding, listening. A cigarette waiting in an ashtray burned down to the ash.

After a particularly decent playback, Dennis murmured, "We should call this 'Least Worst Song on the Album,'" and that's when I started having fun. That's when I decided it was worth it to have jumped into two dudes' pissing match—not because it was any great accomplishment to take this song from terrible to almost good, but because this man was a professional, a recording music professional, and he was on my side.

Flying home, I considered the least worst ways for Joe to find out. Through the Brooklyn grapevine? From Luke Skinner himself, in some aggressive text or barroom brag? The answer was clear. When the rough cut of the song landed in my inbox the next day, I forwarded him the file with what I intended to be a brief, classy, and not-sorry intro: weird, I know, but he asked and I saw my chance to produce, etc.—ended up sounding not too bad!

I did not anticipate his response to be silence. It truly hadn't occurred to me. It was worse than Raj's scathing email because it was a thousand cuts, every inbox refresh a new laceration. At the same time, I resented how much I cared. Let him be pissed, I reminded myself constantly, before checking my email again.

After two weeks of this, on a cold Sunday night, I made Zoe call him. They had been in closer touch since Joe's SF show, and Joe had resumed his tradition of joining the Gutierrezes for their Christmukkah, though I had taken over his spot for Thanksgiving. She went on a walk with her phone and returned a half hour later with a tight expression. I met her in the hallway between our rooms.

"Who needs him?" she said curtly, almost brightly.

"I didn't say I needed him," I said. "I just need to *know*. Now. Please. What he said."

She sighed and tossed her cardigan into her room. "First it was about Luke Skinner, my god, he *really* hates that dude. And your standards are what he's always loved about you, it's like he doesn't even know you anymore if you'd work with Skinner, blah blah. Then it got deeper, like, 'Why not me? How could she refuse me when I ask her for help, but say yes to him? *Strong & Wrong* could've been so much better!' After that he changed the subject. We talked about my parents the rest of the time, which was a relief, because that was awkward as fuck for me, dude."

A knot was rising in my throat. "Sorry," I managed. "But did you like, stick up for me? Because it was different with Luke, it was business—it wasn't—"

She clapped a hand on my shoulder. "I tried, I promise, though perhaps not valiantly given his complete lack of interest in hearing it."

"Also what about how this feels for me? It really sucks that I produced a song and it's still got that asterisk on it. Like I'd be nothing without him."

"So?" she said. "He'd be nothing without you either. Let's focus on the good news here, which is that you can release yourself from Joe Morrow's grip now, as he has from yours. Our long national nightmare is over. Honestly, how many different ways is it even possible for the same two people to break each other's hearts?" She gave my shoulder a squeeze, a squeeze that said she knew it hurt, she really did, but she was done. "Hey, if I order in will you split with me?"

She wandered away and I lifted my hand to the spot she'd squeezed. I knew she was right: it was time. And I did feel a fledgling sense of liberation. It was buried, but it was there, rising slowly as dough.

What Makes You Think You're the One

A happy distraction arrived at work the next week when we got a call from our biggest client, a global conglomerate that owned half the brands in your average bar—the cheap vodkas, the expensive vodkas, the old-school scotches you thought were made by monks—asking us to hold an "informal focus group" with our trendsetters in New York during the CMJ Music Festival. CMJ was technically a music-business conference but functioned for fans like an urban festival, held in small venues across Lower Manhattan and Brooklyn. One of our client's brands was a sponsor, and they knew it was a hotbed of trend information, but they wanted more than they got from our reports.

"Your reports tell us what music they love," explained the insights director, speakerphoning into our SF office. "But *why* do they love it?"

"We always strive to cover the why," I said smoothly, raising my middle finger at the phone.

"We just feel like we could get deeper," came the voice of the insights guy. "If we were in the same room with them."

"Of course you could," said my boss, swatting away my finger. "The Why is a bottomless ocean. We'll write up a proposal."

The Why: always the golden question. If marketers could understand *why* kids liked Arcade Fire, they figured, they wouldn't have to pay for the rights to an Arcade Fire song in their ads; they could commission their own knockoff version for similar effect. They wouldn't have to buy up small-batch distilleries; they could capture the essence of Arcade Fire in a brand, slap the label on a bottle of generic rotgut, and stick it on the shelf next to Grey Goose. The Why was where the real money was.

"Beautiful," the client was saying. "Find a nice restaurant with a private room. Figure budget for drinks. Dinner too. Maybe we'll catch a show afterward—we can get passes as long as it's not too buzzy."

I was very much liking the sound of this, but my boss's expression had started to shift. "Will the trendsetters be sampling product?" she asked coolly.

"Oh, we may let them sip a new ultra-premium rum we just launched," he said. "But the goal here is the Why."

"Mm-hmm," my boss said, pursing her blue-red lips. I wasn't sure what was going on; buying our trendsetters dinner was not remotely typical, and I'd never seen that look on her face during a new project call.

He rattled off a few other demands—"Percy should moderate, they'll feel more comfortable talking to one of their own"; "Let us know when you've picked the show, we'll make sure they carry our rum at the venue"—and then said it was great chatting with us ladies.

My boss ripped off her headset and pronounced, after a guttural grunt, "Fake research."

"What does that mean?"

She grunted again and typed lightly on her laptop, telling me to hold my thought by way of one raised eyebrow. I waited. She was the founder of the agency, but we were small enough that she still had her hands in everything. I liked her as much as I could like a treadmill capitalist who needed a half Xanax and Norah Jones to sleep at night, which, it turned out, was a fair amount. She was smart and tenacious and she managed me with respect.

When she was done typing she looked at me steadily. "This

isn't about the Why, honey. They already pay us plenty for the Why, they've got Why coming out of their ears. This is about seeding their new rum with influential scenesters during CMJ, to get them to tell all their friends."

I was confused. "Why don't they just pay them to be brand ambassadors?"

"Their budget was probably earmarked for insights. Plus it's inauthentic. This isn't Red Bull, this isn't the nineties. Everyone knows when a brand is paying for ambassadorship now."

I nodded. "Okay, so it's fake research. Does that . . ." I wanted to say *matter*. "Upset you?"

"Of course it upsets me!" She clamped her thumb and forefinger onto the edges of her forehead and moved her pliable, fiftysomething skin in circles. "It upsets my integrity as a researcher!"

I caught my eyes before they rolled. We'd had this conversation before. I didn't understand the concept of integrity in an industry like ours, which existed solely to help corporations sell young people products they didn't need. I thought we were all swallowing whatever sad excuse for integrity rose up in our throats every morning, but apparently that was just me; my boss and co-workers felt they were playing a vital role in the system, making products more relevant for a consumer who was often misunderstood by the business world. There were times I could see their point. "So, what, we're going to turn him down?"

She looked back at her computer, where she was filling in our project costs spreadsheet. "No," she said, narrowing her eyes at the screen. "We're going to charge double."

New York had shifted into a premature winter in the few weeks since my visit to the studio, brittle leaves barely clinging to the trees on lower First Avenue. I found the restaurant our office manager had booked—Peruvian inspired, inoffensively trendy—and introduced myself to the hostess. "People love this shit," I muttered under my breath as I made my way to the private back room. The client was already there.

"How was your flight?" he said as he shook my hand. He'd clearly put effort into dressing down for the event, wearing a pair of dark-wash boot-cut jeans and sneakers, and was twisting the expensive watch on his wrist as if he knew it gave him away. I set my backpack down at the head of the long table and gave my standard answer about getting so much work done on the flight.

The brand manager arrived, and I knew he was the brand manager because he was wearing a fleece vest with the fucking name of the rum on it. "Hey!" he said, barreling toward me with his hand outstretched. "I'm Kyle!"

"Hi, Kyle!" I said. "Can I ask you to please remove all logos from your clothing? We don't want to bias the respondents."

"Oh! Sorry!" He stripped off the vest, revealing a button-down that also had the name of the rum on it, embroidered just above the pocket. He looked at it, then up at me. A server appeared at my shoulder and asked me to review the prix fixe menu.

"I'm going to trust you can figure this out," I said to Kyle with a smile before turning to the server.

Trendsetters were trickling in. Two greeted each other with recognition, but two wasn't bad. I fanned out an assortment of discussion stimuli on the vintage credenza, mostly CDs of bands playing CMJ as well as older artists I considered key influences. A proliferation of tabletop candles sent warm shapes moving on the walls and I felt something I recognized, curiously, as excitement. It was nice to know what I was doing, even if it was all fake.

I started by going around the table for introductions, asking each for their name, job, hobbies, and favorite bands playing CMJ. Everyone was obsessed with the Decemberists, whose showcase had already become an impossible ticket, along with several smaller bands whose names I pretended to recognize. The server moved smoothly behind the trendsetters, delighting them one by one with their choice of red or white. Kyle reentered the room wearing an ill-fitting EAST

VILLAGE NYC sweatshirt and leaned against the credenza next to the insights guy.

"Nobody's mentioned Girl Talk, who played yesterday," I said, holding up the mash-up artist's CD. "Any thoughts?"

The trendsetters fell over each other to answer:

"I was there! It was the best!"

"He ended up practically naked, we were all dancing onstage!"

"Sampling is so exciting, so democratic!"

"Plus it's all hooks, you're never bored!"

I took notes on a yellow legal pad. Songs aren't supposed to be all hooks, I wanted to say, and for a moment I felt old. "What about Beach House, who we're going to see tonight?"

"Magical," chirped two in confident unison, and another elaborated: "That's the opposite of Girl Talk. Beach House is closer to the Decemberists—otherworldly."

"What's appealing about otherworldliness?" I asked, knowing full well what was appealing about Beach House's mystical, mind-expanding sound.

They explained enthusiastically. Only one stayed quiet: a boy I'd plucked from the deep center of a warehouse dance floor largely for his striking resemblance to Billy Corgan of the Smashing Pumpkins, except younger and with hair. He was sitting directly to my left. He'd already finished his glass of wine and was looking around for a refill.

"What about you?" I asked him. "Any thoughts on Beach House?"

"Eh," he said. "I'm sick of all that whiny shit—it all feels very post-9/11 to me, very soon-to-be dated. I just want to party, man. Give me Girl Talk any day."

"What about last year's CMJ breakout, Clap Your Hands Say Yeah?" I asked. "That's very danceable."

He made a face. "Dance music for whiners," he said, which drew a laugh from the credenza. The server refilled the boy's chardonnay and he gulped it like lemonade. "My favorite thing about CMJ isn't the shows, actually, but just the energy of the week, how there are so many people in town, musicians everywhere. You know that band Caroline?"

Something wild reared up in me, about to buck—it felt violating, that word in this context—but before I could react, his gaze slid off me and onto the trendsetter who was nodding the hardest, a blond girl seated across from him. "They were at this party I was at last night," he told the blonde. "Some other band was playing, then the Caroline guy got up, totally wasted, and sang a Fleetwood Mac deep cut. It was amazing." He turned back to me. "That's the kind of stuff that happens during CMJ."

"The lead singer of Caroline," I confirmed. "Interesting. Which Fleetwood Mac song?" I held my pen poised above the paper. I could feel my heart in my fingers.

"I dunno. Lots of drums."

"Mmm." I nodded. "A faithful cover? Or did he add his own spin?"

The clients bent heads, whispered. Billy Corgan looked at me like I was insane. "It was a party," he said.

Kyle pushed himself off the credenza and held forth a tall, square-shouldered bottle. "Who wants to try some rum?"

After dinner our whole motley crew walked to Cake Shop, the venue for the show I'd chosen, Beach House. The clients were happy because the trendsetters had been universally effusive about the rum (not exactly shocking given that they'd been warmed up with wine, food, and a glowing backstory from Kyle about the organically farmed sugarcane used to make the base—he may as well have kept his vest on). And Cake Shop won me extra points for authenticity, with its sweaty, airless venue hidden underneath a bakery. "Put pictures of this in your report," the insights guy whispered as we descended the stairs. I dutifully snapped a pic of the crowd with my digital camera.

But Beach House was the wrong choice, too mellow and far too beautiful for the crass context of our evening. They put the audience under a hushed, introspective spell. Both clients French-exited almost immediately, which I tried not to take as an insult—they probably had trains to catch, kids up at six. As soon as they were gone my work persona slipped from my body, and the suddenness of the evacuation left me feeling wrung out. I couldn't stop thinking about Fleetwood Mac. Every tall, curly-haired dude looked like Joe until he didn't, until a quarter turn of the head revealed him to be a pale simulacrum, weak in the jaw, tight in the smile. Had he really been wasted? Joe could put back the beer, but he always stopped before his gait started to stagger like his dad's. Had he been depressed about Caroline's low profile at CMJ, their decidedly un-buzzy afternoon set? "Britpop Night" had faded quickly from dance floors with the end of summer, and album sales were slumping. Was he okay?

The boy with the Billy Corgan face stood alone at the edge of the crowd sipping the client's rum neat—they were all ordering it, unbelievably, with their own money—his nose aloft like a dog on the scent of a better scene. I wanted to corner him with all the questions in my head. Who else was at the party with Caroline? And what did he mean by wasted? But of course young Billy didn't know any of this; he just wanted to party, man.

I slipped up the back stairs, spun my iPod wheel to Fleetwood Mac's *Tusk,* and carved a jagged route back to my hotel room. And then, with my laptop on my lap in an uncomfortable chaise overlooking Lower Manhattan, I wrote my strangest blog post yet.

What Makes You Think You're the One

The Drummer bangs hard on the snare to kick it off— one, two, three, four, one. The Singer receives each snare hit like bullets to his torso, staggering, arms draping off an invisible crucifix. And then he sings.

She isn't here, the girl who thinks she's the one. But with his eyes closed, in the carousel of his drunken mind, the Singer sees her face vividly, prismatically. It slides into focus at the end of every measure and then it spins away again. It's a face he hasn't seen in a while; the song has conjured it.

What makes her think she's the one? He shouts the line with a level of indignance he dimly acknowledges as wrong for the setting, which is just a party, after all. But it's a punk song, practically; it's Lindsey Buckingham raging harder at Stevie Nicks than he ever had before, the kind of rage that comes only when you know you're guilty too. It's Mick Fleetwood fully unleashed. It's a lyric that must be spit, that must be spat, a lyric aimed at shoving someone out of her own head, hard.

He opens his eyes and oh look, he owns them all—even the dudes have arrested their beers midraise, mouths hanging, though it's the girls who look like they're on the verge of melting into their cans of Sparks. He can tell they haven't heard the song before. *Rumours* and "Rhiannon," that's as far as they ever went on the Mac. Fair enough. He's no deep-cut snob. Neither is the girl who isn't here; it's something they've always had in common.

But the truth is, she's just as bad as the rest of them. He shuts his eyes again, sings menacingly at her careening face. See, she used to get those same melty eyes when he sang. It wasn't until he got good—until she looked around at his shows and saw other girls with that same dumb look—that she started going cold. Now, no matter how much she smiles or claps, her eyes harden when he sings. She wants to be the only one. She wants him as her deep cut, a B-side unearthed from a rarities bin, proof of her own specialness because she's the one who discovered it, because she doesn't know how to sing her own damn song.

When I woke the next morning, the post had earned only a handful of likes, along with a smattering of confused and occasionally hateful comments. My beloved Alma had written, somewhat hilariously, *I do not know these people?* I deleted it instantly, mortified, even as I hoped, with some small piece of my pathetic heart, that Joe had seen it, and that he'd received it as I'd intended—as an apology.

Someone Great

Skinner's album was released in early 2007 to a full-throated pan on *Pitchfork*—2.3 out of 10!—that unceremoniously dumped all of Luke Skinner's dreams into an industrial-strength incinerator. "Least Worst Night" had been given prime track four placement on the album at the last minute, but who cared after that review. The night it posted, Zoe and Melissa banged on my bedroom door with a bottle of tequila and a rented *High Fidelity* DVD to cheer me up, but I felt oddly fine. There was justice in that 2.3, proof that labels couldn't turn shit into money through force alone, which pleased me even though that shit had my name on it.

I would not have handled it so well if it weren't for the fact that "Bay Window" had just been released as a belated second single on *Strong & Wrong* and was enjoying a slow, halting ascent up the alternative charts. Shortly after the Skinner release, it was featured in the pivotal love scene of a lauded indie film—Joe and the Curlers' bassist were photographed on a red carpet at its Sundance premiere, arm in arm in long, expensive-looking coats—at which point it leaped twenty points up the alternative charts and into the Hot 100.

Two weeks later, Joe sang it alone at a white grand piano on a late-night talk show. It was a particularly arresting rendition, complete with a sudden if brief appearance of tears on the line "the phone rings, but it's always for her"—tears I knew were for his dad, not me, though the audience probably thought otherwise. Zoe and I both teared up too, watching it—how could we not? How could anyone not? Sure enough, the internet started talking. The clip enjoyed a second life online, passed around among friends and then embedded into Tumblrs and cultural roundups.

I was not chill about it. I read everything, every post, every comment. This was my favorite, on a big music blog:

Song of the Year Contender: "Bay Window," Caroline

Caroline's Joe Morrow seems at times more like a pop star than an indie front man, and this isn't a slag. "Pop" is a complicated word. Morrow crosses over not when making his audience dance, as on the impossibly catchy yet decidedly still indie "Britpop Night," but when he makes them *gasp*, as on the late-breaking follow-up single "Bay Window." The way he croons about watching the Twin Towers fall on TV with a love interest, it feels too universal to be anything but pop. Especially when, in the bridge, he shoves her into the friend zone. Ugh, how it hurts this listener, every time. Why does he do it? Because he's scared shitless, and that's what we do when we're scared shitless. We run. "Bay Window" will never be soundtracked to 9/11 anniversary specials because it's not how we want to see ourselves behaving in the event of tragedy. It's about how we actually behave. How we turn the tragedy inward and make it our own.

"Actually he did it because he'd only slept with a lesbian and I'm a pain in the ass," I said to the screen, but I bookmarked it and emailed it to my mom, and then, I couldn't help it, I sent it to Joe. I was starting to think of us as a divorced couple with a successful grown child—shouldn't we experience that success together, in some small way? I left the email empty beyond the link, no pleasantries, hoping the subtext was clear: You won, I don't care, this is fucking cool. But Joe never responded. I tried not to obsess about it this time, but his silence felt like a hard punch on a still-tender bruise. He didn't need to celebrate with me; he had a girlfriend, a bed full of guitars. After that, I kept the links to a bookmark folder.

Video: Caroline Live on *Late Night*

Caroline's first late-night appearance last summer went as expected: they played their new album's obvious single, "Britpop Night"; the band sounded great; lead singer Joe Morrow oozed his usual talent and charm. The song was a critical darling and a feel-good hit of the summer in certain scenester circles. But nobody expected Caroline to be back again on TV many months later singing a tearjerker ballad your mom would love, nor that said tearjerker would outpace the success of "Britpop Night." Watch Morrow sing the shit out of "Bay Window," and grab the Kleenex . . . and your mom.

I knew Joe wouldn't mind being labeled pop, but I did start to worry a bit when the commentary took this "your mom" slant. Was this my influence? Oh, how they'd mocked me at Amoeba for my love of k.d. lang.

I was right: from "your mom," it was a quick line to backlash. From one of the bloggers in my network:

RIP Caroline. *Funny Strange* remains one of my favorite albums of the decade, but they are jumping a big fat shark right now. *Strong & Wrong* was nowhere near as good, and now they're everywhere doing this sentimental snoozefest about 9/11? You're eating black beans, congratulations dude. Their lyrics used to be way cleverer. Pass.

Then it hit the culture warriors. From a major New York media site:

As the clip of that 9/11 torch song "Bay Window" makes the rounds, we feel compelled to point out that bay windows aren't particularly common in New York. Or New Jersey. But you'll find them all over the San Francisco Bay Area, including Berkeley, where the band Caroline was formed in 2001 as the college project of lead singer Joe Morrow. In the chorus, he describes himself watching "the world begin to end" (fair) and "the good give up again." Wait, what? Is that what it looked like from the West Coast—giving up? Because our memories of NY1 that day are of firefighters running into burning buildings. Cops pulling bodies from rubble. Stories of the man in the red bandanna escorting people down the stairwell of the South Tower, or the passengers of Flight 93 fighting back against the hijackers. Are these people not "the good"? Because they sure as hell weren't giving up. Probably Morrow is attempting some sort of anti-war message, which we support in theory, obviously. But maybe when we're talking about a real day with real acts of unbelievable heroism, we can be inconvenienced to choose our words more carefully, or else leave it to the people who were actually there.

"The good were the people who could've stopped the Iraq War!" I told the screen. "Who voted for Bush's reelection because he made them feel safe! How is that not obvious?"

But the worst was when, just a couple weeks after it had started, the backlash stopped coming. The praise stopped coming too. The internet moved on.

For weeks I felt restless, and a bit crazy, like I'd dreamed the whole thing. Every night I checked my bookmarks for reassurance, tallying up the positive mentions and the negative. How would "Bay Window" be remembered—as profound, universal pop, or problematic adult contemporary? Or would it not be remembered at all?

Around this time I found myself in a throng of dancing bodies at an LCD Soundsystem show. I'd come alone because Zoe and Melissa had started going to bed early in their "old age," and because the expectation of socializing at shows had always annoyed me anyway.

It was late spring or early summer, or maybe midsummer; the days swam in San Francisco's seasonless muck. At work I'd been given a promotion and a twenty-two-year-old girl to send crisscrossing the country in search of trendsetters, which was clearly a good thing—one more 3:00 a.m. breakdown in a hotel might've sent me out a city-view window—but I found myself longing for a swampy Miami cab ride or a bracing winter walk through Manhattan, anything to shock my system and mark the time.

When the dancing bodies began to tighten around me, I chastised myself for drifting so close to the stage. I started fighting my way out, my eye on the exit to a mezzanine, but then I noticed the faces of the dancers. Several local musicians I respected, one of whom had opened for Caroline on the *Funny Strange* tour. The owner of a legendary SF studio. An electronic artist and DJ I'd recruited as a trendsetter years earlier. I felt a hard snap of loneliness: I still wasn't in the club.

The band started playing "Someone Great" and I decided not to fight the throng. I closed my eyes and let the sweaty flesh bounce off my own. Elbows skimmed my forearms; heels jammed my toes. After spending weeks untethered on the internet, the physicality felt good, even as it scared me a little, even as it sharpened my loneliness to a point. Luckily it was the perfect song to be lonely to.

"Someone Great" is about loss. Actually it's about the death of James Murphy's therapist, but we didn't know that then, or at least I didn't; Murphy was cagey in interviews. To me it was about how it feels when you've lost someone, and the one person you want to talk to about it—the one person who could help you grieve—is the person you've lost.

It hit me hard, as Murphy sang, how badly I wanted to talk about "Bay Window" with Joe. How cruel it was for him to deny me that.

I could feel the song's groove in my blood, the jumpy electronic melodies that had no business being as emotional as they were. I remembered learning in school that the human heart has an electrical system: that was the sound of "Someone Great." Each skittering beat and record-scratch squeak corresponded to the flares my heart sent up when I thought about Joe—the love, the jealousy, the anger—but they didn't build to a crescendo. They flickered off, and on again. They kept coming.

I opened my eyes and watched Murphy onstage, singing with his chin raised, clutching the mic like a life preserver. His bandmates twisted knobs, tapped keys. Gray tufts poked out of his temples. He had lost someone great, but he was someone great too. And his pain over this loss would keep coming until the day it stopped, when someone great would be mourning him.

Envy arrived, almost by habit—how lucky Murphy was to be able to express this pain, achieve such catharsis—and suddenly I felt so incredibly bored with myself I wanted to jump out of my skin. I wanted to pull the plug on my own damn heart. I had my name on a *Billboard*-charting hit, and I still saw myself as a musical idiot. Was I no better than Luke Skinner, dumbing my life down to fit the limitations of my talent? Why couldn't I follow the advice I'd given him? Why couldn't I be someone great?

The next day at work I hired the agency's designer to help me fold my blog into a professional website. I sketched out what I wanted:

Percy Marks, Song Jerk, in old-school soda-fountain lettering to clarify the pun, with three buttons: *Songwriting, Producing, Writing* (where the blog lived). It still felt ballsy to call myself a songwriter and especially a producer—no matter how little musical talent Rick Rubin had, I was certain I had less—so I didn't tell anyone about the site. I just let it sit there, waiting for someone to google me, or more likely to google "who wrote Bay Window."

While I waited, I bought myself a keyboard, which I set up in the window of my bedroom next to the desk, and my own marbled composition notebook. I used them to finally scratch a lifelong itch: jotting down a line here, a couplet there, molding them into melodies. I sat in my window every morning before work as I drank my coffee, brutishly picking at the keys. My activist ex was now working for the Obama campaign and had given us a stack of Shepard Fairey posters, which we'd plastered in our windows to such a degree that the morning sun sent a pleasant blue-and-red cast over my room.

And then, while I was visiting Indiana for the holidays, sitting on my brother's bed, it happened. I got an email through the site from Meg Vee, an objectively badass indie front woman I had admired for years.

> *Hi, so, I don't know if you've ever had a boyfriend-slash-musical-collaborator but it really sucks to find out he's been cheating on you with your fans so you kick him out of your band and then you have nobody to write with. And everyone in Brooklyn's already in bed with each other song-wise. So I was asking around and Dennis from Lowtop Studios mentioned you, then I looked you up and was like OH HER! I've come across your blog a bunch of times, always so good. Any interest in punching up a few songs for me? Might be nice to make music with a woman for once in my damn life.*

I dropped my laptop and screamed into my brother's pillow.

Comfy in Nautica

I arrived in the lobby of the denim company at 8:55 a.m., sweating in the only outfit I owned that checked both the hipster box and the corporate-hotshot box: a pair of high-waisted slacks, a cashmere shirt that was 75 percent off at Loehmann's and still the most expensive thing I owned, and woven oxfords from Goodwill. It wasn't technically uncomfortable, but I could never put it on without counting the minutes until I could return to my jeans and black T-shirt.

I hated pitching new clients in the best of circumstances, and this was the worst. It was September 2008 and the economy was in a free fall, though projections varied; nobody was sure if the entire fantasy of America was grinding to a halt or if it would just be a slow fourth quarter. All our pitches had been canceled except this one, and a third of the agency had been canned, including my beloved twenty-two-year-old employee. I'd be lying if I said I wasn't nervous. I had co-written a song for Meg Vee's upcoming album, likely a single, but I knew better than to expect it to provide a livable income. I'd received two royalty checks for "Least Worst Night of the Century So Far," one for songwriting and one for producing, and neither could buy me a bag of groceries. Even the "Bay Window" checks hadn't covered rent. I needed this stupid job.

My boss was waiting for me in the lobby, all sharp angles as usual, blazer and flat-ironed bob and those permanently pursed neon-red lips. She was wincing at a TV screen mounted above the receptionist's desk. FEDS SEIZE WASHINGTON MUTUAL, read the ticker.

"Less than ideal pitch conditions?" I said, coming up beside her.

"This is a farce," she said grimly. "I can hear research budgets going through the paper shredder as we speak." There were dark moons under her eyes under a too-thin veil of cover-up. She shuddered like a dog shaking off the rain and turned to me brightly. "Shall we kill it anyway?"

I mimed violent stabbing. She called me a millennial and summoned the elevator.

"You know, they keep changing the cutoff year," I said as we stepped in. "I think I'm Gen X now."

She looked alarmed. "That never leaves this elevator."

When the doors opened, a bald man stood waiting with his hand extended, and talked about the weather and the bailout package as he led us down a glass-walled hallway to a conference room.

We busied ourselves setting up the projector, fumbling over the inevitable Mac-to-PC transition. We were presenting an abridged version of our 2008 trends package, including a hastily developed slide about the trendsetters' response to the economic doom ("Break It Down Again," I'd titled it). It was all a teaser for the annual subscription that we were hoping they'd purchase, that we desperately needed them to purchase. The bald man provided introductions as the clients filed into the room, carrying plates of bagels and coffees—a breakfast meeting, ugh. I prepared myself mentally for the discomfort of watching twenty people chew. And then a girl sauntered in, a girl who was younger than me, and much cooler.

"This is Casey," said the bald man. "Assistant brand manager."

Casey had long dark hair in a hand-raked side part so aggressive it created greasy, individuated strands across her forehead. Smudgy eyeliner traveled well below her eyes, as if it had been applied the day before. She took a seat near the back of the long oval table.

As I started presenting, Casey's presence became comical to me, helping me tolerate the symphony of chewing noises. She probably knew most of what I was saying! They could just ask this hungover kid! But she took notes through the first section on macro-trends. She nodded gravely during the "Break It Down Again" slide: trendsetters don't see the economic collapse as a bad thing, necessarily, I said; they see it as an opportunity for our culture to reprioritize, start over. Casey's elders grimaced.

During the segment on nightlife and socializing, I went to great pains to avoid looking at her. I was just about to move into fashion when a man interrupted.

"I have a question about sourcing." He was in his thirties and wore a blazer over a hoodie, facial skin glistening with product. "I know you get this information from a panel of trendsetters, but how do you find them? Who decides what constitutes a trendsetter?"

We kept a slide hidden at the back of the deck for this question. My boss quickly navigated to it and gave him a quick rundown of my recruiting process.

"So it's her, basically," the man said, looking at me. "You're the arbiter."

"My mother is very proud," I deadpanned, and they all laughed. I saw some of them sit up straighter, the women adjusting their blouses, the men smiling a little too hard. It always happened: they wanted to impress me. I was the arbiter.

But the shiny-faced man wasn't smiling. His squint moved from me to the projected slide, where I had assembled snapshots and bios of a handful of trendsetters. Jesse Jams, DJ, Miami; Liv, writer and eBay reseller, NYC; Jorge, hairdresser and activist, SF. Jorge was my favorite, with his pink braids and intense gaze; he was a vocal opponent of Proposition 8, the anti-gay-marriage legislation that was on the verge of passing in California, and had cofounded a "No on 8" organization to which Zoe was currently devoting the majority of her free time.

The shiny face looked around the table, then back at me. "But your trendsetters don't seem cool to me. They seem more . . . granola."

"That's why you hire us, though," I said. "Because you don't know what cool is."

My boss inhaled sharply and I felt myself pale, like she had sucked out my soul. The man didn't try to hide his shock.

"Excuse me," he said. "We're on the cusp of an actual depression. This time next year, you think anyone's going to care what these hippies think about anything? Shouldn't we be asking the people with money what they think? People can be cool and still have money, you know."

Casey raised her hand, then used it to flip her aggressive side part to the far opposite side. "Coolness is having courage," she said.

"Right!" I said desperately, pointing at her with both forefingers. "Panda Bear!"

The man got over his shock and began to look enraged. "Panda Bear?"

My boss was staring at me icily, but I kept going. "It's a song lyric, but I think what Casey's getting at is that the leaders of today's youth culture might not conform to your white-collar idea of what's aspirational," I said to the shiny man. Casey shrank in her seat. "Trendsetters tend to reject the 'comfy' path, and that takes courage." Color had rushed too swiftly back to my face after its earlier departure; my lips throbbed with heat.

"Hey," said the guy, fingering the drawstring at the neck of his hoodie. "Watch who you're calling white collar." The man next to him laughed.

I had the perfect comeback. It would be dropping a grenade, but that Panda Bear quote had flipped a switch in my brain. I wanted out. So I said it: "A hoodie under a blazer is the worst collar of all."

His eyes widened into white-hot circles.

"Let's move on!" my boss chirped. "Percy, shall I take over?"

My boss drove me home in dead silence. When I could stand it no longer I said, "I think you finally just met the real me."

"Were you trying to get me to fire you so you can claim unemployment?" she said. "If so, congratulations. You're fired."

I felt both panic and relief. My mind spun with numbers: rent, loans, the moderate total in my savings account. Nobody was hiring. "This job has always been bad for me," I said.

"Everything is bad for you. I just read that walnuts are bad for you."

I wanted to explain myself in a way that would make sense to her. "When I was presenting the 'Break It Down Again' slide, all I could think was man, if society is really collapsing, I don't want to be on the side with these jerks. I want to be on the side with the granola kids. You know?"

She didn't know. She merged into the Broadway Tunnel.

"I'm sorry."

She accepted my apology with a nod. "I did enjoy the look on his face when you started talking about Grizzly Bear," she said, with the crack of a smile.

The image returned to me: a patchy redness blooming through his moisturizer. "Panda Bear, but yeah. How dare I humiliate him with my hippie rock 'n' roll! Do you want to hear the song that girl was talking about?"

She nodded, barely, and I plugged in my iPod. The militaristic rhythm of "Comfy in Nautica" filled her SUV, followed by the glorious contrast of layered vocals. When Panda Bear sang about courage, he meant the opposite of how the shiny-faced man would define the word. He meant being softer inside. He meant remembering to have a good time—to resist the lockstep, percussive world that pulsed behind his singing. To resist the percussive world that maybe pulsed inside yourself.

She pulled up at my building just as the song ended. "Are you under the impression that you just communicated something significant to me through that song?" she asked. "Because I couldn't understand a word that boy was singing."

I smiled. "I won't leave until you find my replacement."

"Hah," she said bitterly. "Replacement, that's funny. No, you'll leave immediately—after you do one more thing for me."

She told me she was finalizing a deal with the alcohol company in New York to sell them our trendsetter panel. They wanted to call them "influencers" now, a subtle but important shift that meant less research, more marketing. For our trendsetters to survive in this economy, my boss explained, they had to evolve downstream, closer to the sale.

"Gross," I said. "But okay. What do you need me to do?"

"One last recruiting tour. I promised them a round of fresh blood. But none of your intellectuals this time. Give me bloggers, big Facebookers. Kids with clear ROI."

The fact that she didn't realize I could find these people online was probably one of the reasons her company was about to fold, but I wasn't going to turn down my last paid loop around the country. "On it," I said, and added, sincerely, "Thank you." Then I clamored out of her car, my legs shaking slightly under me as I looked up at my building, its windows screaming at me in block letters: HOPE, HOPE, HOPE.

Heartbeats

My final tour was startlingly unpleasant. I was given only two nights per city, less than half the time I was used to, and my hotels had been downgraded to whatever level is well below room service but just above bedbugs. I spent Miami and LA mostly in the hotels, messaging trendsetters online and half-heartedly searching job bulletin boards.

In New York they put me in Times Square. I met about half my quota online the first day, sitting at a microscopic desk with a view of a giant Planet Hollywood sign, but the next morning I was dying to get out. I met Nomi for lunch at Dojo, a cheap NYU-area restaurant that just a month earlier we would've thought ourselves far too mature and successful to patronize. Nomi had ascended to *Vogue,* but magazines were the worst place to be, and she knew her days were numbered. She showed up in all black, dressed for the funeral of her industry.

Halfway through our four-dollar plates of noodles I asked, spontaneously, if she wanted to make some extra cash as a trendsetter— like many journalists she'd been hustling to amass a following online; I'd been enjoying how well the snitty comments she used to make in the margins of my stories translated into the language of social media—then remembered with a wave of horror that she was well into her thirties now, far too old for the panel.

She rolled her eyes. "I'm too old for this conversation. Keep your blood money."

We talked a lot about how the other creatives in our orbit were faring, hunting for clues about our options. She told me Raj was writing a book about spices, had been paid a decent advance for his proposal. Harrison had ended up in tech. Nomi wasn't ruling anything out.

"What about your guy, the wedding singer?" Nomi asked as we descended into the West Fourth station.

"I wish I knew," I said.

We stopped at the entrance to her platform and she noticed my expression, which I could feel was suddenly unsettled. "People will always go to shows," she reassured me as we hugged goodbye.

I waited a long time for my train. Commuters moved through the station with a different energy than usual, slower, on edge. A busker played a minor-key tune on a violin that ricocheted off the white-tiled walls and hit me on a cellular level. I knew Nomi would be fine; she would seize her impending free time to design a new, more interesting career path for herself. I'd be fine too, eventually. But Joe didn't do well in times of upheaval. I told myself he had a reliable if modest source of income, not to mention a girlfriend—he didn't need me. But by the time my train arrived, I'd decided: I wanted to see him. I wanted it for me. The thought sounded profoundly comforting, and it sounded, now, like something I could handle. It had been more than two years since I'd seen him onstage at the Troubadour, five since the night on the Brooklyn rooftop.

But only one since my last unanswered email.

Back in the hotel I logged in to Zoe's Facebook account and searched his name: still living in Brooklyn, not currently touring. That very night he'd been tagged in an invitation to a show at Union Pool, a Williamsburg mainstay where I could probably find a few trendsetters, though he hadn't responded to the post. Scrolling further, I saw he was regularly tagged at Union Pool. There was even a shot of him behind the bar.

I played the scene out dozens of ways as the afternoon crept by:

he would be with her, in all of them, and I would be ready. I would be cool. That's what I wanted, more than anything: a low-pressure way to say hey, we're cool, how are you. No need to be weird anymore; we're too old, and the world is too fragile.

Williamsburg had gentrified visibly in the past year. A nearby diner had been given a shiny makeover that seemed both incongruous and perfect for the times, a garish embodiment of overspending. But inside the bar, everything felt worn and comfortable. Ceiling tiles in a random pattern of turquoise and white evoked the building's original purpose as a midcentury pool supply shop, and looked, in a few spots, like they might fall on our heads.

I did a quick loop: a meager crowd for a Thursday; loud, unfamiliar music; no Joe. I allowed myself a drink and then got to work, but the pickings were slim. People were staying home, saving money, watching the news. Finally I found a brash twenty-five-year-old girl named Liza-Beth—not Elizabeth!—who thought trends were "beautiful proof of human frailty." She wasn't on Facebook, but I took her info down anyway in case I got desperate.

I was reviewing my quotas at a corner table and beginning to accept it wouldn't happen when it did: the silhouette of his upper half materialized against the warm lighting of the bar. The soft curls and square shoulders—my adrenaline surged before I was even sure. He was talking to someone, mid-nod, when our eyes met. He froze briefly and then resumed his conversation, his gaze returning to me every few seconds, then flicking away again. No wave or expression of shock, which seemed strange, though I realized I hadn't done either myself. It was hard to know what kind of greeting would be appropriate for a history like ours.

The people he was talking to, two girls and a guy, appeared to have intercepted him upon entering; he didn't have a drink, and a light pattern of raindrops dotted the shoulders of his denim jacket. One of the girls talking to him was Liza-Beth. I stood and moved through the crowd to their group. His darting eyes monitored my journey.

"Oh hi," said Liza-Beth when I arrived. "Guys, this is—uh, I'm sorry—"

"Percy," I said.

"Right! You guys, Percy works for this company that will pay you to take surveys about bars and music and stuff. She's legit." She clamped her mouth down on a cocktail straw, took a slurp, gave me a side-eye. "I mean, she bought me a drink, so I'm assuming she's legit?"

"How much?" said the guy who wasn't Joe.

"Payment varies by assignment," I said. "But unfortunately we've met our quotas on white dudes for the year."

Joe laughed.

"You look familiar," I said to him.

His head tilted. "Do I."

"He's the lead singer of Caroline!" Liza-Beth gushed.

"Oh? Is that a band?"

"Come on," she said. " 'Bay Window'? You're making me doubt your legitimacy, Percy."

"Joe," he said to me, holding out his hand. His grip was firm, practiced. The markings on his inner forearm were indeed a tattoo: one long musical staff, treble clef, no notes.

"Can I buy you a drink, Joe?" I asked.

"I thought you had too many dudes," said the other guy.

"Well, for a *lead singer,*" I said, aping Liza-Beth's reverence, "we might be willing to go over quota."

"Why not?" He gave his friends a nod, and we wedged into two empty stools at the bar. I ordered us Budweisers for old times' sake. I felt unreasonably excited. He was wearing a Serious Moonlight Tour shirt, vintage to the point of threadbare, and one of those jean jackets with a nubby white fleece collar. He'd shaved off the beard and reined in the curls, which sat above a slightly higher hairline. I unzipped my backpack and took out a blank screener.

His eyebrows went up at the sight of the formal document. "Quite a job you have there, Percy."

"I'm aware," I said, raising my voice over the chatter and the clinking of glass from behind the bar. "Okay—age?"

"Twenty-eight."

I had already filled it in. "Do anything for work besides music?"

"Odd jobs, when we're not on tour."

"Really," I said, writing this down. "Like what?"

"I fill in here behind the bar," he said. "Donate blood. Dog-sit."

I smiled. "Hobbies, interests, passions?"

"Songwriting," he said. "Piano tuning. You seem too smart for this job."

I stopped writing. I couldn't quite read his tone: it seemed both familiar and chilly. "Maybe that's why I got fired last week," I said.

He gave a small, sympathetic grimace. "Not because capitalism is failing?"

"That too."

"What's your plan?"

I bit my lip. "I don't know. I'm also a music journalist and a songwriter, but, you might know this actually, turns out there's no money in indie rock?"

He laughed and crossed his arms, then one leg over the other; he was wearing Beatle boots, worn but nice. "You have to tour to make money."

"So you're okay?"

He nodded with a self-assuredness that surprised me. "As long as I can get on a stage with a microphone, I can make a living. How'm I doing, by the way? Am I trendy?"

I made a still-deciding face, tilting my head from side to side.

He laughed. "Journalists always say I'm gangly."

"I wouldn't use that word," I said. I clicked the pen in my hand a few times, happy for a prop. "I enjoy the way you . . . inhabit space."

He bounced the foot of his crossed leg, considering this. He was smiling, having fun now. "Are you going to write that down?"

I clicked my pen back on. "Candidate has an enjoyable way of inhabiting space: slightly awkward without being self-conscious."

He laughed. "Candidate is awkward but doesn't know it, basically?"

"Right. And is therefore not, in fact, awkward."

"Nice try," he said. "I just get a pass because I can sing."

"Ah," I said, holding my pen up. "But I've never heard you sing."

He gave an exaggerated nod. A band started playing from a back room and the main bar emptied significantly, quieting down. He made no move to join them.

I wanted to talk about "Bay Window" without losing the protection of our little game, so I said, "Are you the one who sang that problematic mom-rock song about 9/11?"

He laughed. "Blame my co-writer for the problematic bits."

"That must've been hard, though," I said.

He looked surprised. "Are you kidding? It was amazing. Biggest hit of my career, and the fact that it was a curveball makes it even better. People don't know what to expect from me now. I can do anything."

This was a good point that hadn't occurred to me, but all I said was "Must be nice."

He leaned forward. "I'm very grateful for that song."

I felt a tiny sting in my eyes. I nodded.

He leaned back again. "I live just up the road," he said. A new note in his voice, tentative. "If you want to hear me sing, that is. I could play you some things I've been working on."

I shrugged. "I don't have a lot of opinions about music."

He broke character, laughed abruptly and boisterously.

"Okay, say I did." I restrained my own smile. "I've learned it's not a good idea to become involved with other people's work, at least not people you're attracted to. Makes for a weird dynamic."

The eyebrows. "So you're attracted to me?"

My cheeks burned. What was wrong with me? "Everyone is attracted to you," I backpedaled, with a sweeping hand gesture intended to indicate both Liza-Beth and the redheaded bassist, wherever the hell she was. "It's nothing special."

He looked at me carefully. He was waiting for me to say just kidding, of course I'll go to your apartment with you, of course I'll listen to your genius songs. He was thinking—I was certain, I could see it in the edge forming around his mouth—of Skinner.

Before he could speak, I asked the next question on my screener: "How would you describe your social scene?"

"Broken." He motioned to the bartender for another round, then narrowed his eyes at me. "Hey, are you the one who blogged about me singing 'What Makes You Think You're the One' at a house party, couple years ago? How the hell did you know that?"

He'd seen it. I held back what would've been a terribly inappropriate smile. "From one of my trendsetters."

"Oh really!" The chill in his voice came back, hardening now to ice. "So it *is* a useful job for you!"

"I just guessed at the song, though—was I right?"

He let out a half laugh, nostrils flaring. "It would've been a lot less creepy if you'd been wrong."

"Wow. I'm sorry if that felt invasive—"

"I was in a bad place, that night—our CMJ show sucked, my girlfriend was mad at me—"

"But the piece wasn't about you, really."

"That's true—it was about the author, right? How she always tries to own the singer's accomplishments? Interesting."

Suddenly I hated him all over again. My right palm let out a throb of phantom pain. "Calm down," I muttered. "I deleted it five seconds after I posted it."

"Yeah, thanks for that. Made me think I'd hallucinated it." He stopped and sighed, rubbed his forehead. "Never mind."

ANGER ISSUES, I wrote on the screener, cupping a hand so he couldn't see.

Then, bizarrely, he laughed. "Ancient history, though, right? Kinda weird how much I still care sometimes."

"It keeps coming," I said, "till the day it stops."

He lifted his head, eyes brightening at the reference. "Percy, have you ever noticed that talking to most people is boring? Easier than this, but boring?"

"Yes," I said. "But why are we talking like this at all? Didn't you just say you had a girlfriend?" When he didn't answer right away I looked back down at my screener, nervous.

"No girlfriend at the moment," he said.

Panic rose inside me. I looked down at the page, which went red for a half second, then black. Then my vision restored. *NO GIRL-FRIEND*, I wrote. "What happened?" I asked, keeping my voice even.

"She's amazing," he said, and I wished I hadn't asked. "But she's older, and—well, there was a biological clock issue."

This didn't shrink my jealousy, but it gave it a different shape. He was a complicated shadow on her life too, a heartless waste of precious time. I felt an obscure kinship with her, even as I hated how grown-up their relationship suddenly seemed, how weighty and real their problems. Music was playing again in the bar: Hot Chip's "Ready for the Floor." Two girls began to dance.

"And you?" he asked, taking a small drink of beer. "Any smart young politicos in your life?"

Zoe must've told him about the Obama staffer. "Nope," I said. "Honestly, I've only had one real boyfriend, and that was years ago."

"Oh yeah? What happened?"

"I cheated on him."

He thought about this. "And you just told him? Right away?"

I nodded. "And he dumped me right away."

His face registered this slowly. After a minute he said, "Poor guy."

"Eh," I said. "He's married now. I did him a favor, really. You don't know how insufferable I can be."

He leaned forward suddenly, moved his knees so they parted mine. "Come over," he said. "I want to suffer you."

I looked down at our legs, four alternating stripes of denim. "But you hate me," I said.

"Not as much as you hate me."

"Jesus," I said. "I'm sorry about Skinner, but not everything is about you, you know?"

He leaned back slightly. His knees were still touching mine. "Here's the apology I want. Come over. Work with me."

I looked away. "Heartbeats" by the Knife started playing. Angular synths cut the air between us, followed by Karin Dreijer's sharp, dramatic voice. The song had come out after we'd stopped talking; we'd never heard it together, never discussed it.

"The Knife is the perfect name for their sound," he said quietly.

"Totally. They're the aural equivalent of a meat cleaver."

He smiled. We watched each other listen to the song, his smile slowly fading. It's a mysterious song about an intense romantic encounter, a true and astonishing episode of love—but something goes awry in the bridge, and all Dreijer is left with is a conviction that after this experience, divinity will never come from above. Not for her. Only earthly bodies, pressed so close they're sharing heartbeats, could ever be divine.

When the last biting synth chord lifted, I found all my temper flares had been tamped out. They seemed idiotic in the face of the song's grandeur. It was a song I understood only because of Joe, and now here he was, inches from my face, breathing slow and shallow. His knees were closer now, squeezing mine.

Then wordlessly he stood and led me to the bathroom. As we crossed the room it felt oddly quiet, almost still, like those fantasy sequences in movies when everything pauses except the main characters. We joined a silent line of people waiting and stood together leaning against the wall. Our pinkies hooked.

"Do you ever think about that day at the wedding?" he asked in a hoarse whisper.

"Yes. Zoe once told me that was the whole point of that day."

"I start with the knock on the door," he said.

"I start with your hand on my shoulder."

He turned swiftly and kissed me. It was shocking but also sooth-ing, like falling backward into a warm pool. His hands were in my hair, the pads of his fingers cradling my skull, and then his palm slid down my back, pressing me so close I could feel his ribs on my breasts, the thump of his heart inside my own, just like the song de-scribed. Nobody in the bathroom line said anything. Or maybe they did and I didn't hear them. When he finally pulled back, he wore an expression of deep satisfaction, like the world was right again. I was woozy from the kiss, but that look made me want to clarify something.

"No songs, okay?" I said. "Just us." I leaned in again.

He turned his cheek.

I froze. "No, don't—it's just—"

Wasn't it obvious? Wasn't it obvious that working on his stupid songs would ruin everything?

"It's important that I do my own thing," I finished.

"Was Skinner your own thing?" he said, his face still at an angle.

"Kind of, yeah. Because it wasn't you."

He scoffed.

"Okay, do you want to *just* do music?" I challenged. "Strictly business?"

He flinched, his face inching even farther away.

"Yeah, me neither," I said. The volume seemed to have been turned back up on the bar sounds, and the bathroom line had lengthened behind us without shortening in front of us. I waited for him to say something, but he was still drifting away from me. Then he leaned back on the wall and folded his arms high on his chest.

I sighed. "What was I thinking?" I said, and it was a question that truly baffled me. Fucking "Heartbeats." We'd gulped down that song like a couple of drunks, recklessly chasing euphoria. And now, instead of the mature resolution I'd been searching for, I had re-wound myself back into my early twenties.

"You can go if you want," he said.

"No, I can't. I need two more trendsetters and I fly out tomorrow morning."

He nodded, still not quite looking at me. "I'd help you, but"—he lifted his shoulders—"I don't want to."

"I don't blame you," I said, and walked back to the barstool, where my backpack was waiting on the floor. He stayed in the bathroom line. A few minutes later I saw him leaving. He gave me a small, resigned smile as he pushed through the glass door.

The next morning, on the cab ride to JFK, I got a text from him. He was going to be in the Bay Area next month for a benefit show, and wanted to know if he could come to Thanksgiving dinner at the Gutierrezes'. **Zoe says you get priority,** he said.

Sure, I responded, and felt so relieved I almost cried. Maybe in the light of day, away from barstools and banter and that song, we could be cool.

A few minutes later, he texted, **BTW how good is the new Shins?** I looked out the window with the phone on my chest for the remainder of the ride, just enjoying the feeling of having Joe to respond to.

The Girl in the Bridge

Thanksgiving at the Gutierrezes' was jubilant and cozy. Zoe had lost her job and I still hadn't found one, but Obama had won the election and it was hard not to be optimistic. After dessert Joe played guitar and sang Bowie's "Kooks," and Zoe's parents began dancing, then Zoe and Melissa joined them. I excused myself to the kitchen to do dishes. I'd been making it work, pretending to be comfortable, pretending it was easy to share this evening with Joe—but "Kooks" was too much. I leaned into the noise of the running faucet and clanged pots and pans with abandon.

By the time I rode the train home I felt drained but okay. Joe had been awkward when addressing me directly but otherwise relaxed, so obviously happy to be back; I didn't want him to be shut out of the Gutierrez home any more than I wanted myself to be. I could do this once a year.

The next afternoon I was at my desk writing when I saw Melissa's car pull up out front to drop off Zoe. After Zoe got out, Melissa rolled down her window for a goodbye kiss.

Zoe came straight to my room and fell on the bed. "Thanks for last night. I have two things to tell you."

I turned in my desk chair. The moment I saw her face, propped up with her chin in her hands, I knew. "You're moving in with Melissa."

She looked relieved, though her brow stayed creased. "It would be insane not to, right? I have no income, and our rent is higher than hers, plus—"

"Plus it's time," I said. I'd been playing whack-a-mole in my head with this possibility for weeks, ever since the passage of that repulsive Prop 8, which Zoe's dad's Catholic church—though not Mr. Gutierrez himself—had vocally supported. I knew Zoe and Melissa weren't ready for marriage, but there was something about being denied the right that seemed to make her want to lean further into domesticity, to prove the stability of their union. I totally got it.

"I wanted to wait until you were ready, but—"

"I'll be fine, Zoe," I said, and I meant it, even though my stomach had dropped through the seat of my chair. "I'm making a little money. I'll turn my blog into a book. I'll get a roommate."

She scooted off the bed and sat on my lap, hugging me. "But there will never, ever be another me."

I held her tightly, as if I could squeeze all the love I owed her into her body by force. "Never."

"Ow," she said, pulling back. "Second thing. Joey's coming over later and I don't want to hear any whining about it. It's the anniversary of the first time the three of us ever hung out—remember?"

She knew what she was doing, telling me her moving plan first; now I was sentimental and primed to please her. I nodded mutely. And it did make me smile to remember our day-after-Thanksgiving 2000—the strange, clean expanse of those wide suburban streets; the way my life had seemed like an uncrumpling ball of paper, smoothing out as the night went on. It occurred to me that Joe and I weren't together then either, and it was one of the happiest times of my life.

A few hours later he showed up with a bottle of wine, a gallon-sized Ziploc of leftover turkey from the Gutierrezes, and a recipe for potpie.

I drank a full glass of wine in minutes. We took turns playing from the kitchen table iPod dock. Joe made the dough while Zoe assembled the ingredients and I cleared off our kitchen table, which was covered in books and magazines and Zoe's various fundraising paraphernalia. Halfway through my second glass of wine, I was enjoying myself.

"Play the best song about moving," Zoe said when we sat down to eat.

Joe dove for the iPod. When "Packing Blankets" by the Eels started playing, I couldn't hide my disappointment.

Joe sighed. "I need more wine before I hear whatever Percy is about to say."

"Above the fridge," Zoe said.

"I have no objection to this song," I said. "I just can't believe you didn't play 'New Slang.'"

Joe pulled a cork and then pointed the bottle opener at me accusingly. "You didn't know 'New Slang' was about moving until we read that interview with James Mercer in *SPIN*."

"So?"

"So, disqualified," he said, sitting back down and topping off our glasses. "Also I forgot."

"How could you forget that album? Did you *Eternal Sunshine* it out of your mind because it reminds you of our nonexistent college affair?"

"It's just very important to me that you know I don't think 'Packing Blankets' is a better song than 'New Slang.'"

Zoe was smiling widely. "If you freaks ever let me have my turn, I'm doing 'California.' I listened to that daily in Africa."

"Ooh, let's do best Joni songs next," I said. "Joe, if you play some meandering jazzy thing I'm leaving."

"Come on," he said. "Obviously we'll both choose 'A Case of You.'"

I smiled.

Zoe's pick was "Big Yellow Taxi," and I think that was her last contribution, because it led to Joe and me making fun of the Counting Crows' cover of "Big Yellow Taxi" and then a lengthy round of worst covers ever, followed by best Christmas songs ever, at which point Zoe got up to do the dishes.

"We're being annoying," I said quietly to Joe, who was scrolling through the iPod to find "2000 Miles" by the Pretenders.

He clicked the song and turned to look at me. We were inches apart. "So? I've been annoying Zoe since the nineties."

I looked over at her, her hands in the sink, shoulders swaying slightly to the song's repeating guitar line, which whirled through the room like snow. "She's leaving me," I told Joe.

He winced, nodded. His hand reached out, but didn't seem to know where to land; eventually his fingers rested, briefly, on my forearm. I felt the music slow and wobble, like a needle passing through a warp in the vinyl. Then he thumbed the iPod to a Bowie shuffle and announced, "I'm drying!"

We ended up in Zoe's room, looking through old photos and laughing harder than I could remember ever having laughed, and then Zoe started explaining all the factors that had gone into the economic collapse. It was almost midnight when I realized Joe had drifted into my room.

"The CDs are gone," I said as I followed him in, picking clothes up off the floor.

He was standing in front of the synth. "I can't believe it."

"Zero chance I'm playing that thing in front of you," I said.

But now he was looking at my notebook on the desk, open to a page of verse. "Is this for Meg Vee?"

"Yeah." I watched his face carefully.

He nodded slowly. "People are talking about it. Heard you turned a weird dirge into a lead single."

I felt an explosion of pride so strong it must've been obvious on my face, but he was still looking at my notebook. "Does it bother you when I write with someone you don't hate?" I asked.

"Not as much," he said distractedly. He was touching the notebook with his fingertips, reading the lyrics. I didn't mind; they were good.

"Hey," he said suddenly, looking up. "What if we started with your idea?"

"For a song?"

"Yeah. Surely you don't just fix other people's songs, or write about them. What would *your* song be about?"

"Joe," I said. "That won't solve everything."

But I did have an idea, a big one, so big I already knew I'd be powerless to resist telling him. I sat on the edge of the bed. "Fifty percent," I warned.

"Deal." He sat next to me, his hands folded between his legs, one of which was bouncing slightly.

"It's called 'The Girl in the Bridge.'" I watched his face slowly process the "in." "Someone said that to me after the Troubadour— 'You're the girl in the bridge!' Very surreal moment for me."

"Wow. So it's about you?"

"Only the bridge is about me. Something similar to that Fleetwood Mac post, remember, about how I'm basically the worst?"

He kissed me on the lips, fast and firmly. Then his eyes widened. "Sorry. Carry on. You're not the worst. Carry on."

I felt my body rocking slightly on the bed, shocked. "Joe," I said.

"Won't happen again." He jerked his hand horizontally as if striking it from the record.

"Good," I said sternly. "We went through this, remember—"

"Oh my god Percy I take it back, please, it was an accident—tell me about the song!"

I almost laughed, but I didn't want to undermine my point. I took a breath. "Fine. The rest is your part of the story. The girl only appears in the bridge."

His eyes rolled back in his head. "So fucking cool." Then they snapped back, brighter than before. "Wait. I have the perfect music for this." He bounded out of the room, and seconds later he was sitting next to me again with his iPod and a pair of over-the-ear headphones. "Do you have lyrics?"

"Some." He looked over at the notebook on my desk, but I shook my head. "They're not ready."

Zoe rapped on the open bedroom door. "I'm heading to Melissa's, freaks!"

We jumped off the bed. "What?" I said. "No!"

But she was already pulling on her coat. "I can't handle the sexual tension in this place," she said, giving us each a hug. "I feel like I'm about to get electrocuted."

Something about the way she said it so plainly, loaded with tacit approval, made my last layer of defense against Joe crumble. Just one night, I decided. There's only so long you can hold out against a force so strong the whole room can feel it.

"Zoe, I love you," I said, then added, "More than Joe. I love you more than Joe."

She laughed. "I love you more than Joe too."

"I'm right here," Joe said.

We walked her out, waving like parents as she descended the stairwell. When the door shut there was an uncertain second and then we were attacking each other, pulling off clothes, stumbling down the hallway. My brain wanted to get back to the song, but my body kept winning.

"Is it up-tempo?" I asked as we fell on the bed.

"Mid," he said, and put my breast into his mouth.

We rushed the sex, somehow, clamored through it like teenagers. Immediately afterward he grabbed his iPod from my nightstand and handed it to me.

I clamped on his giant headphones. He was still inside me; I was sitting on top.

"If you don't like it, we'll find something else," he said. I nodded, and he held my gaze as he pressed play. A syncopated snare beat. Rhythm guitar established the groove. Then some strange instrument—an electric guitar, I realized, processed beyond recognition—began playing two phrases over and over. The first phrase was tense, withholding, repeating; the second was an explosion of sixteenth notes, a burst of melodic inspiration that brought us nowhere but right back where we started. Tense, repeating; melodic. Tense; melodic. "You'd just sing right over this loop?" I asked, inaudible to myself. He nodded. A smile spread over my face. I felt him get a little hard again. The loop kept going, and other things were happening now too—more drums, synths, some sort of crunching machine-produced noise deepening the groove.

"The melody will need to be simple over all this," I observed. He pushed up on his elbows and motioned for me to pull off an earphone; I complied, stretching it out so he could hear, and he sang a wordless melodic line over the loop. I nodded. It worked, and it was amazing—an entirely new direction for him.

We were in the bridge now: the loop dropped out, the rhythm destabilized. I pulled off a headphone so I could hear myself, then sang, "He met his match but couldn't light it." Instantly I felt Joe become very hard. "She was always wet. She'd draw his blood while clawing her way . . . to get a little respect." The melody, which had come to me from nowhere, rose and fell like a swan dive, smoothly threading the density of his instrumentation. "Her worst brought out the best in him, but she wanted it better. And every time she found perfection, he was always better."

The loop returned; the groove settled back in. He sat up to kiss me, and this time we made it last.

I woke first. My first thought was panic that I'd forgotten my beautiful bridge melody, but I found it waiting calmly at the edge of my mind.

A white sky through the window filled my room with a soft, even light. Joe's mouth hung partly open on the pillow. I could see now what he had seen at Union Pool: that separating the songs from the sex was a ridiculous notion. Neither would be as good. I remembered Alma's comment about music infiltrating our physical lives, and wondered if that phenomenon worked both ways—if good music came straight from the body itself, sometimes. If the best stuff happened when you kept the borders between your mind and body as open and porous as humanly possible.

I was staring at the ceiling and starting to drift off again when I heard his voice, throaty with morning: " 'He was always better'—is that true, or just a good line?"

I rolled onto my side. His eyes were half open, flakes of sleep in the lashes. "It's true," I said. "But 'better' cuts both ways, doesn't it? Or maybe you don't know what it's like to have someone be constantly better than you."

He put a hand on my hip. His eyes were fully open now. "I do, actually."

We looked at each other a long time. Then he rolled on top of me and disappeared under the covers, kissing a trail down my sternum, exploring with his hands. Each touch lit up multiple parts of my body, fingers and lips and random patches of my arms and legs, and the effect was dizzying; I couldn't tell which touch was real. He bent my knee and kissed a line along my inner thigh. Somewhere in the heat map of my mind I had the clear thought that I couldn't wait to do what he was doing, to explore his body this way. When it was my turn I pushed him over, giddy. I checked for the mole on his collarbone: still there. I bit the nipples I'd seen through T-shirts, under an open coat on his Berkeley porch. I licked the length of the muscles in his forearm that flexed when he played guitar, and held the thighs I'd felt shaking with excitement on the Manhattan showroom piano bench, shaking now again in my arms.

Afterward we moved seamlessly into "The Girl in the Bridge." I brought toast and coffee on a cookie sheet into the bed. We worked on the keyboard and in the notebook, fitting words into our melodies, iterating on every note, every syllable. It was clear to both of us that Joe didn't get final say anymore, which led, eventually, to a standoff over an awkward verse rhyme; he capitulated to my edit, but not before muttering something obnoxious about seeing how it sounded on tape. "How about we go out to lunch before I bludgeon you with a cookie sheet," I said, and he kissed me, which was a reasonably effective apology not previously available to us.

While he showered I stayed in bed, checking my email and the job posting boards. He returned with a towel around his waist and peered at my screen curiously. "Do you actually want any of those jobs?"

"Of course I don't," I said. "But this apartment isn't cheap."

"Can you get a different one?" He pulled on his boxers and let the towel drop. "A cheaper neighborhood, or city, even? What's keeping you here?"

I looked at him. There was Zoe, of course, but I knew our friendship could survive any distance. "It's a good question."

"Right?" he said, and joined me in bed.

But where would I go? Not New York, which was just as expensive. Not Indiana. The laptop was burning hot against my knees. "When you were touring the States for *Funny Strange,* you used to send emails from all these little cities—"

"Missoula, Montana." His eyes were dancing over my face. "New Orleans. Both Portlands."

I was already searching. Within a minute I'd found a charming attic unit in a house in Maine for less than half my share of the San Francisco apartment. The photos seemed to glow with all the extra hours that rent could buy. I could write all night. I could drive to New York to meet my collaborators. I tilted the screen to show Joe.

He pulled the laptop onto his own knees and started tapping at the keys. The look in his eyes reminded me of our "Sara Smile" night so many years ago, when the lights came on in the bar and I'd seen it for the first time, that wounded, galvanized intensity. Then I peeked at his screen. "Joe—"

"Shut up." A minute later he turned the laptop toward me proudly. It was a small house for rent in Montana. He clicked through the photos: two bedrooms, a dining room with wainscoting, and, in the back corner of the yard, a freestanding studio, already sound-proofed by the owner.

"Come on," I said. "Caroline is a New York band."

"I could use some space from those guys, honestly," he said. "You heard what I'm doing these days. I need a studio."

The possibilities crashed over me like a breaking wave.

"So do you," he added, and his voice was tender with pride.

I pushed off the covers and stood. He looked up at me, his mouth quivering at the edge of a smile. On the screen between us, the little studio was lit from within, its windows warm and yellow. "It's a fairy tale," I said. "With two cats in the yard."

Annoyance flashed on his face, like the point was too obvious to even mention. "It's just a month-to-month lease, Perce." He rose to his knees on the bed. "Have we ever even really tried?"

That old "Surf's Up" sensation rose in my chest: door after door after door, endlessly opening. I felt an overpowering desire to run through them all, to see how far they went, even as I knew I'd be clawing my way, drawing blood, through every one.

"You think you know everything." He crossed the bed toward me on his knees. "You think the songs will come between us again."

"They will," I said. And then I grinned, took his face in my hands. "But they'll be so good."

Acknowledgments

This book could not possibly exist without Dan Lyon, whose support took countless forms: giving notes on early drafts, explaining diminished chords, playing versions of "Bay Window" on the piano at night. When my obsession with writing this book upended our lives, he never once complained or doubted the payoff. I love you for that, Danny—and for so much more.

Nor could this book exist without my dad, the poet and songwriter Chuck Brickley, who taught me almost from birth how to listen deeply to a pop song. Thank you, Dad, for every cassingle and CD you brought home for me from A&B Sound, and for showing me by example how to live a creative life in the real world.

To my mom, Kim Brickley: your fierce belief in me and open-hearted love built the foundation for all my work, beginning with those first stories you helped me build out of cue cards. I am so grateful. Meanwhile, my envy of your talents could be the subject of a whole other book—and might be, someday!

Rachel Swaby, my forever first reader: when your enthusiasm for this story seemed excessive even for you, I knew I had to fight for it. Thank you for knowing when I need a push.

Anna Stein, the word "agent" sounds too small to describe what you do! Thank you for fixing the bridge—of the book, and of my life. Big thanks also to Karolina Sutton, Jiah Shin, Julie Flanagan, Claire Nozieres, Zoe Willis, Blythe Zadrozny, and Jamie Stockton.

Amy Einhorn, thank you for your nuanced editing, and for throwing your spectacular might behind this story. To the rest of the Crown team, including Lori Kusatzky, Dyana Messina, Stacey Stein, Julie Cepler, Chris Tanigawa, Liza Stepanovich, Abby Oladipo, Philip Leung, Amani Shakrah, Michele Giuseffi, Chris Brand, Chris Allen, Annsley Rosner, and David Drake.

To Beth Coates, Jo Thompson, Amy Perkins, Maud Davies, Holly Martin, Emily Merrill, and everyone at The Borough Press in the UK: you have found every opportunity to blow me away with your passion and ambition for this book! And to Bhavna Chauhan, Amy Black, and everyone at Doubleday Canada: thank you for bringing me home.

To Ken Brickley, greatest brother in the history of brothers and the original King of Fun. To Sue Lyon, dream mother-in-law and my favorite reading buddy. To my beloved grandmother, Dortha Brickley, for the gift of our Indiana home. To all my loving, musical, and delightfully opinionated family: Tim Brickley, Pat Brickley, Catherine and Thomas Harris, every Kramer and every Lyon.

Thank you to Claire Campbell and Patrick Maley for reading early drafts, and Ramesh Pillay for reading a different book that helped me get to this one. To Angela Cravens—could I have survived the query trenches without you? To Alexander Reubert for digging me out of those trenches. To Sarah Ramey and Dan Kois for your help with the agent search. To Karen Thompson Walker for advice and perspective about everything that came next.

To the Berkeley crew who could talk about music and books forever, especially Ricky Mills. To my SF friends who showed me the joys of the dance floor, especially Kelli Townley and Anshuman Duneja. (Kelli, the dance floor was just the beginning, of course; it would take pages to acknowledge you properly!) To Matthew Bice for the Shins EP, Brian and Krystle Moyers for the library, Tim Leong for the designs, Warren Boothby for the bars. For assorted inspo: Christian Lyon, Kelly Cloutier, Aaron Poser.

To Barbara Bylenga, who gave me a career in research but always saw me as the writer I really was. To Courtney Leeds for the "judging people for a living" line, and Black Bamboo for seeing me through some crazy cultural plot twists. To Steve Kantscheidt and Portland for giving me the balance I needed to write again.

Thank you to the teachers: Mark Slouka, Christine Schutt, Sigrid Nunez, Ron Loewinsohn, Tom Farber, Lenora Poulin, Chris Crosgrey, Duncan Mason, and, again, especially, Dad.

Thank you—of course, of course—to all the real musicians who appear in these pages.

Maisie and June, this is what I was doing on my laptop at all those playspaces and trampoline parks. Sorry you're not allowed to read it until you're teenagers. Thank you for being such cool, independent, creative kids. I can't wait to watch you discover, through whatever passions might strike your hearts, how big life can be.

ABOUT THE AUTHOR

Holly Brickley studied English at UC Berkeley and received an MFA in fiction from Columbia University. Originally from Hope, British Columbia, she now lives in Portland, Oregon, with her husband and their two daughters. *Deep Cuts* is her first novel.